DRAGON MAGE

The First Dragon Rider Book Three

AVA RICHARDSON

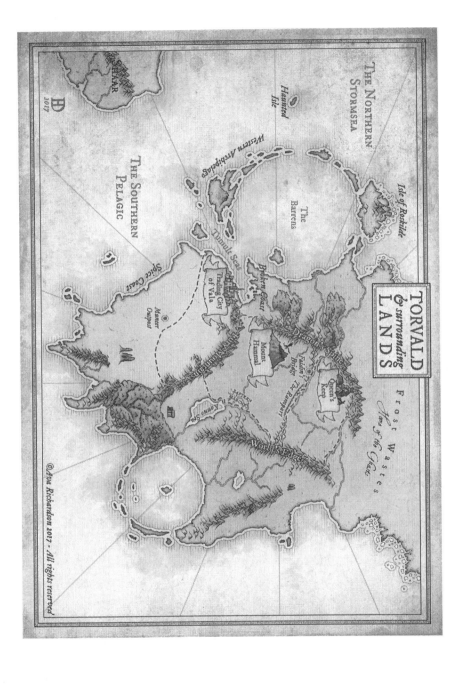

TORVALD
& surrounding
LANDS

THE NORTHERN
STORMSEA

THE SOUTHERN
PELAGIC

Frost Wastes
Home of the Glaciis

Isle of Rocklite

The Barrens

Haunted
Isle

Western Archipelago

Tsunula Seas

Spice Coast

Manor
Outpost

Trading City
of Vala

Bitter Glaar

Mount
Hammal

Dragon Spine Range

Valdin's
Bridge

Til Rampart

Queen's
Keep

World's Edge

CONTENTS

THE FIRST DRAGON RIDER TRILOGY

Dragon God

Dragon Dreams

Dragon Mage

THE FIRST DRAGON RIDER

DRAGON MAGE

AVA RICHARDSON

MAILING LIST

Thank you for purchasing 'Dragon Mage'
(The First Dragon Rider Book Three)

I would like to thank you for purchasing this book. If you would like to hear more about what I am up to, or continue to follow the stories set in this world with these characters—then please take a look at:

AvaRichardsonBooks.com

You can also find me on me on
www.facebook.com/AvaRichardsonBooks

Or sign up to my mailing list:
AvaRichardsonBooks.com/mailing-list/

BLURB

To unite a fractured kingdom, a reluctant hero must rise.

Neill has been charged with the impossible task of bringing the Middle Kingdom together to fight the burgeoning threat posed by the rogue sorcerer Ansall and his dragon Zaxx. Neill longs for his old life as a mere foot soldier for his father responsible only for his family's wellbeing, and is unsure about whether he is fit to lead an army. Neill's contemplative nature forces him to consider every aspect of the problems he faces, but often makes it difficult for him to take action—and failure to act could mean the deaths of many.

Now, echoing Char and their dragon Paxala, his duty beckons him to lead the Dragon Riders—and take his rightful place as king—but with doubt and new enemies creeping in, his resolve will be tested. When the mysterious Dark Prince arrives with an offer, Neill will have to make a decision that could change the course of history.

As Ansall grows in strength by harnessing black magic, Neill must choose between his own desires and the welfare of the entire kingdom. Can he rise to the challenge before it's too late?

PART I
END OF AN ERA

CHAPTER 1
NEILL, THE PURPLE & GREEN

I watched as the small blot on the landscape became a figure on a horse, moving fast, and surrounded by its own trail of flying dust and scattering rocks. The wall scouts atop the Draconis Monastery where I now stood had seen the shape not a quarter of a watch ago, and summoned me, of all people, to make a decision about it.

"Do we let them in?" muttered Lila Penn at my side, screwing her eyes against the sun's high glare. She had grown both in height and stature it seemed to me. Or maybe it was that the yoke of the old Draconis Order had been thrown from her shoulders, and she could stand tall, no longer burdened with the cruelties thrown at her because of her skin color, her gender, and her pirate heritage.

Gone were the heavy, cumbersome black robes of the Order, and gone the silly cloth and leather sandals that had done nothing to protect the feet from the chills of the towering Mount

Hammal. Instead, Lila, like myself and all the other students who still lived here at the monastery, had reverted to donning part-robes and far-sturdier attire that we were all more used to. Lila wore the leather cuirass that she had arrived at the monastery with, along with her bright orange headband, and her boots were now the reinforced, inter-woven leather greaves that most of us wore.

"I've got him," Lila murmured, sighting down the short bow that she held straight towards the rushing figure.

"No, wait a minute, Lila – let's just see what he has to say, first, right?" I said uneasily.

It has been a little more than a moon's cycle since we had taken the monastery from the Abbot Ansall and the others of his ilk. The old ways of the Draconis Order were upturned and thrown over, and everything was still in chaos behind us.

The wall that had collapsed on the Golden Bull Zaxx was still down, though we had managed to convince one of the Great Whites to shift and nose the masonry blocks into a rough and disheveled embankment where the wall had once stood. The tunnel through which the Golden Bull had wormed his way into and escaped was still a visible sink hole on the other side, and every time I caught sight of it I shuddered.

Another thing to worry about, I thought, my anxiety only increasing as I watched the rider.

"He could be anyone. From anywhere. It could be the Abbot, come back to try and mesmerize and curse us again..." Lila growled. "Don't forget what happened to Dragon Trainer Feodor," Lila almost spat, keeping her bow string taut.

"Lila!" I admonished her. How could I forget the terrible sight of Feodor – one of the few actual dragon monks here aside from Jodreth whom I actually liked and could call a friend— fried to a crisp by the Abbot, all for having the temerity to defy him. Burying Feodor had been one of my first priorities, and the ceremony had been short, awkward, and grey.

This is not the sort of future I want for this place, I thought. So far, all that it had been were worries and funerals and then more arguments between the remnants of the 'true' Draconis Order monks who had stayed behind, and us students who were trying to work out just what on earth we were doing.

The Draconis Monastery still stood, in part (despite the dragon's constant smashing of roof tiles and gouging of rock as they soared and perched on the walls to investigate) – but the Draconis Order was no more. With the disappearance of the Abbot Ansall and his most-loyal followers, the older monks left here had wandered in a sort of daze for the first week or so. I could see each of them asking themselves and each other the same questions every time that they saw each other: *What do we do? What are we supposed to do? Why are we here at all, if not to control the dragons?*

I couldn't give them the answers, and so instead I tried to remember what I could do being a Son of Torvald and help by being a leader, a warrior. Of all of the students here I probably had the most strategic experience, thanks to my father's tutelage.

Which was why Lila had called me, here and now, to deal with this fast-approaching rider.

"We haven't had anyone visiting the monastery since..." I

said under my breath, my heart hammering as the figure approached. It felt in my heart that it wasn't just one person on a horse, but a storm…

"I know we haven't. It could be anyone – it could be a message from Prince Vincent, from Char's father the Northern Prince, or even from Ansall himself!" Lila said at my side, as two more of our ad-hoc wall guards appeared – the tall and broad Terrence, student son of Prince Griffith the King-Prince of the South and, surprisingly, Dorf Lesser, my generously framed friend and one-time room-mate. They each carried short swords and spears – with Terrence looking as regal and as comfortable as his father, and Dorf looking slightly ridiculous in the helmet that didn't fit, and an oversized shield strapped to his back that made him look a little like a turtle.

"Terrence," I nodded, greeting the student who had once been my rival. Like Lila, the nobleman's son had changed in just the short month since the wall fell. When he had seen the Abbot's complete perfidy and lack of respect for the students, Terrence became quieter and less disruptive, and ready to accept our new way of working with the dragons.

"Torvald," Terrence nodded back– still managing to inflect just a little bit of that sarcasm he always had when referring to my lowly warlord's family – not even a noble – but he grinned in the next breath, showing that he had accepted that he had to deal with a 'commoner' like me, Dorf, Lila and the others.

"Who is it?" asked Dorf, his usually round eyes squinting. "Do you think that it's from the Dark Prince?"

I shrugged. It would make sense, though. The Draconis Order

stretched across all three kingdoms, of course - but the monastery sat squarely in the middle of Prince Vincent's Middle Kingdom. We were too close and too dangerous for him to leave alone.

There was a flash of color from the rider below, and I heard a sharp intake of breath from Lila. I spun, dreading to see the sure-sighted arrow of Lila Penn arcing ahead of me through the air, but found that I was looking at something else entirely.

The messenger was still riding, but he held out one hand, and from it he clutched a large cloth in the traditional colors of purple and green.

"Don't shoot the messenger," I said urgently. "Those are Torvald colors!"

CHAPTER 2
CHAR, UNEASY

"Neill? Neill – what is it?" I called, still scraping my hair back into its warrior's bun as I jogged into the Grand Hall. One of the old Draconis Order monks had stayed behind after Ansall left and had come to find me out by the dragon crater, where I had been working with Paxala.

"Miss Char? You'll want to be a part of this, I think…" was all that the old man had said, before hurrying me back to the semi-ruined monastery, jogging behind me on his surprisingly spritely old legs.

Maybe he's so healthy because we've lifted the food bans at the monastery, I thought to myself as I jogged. Where before both the monks and the students had been constrained to a diet largely of porridge, gruel, breads, cheeses, and crushed grains – one of the first things Neill and I had decided was to start using some of the store that the monastery had been stockpiling for so long. Salted and cured meats. Dried and fresh fruit. Joints and saddles of meats, a plethora of vegetables available from the little market town at the base of the mountain, plus whatever Nan Barrow could grow in the Kitchen Gardens.

We were trying our best to make the monastery work – only not as a monastery anymore. But we didn't know *what* it was that we were becoming, until we heard what the Torvald messenger had to say.

"Char," Neill said when he saw me, a look of relief easing the furrows of his brow. He stood at the far end of the room in front of the massive fireplaces (where previously the Abbot, the ill-fated Greer, or Olan would lecture at us), and at the side of one of the fires sat a large man with wild red and orange hair, dressed in soft brown leathers and hides. All around them perched others of our unofficial 'council' of sorts: Terrence, Lila, Sigrid, and even Jodreth (still limping from his long-ago battle with the Abbot).

Jodreth himself looked haggard and tired as he rubbed the knuckles on his hands. Even though the monastery had been 'delivered' from our persecutor the Abbot Ansall, I still had barely seen Jodreth, the only fully-ordained Draconis Order Dragon Mage, a couple of time in four weeks. He was always disappearing and returning on mysterious missions, returning each time ever more worried and wan.

"What is it?" I asked again, slowing as the messenger looked up to regard me over his flagon of monastery-brewed light wine and a hunk of cheese almost the size of his fist.

"Char? This is Rudie. He's the Chief Scout for my father's forces," Neill said.

9

"Oh," I said with a gulp. Did that mean that the warlike Sons of Torvald weren't going to be far behind? When they had attacked almost a year ago, the monastery had only managed to fight them off because Neill had taken to the skies on my dragon-sister Paxala, the Crimson Red, and I had been involved in the magical onslaught of the Torvald forces, as directed by the mega-lomaniac Abbot Ansall.

And now that the walls were half down, and we had only a fraction of the defenses we had back then, I thought in horror, we could never hope to hold off a concerted siege by such fearsome and trained armies as the Sons of Torvald! Even with the Great Whites and the other dragons – both Neill and I were wary about petitioning them to work for us in shifting the stones and the rubble. We wanted to build a relationship with them, and not for them to view us as the 'new masters.' Even with the dragon's tentative friendship, I still didn't know how the "free" dragons of the crater would react to being called into battle so soon after overthrowing their old bull. Paxala would fight with us, of course, (she would fight with me, I meant) but would any of the other dragons follow her?

Neill, I could see, shared my apprehensions as he looked at me with wide eyes, but he nodded for Rudie to begin his tale as I took a seat.

"I came to you, Neill, because your father asked me to," Rudie said heavily, keeping a steady gaze upon Neill as he munched on his cheese. This Rudie *looked* like a hunter, to my mountain-people eyes. He had that same, silent, and one-pointed awareness that I had come to associate only with hunters, wolves, and birds of prey.

"My father..." Neill murmured, his look far away.

"Yes," the Chief Scout called Rudie said. "He is still badly hurt. That arrow that he took in his leg, and whatever poisons that little worm Healer Garrett was giving him have turned him into half the man that he was," Rudie growled in his deep voice.

"Garrett," Neill said, and saw him bunch his fists at his side. I knew now (thanks to Neill) that their Clan Healer Garrett, along with most of the healers and scribes throughout the Three Kingdoms, had been trained here at the monastery, supervised by Ansall himself, and so the Abbot had managed to seed the world with his fanatics, spies who spread lies and gathered information. It was one of the reasons he and the Draconis Order had become so powerful.

"Yes. But you don't need to worry about the healer. Your brothers saw to that." Rudie let the implication lie, and Neill nodded that he understood what the Chief Scout meant.

"But your father is a shadow of the man that he was, and now that the Blood Baron is back..." The scout looked at Neill with beetled brows of concern.

"The Blood Baron?" Dorf said. "Who is he? He certainly doesn't sound like a nice fellow!"

"He's not," Neill said. "My father and my older brothers defeated him, but it looks like he had managed to get out of whatever prison Prince Vincent had him in. He was vile, thinking that he might be able to carve out his own miniature kingdom all for himself and his men. He captured villages and towns along the Eastern Marches and demanded that the people paid *him* twice the tax they had paid Prince Vincent," Neill said. "It was my father's job to protect the marches, but Prince Vincent wouldn't spend a drop of money on helping his campaign..."

"Yes." Rudie nodded. "And we thought your father had vanquished the Blood Baron on his own, and for good, until not three days ago the villages of Limsfoot and Endmow were all razed to the ground, with the baron's sign left at the gates."

"What's the baron's sign?" I asked stupidly.

Rudie grimaced, putting his hunk of cheese down and instead turning to the wine. It was Neill who answered me instead.

"The decapitated head of one of the villagers, wearing the baron's red battle helmets, stuck on a pole in front of the gate." Neill shivered. "I thought that those days were over."

"They're only just starting," muttered Rudie, looking around the hall with apparent concern, before finally settling his eyes back on Neill once more. I could sense that these two had a lot of history; Rudie talked to him in the same way that an old colleague talks, one whom had known you all of your life.

"Neill," Rudie said gently. "News of what you did here has spread far and wide, it has reached all across the Three Kingdoms. The realms are in uproar. No one knows what it means. They wonder if you are going to try and seize the crown from Prince Vincent, or whether you are mad, or dragon-bewitched...."

Well, that much is true, I thought.

"It's true," said a new voice at our side. It was Jodreth, nodding slowly. "And, I hate to say this, Neill – but what happens in here, inside these walls, has ramifications out there, outside in the Three Kingdoms. Prince Vincent is already conducting a semi-civil border war with his own brother to the north."

Believe me, I know, I thought. I had witnessed my fathers' troops massing at the borders.

"People are wondering what happens next. When will all of this bloodshed and unrest end?" Jodreth said quietly. "So, there are going to be many little Blood Barons and other criminal-chiefs who think that they can grab what they can in all the chaos."

Neill almost visibly deflated in front of me.

"Master Torvald?" Rudie got up awkwardly from his seat, taking a step forward towards Neill as both Lila, Terrence and I all stiffened, but, to our surprise the large man merely folded down onto one knee and bowed his head.

"Master of the Draconis Monastery," Rudie said formally, although I looked between Lila, Terrence, and Jodreth in alarm. If anyone should be the 'Master' or the new 'Abbot' here – then surely it should be Jodreth, shouldn't it? But he had been away, and had taken little or no interest in the everyday running and rebuilding of the monastery at all, as Neill and the rest of us had.

"Neill," Rudie continued, "your father has heard of how you rode dragons, and is asking that you come to the aid of your people, your clan, and your family. We need the aid of the Draconis Monastery, and your dragons. Help us, Neill."

They're not our dragons, I thought instantly, and was pleased when Neill answered not even a split second later with, "I can't speak for the dragons, nor command them, Rudie." Neill's voice was heavy but sincere. "And I am not the master here, I can only talk to the people here to see who agrees…" Neill frowned. "But, Master Scout – if I can, I will bring everything that I can to help fight against the Blood Baron."

Terence made a loud, exaggerated coughing behind his hand. He clearly wasn't impressed with this turn of events, but I shushed him with just a look.

"Maybe we should let the scout here rest, *Terence,*" I said, throwing him a careful look, "while we all go and discuss matters?"

"Yes…" Neill said uneasily, biting his lower lip as he weighed matters in his own mind. Suddenly he stood up, as Rudie once again resumed his chair by the fire, his wine, and his hunk of cheese. Neill still looked worried and tense, but he had a light in his eyes now. A passion. "I'm going, Char. I'm going, and I would like you and Paxala to come with me."

Beside us, Lila muttered darkly under her breath. "By the stars…." But it seemed that Jodreth was pleased by Neill's decision, as he was nodding thoughtfully.

"Char?" Neill's eyes were still on me. How can you put me in this position, right now? Here? I thought a little angrily, as I nodded to the nearest exit. "*Master* Torvald?" I said through gritted teeth. "The smaller reading rooms, now."

I marched ahead, with Neill the unelected 'Master of the Draconis Monastery,' Terence the Southern Prince's child, Lila the pirate, and Jodreth the only Draconis Monk amongst us following on behind.

CHAPTER 3
NEILL, SURE

"What's wrong?" I looked at Char in confusion, and it did not escape me that she was looking at me in pretty much the same fashion. We stood in one of the small stone alcove reading rooms which were everywhere in the main building of the monastery. They were little more than rounded cell-like rooms, with a narrow stone bench running around the inside where monks and students were supposed to perch with their latest scrolls and reading materials, or otherwise quietly contemplate the mystery and majesty of dragons.

It still seemed odd to me that the Draconis Order had so easily believed the Abbot, when he had taught them to understand the dragons through meditation and contemplation, rather than by actually getting out onto the hills and rocks above the crater and, I don't know, *meeting* them!

But I did know why the Abbot had done so, of course – it was so he could feed his followers his specially crafted, hypnotic visualizations and meditations, making an army of fanatics and keeping the 'real' power for himself.

"What's wrong?" Terence said in mock-alarm. "You've gone crazy, that's what is wrong! I know it's your family, Torvald, but there is no way we can go help them. I'm sorry, but the monastery just isn't ready for that yet."

Oh.

Char slapped a hand to her face. Terence, for all of his change of heart recently about the dragons and the value of other people who weren't princes or prince's sons, was still one of the most brash, brusque, and arrogant of men that I knew. *He was not the one they wanted to start this conversation,* I realized. Char, my closest friend here, looked pleadingly over at Lila, but Lila was only nodding in agreement with Terence.

"I know this is tough, Neill, but Terence is right. The students aren't ready." Lila shrugged, as if that was that.

"Char?" I turned to look at my friend, and I could feel myself glaring at her.

"I…" Char shrugged. "We have only just managed to get Lila and Dorf matched with dragons – and still, their growing link and friendship seem tenuous in my eyes. One bad argument or stupid mistake could set us back another breeding cycle if we wanted to make bonds between dragons and students," she said awkwardly, looking down at her feet and then looking up at me again. "I'm worried about how the dragons and the students will cope."

"*They'll* cope!" I hissed strongly back at them all, and I could see how they were taken aback by the force in my tone. "Can't you see how important this is? Not *just* because it's my father, my brothers, my family – that's not it at all." Lila raised a skeptical eyebrow at me but I kept going. "It's the fact that Rudie rode all the way out here to the monastery and *asked for aid.* That's what you're not seeing. Who would have dreamed to do that in the days of the Abbot Ansall?"

Char opened her mouth to speak, but I barged ahead. "And Char," I reasoned. "You know that you, me, and Paxala can do this. We escaped the north after all, didn't we?" I said. "We fought those wild mountain dragons, didn't we?" The dynamic between Paxala, Char, and myself was working really well at the moment. When we flew together, it was like Char could second guess the Crimson Red dragon underneath her, and occasionally it even felt like we were no longer two young humans riding a greater, larger dragon at all – but that we were a part of one thing entire: a new sort of creature.

I tried to remind Char of this, speaking to her and her alone. "We can do this, I know that we can," I said.

I saw the spark of excitement in my friend's eyes. Like all of us still here at the monastery, she had that same love for adventure and excitement, and the sense of wonder every time she saw a dragon. But then the excitement faded a little from Char's face.

"But Neill... the other student riders...? Are they ready?" Char said. "It can't be just you, me, and Paxala, can it? Against an entire bandit army?"

"No," I said. She had a point, just as she always did, even if I didn't really want to admit it. "We'll need the other dragons, or some of them, at least..." I sighed. "But the thing is, Char,

Terence, Lila, this really *is* important." I tried to explain how I felt to them. "We don't know what we're doing up here. All we know is that we didn't like the way that the Abbot and the other monks were abusing and using the dragons of the crater. We've put a stop to that." I saw them all nod in agreement.

"And now we have to do something *else*, something *different* from what the Draconis Order did. We're not here to just worship the dragons, or study them, or *use* them. We're here for a purpose…" I felt my heart leap to my throat. "And Rudie out there showed me what that purpose was." I looked around my assembled friends in front of me.

"*They* came to *us*. There were those outside the walls who would never normally have dreamed of asking the Draconis Order for help, who are now thinking about what we are doing here, and how the partnership that we have with the dragons might be a good thing," I said exultantly. "We have to honor that, surely, right?"

"Right," Jodreth said with a grim smile. "You always have to honor hope, when you find it. And sometimes you have to put the world before your own concerns. It's the decent thing to do."

"Yes!" I said victoriously. "And we want to be decent, after all, don't we? That's what this was all about – getting rid of the old corrupt Ansall and Zaxx because they weren't decent, and that we were different!"

I stopped at last, a little breathless and giddy with excitement. It was so close, that I could almost *see* the future hanging in the air ahead of us. The Draconis Order could be a place where people come to for aid, for help when no other world power, chief, prince or king could help. Teams of dragons and their student riders flying in V-like flights, screaming their way across the sky, keeping everyone safe...

"I think that *Paxala* might be able to help with that," Char said, tapping her lower lip in thought. I felt excited joy start to coil through me. She was seeing it, too.

"Neill," she asked me, and turning to include the others in the room, "do you remember how Paxala encouraged the dragons to fly against Zaxx at the end of the battle? Paxala had talked to them – even those ones we haven't managed to touch or talk..."

"Yes!" I saw how she was thinking. "You could help the students ride the dragons, I could help with the fighting, and Paxala could help the dragons. She might even be able to call the riderless ones as well."

"It might work," Char said, still looking unsure but breaking into a grin at the suggestion. I knew that she was going to say yes, and I started grinning. The monastery and the dragons had a future, and all we had to do was to encourage it to happen.

"Well, I'll tell Rudie the good news. And I want us able to ride out as soon as possible," I said as I made my way out of the reading chamber.

"Aye, aye, *Master* Torvald," Lila said with a withering dose of sarcasm in her voice. Yeah, I guess I deserved that, I thought. "Please," I added quickly.

CHAPTER 4
CHAR, FLIGHT COMMAND

We flew.

It's hard to describe the wonder of those two small words, if you have never experienced dragon flight. All that it contains, all that it encompasses is just too much. We were soaring at what I considered a medium high height over the patchwork blanket of greens, browns, and blues of the Middle Kingdom below. At this height, everything on the ground looked like toys and far away.

And it was slow! Which was a fact that never ceased to amaze me. When you are flying close to the ground, everything is a blur of roar and speed, but the higher that you go, the world becomes smaller, more indistinct, and slower, as if you are barely crawling along, even though the wind can be whipping through your hair like a gale.

We flew and it was like riding at the crest of a wave, or the tip of a stormfront. Massive vibrations from the winds behind us and from the dragon body beneath us sent a shiver through our bones, making us feel like we were thrumming with power (which I guess we were). The gigantic, leathery wings of the dragon underneath me occasionally snapped, sighed, and roared as Paxala the Crimson Red made minute changes to her altitude and direction.

We flew and it wasn't just the river of sensations from my own skin, eyes, and ears that filled me, but it was also the pulse of information that swam up through Paxala, my dragon sister. Our minds were closer when we were flying than at any other time – even on the odd occasions when I had decided to spend the night curled up, as warm as a bug, under the leather of her wings and against her pyrrhic belly.

Paxala's thoughts were only a breath away, and they filled the background of my own conscious mind like a supporting, joyous chatter:

"Forest, east wind, full-green summer leaves falling into wet mulch; the pink of salmon belly that I can smell in that stream! A cooler patch of northern breeze coming up; distant snows, crisp as crystal and as sharp as blades coming from the top of the world—"

The litany of things that Paxala recognized and sang about in her mind was endless. At the moment, however, she was happy flying at the head of what Dorf called 'a squadron' of the five dragons that we had managed to rouse in Neill's quest.

It's not going to be enough, I thought in alarm (and not for the first time since leaving the monastery, either). Five dragons against a bandit army? How many were in an army, anyway? Were there rules for this sort of thing?

I wish that I had paid more attention to my father's strategy, tactics, and logic lessons, I thought – but Wurgan, my brother, had always been the better at that kind of thing. I just lived for the hunt, and the mountains.

"And the flying, it seems," purred a bright and fresh reptilian voice in my mind, as I realized that the mental praise-chatter of the dragon had died down to a murmur as Paxala instead spoke directly to my mind with her own.

"Yes," I murmured, seeing Neill look up briefly, before nodding and huddling back low down onto the makeshift saddle we had built on Paxala's shoulders and neck, between her spines. He was used to me half-talking to Paxala, both in my mind and with my words, and it didn't appear to bother him at all (although I must have looked odd).

"How are they doing, Pax?" I asked of the other dragons that followed us.

"Morax is doing well," Paxala said, a very slight tail twitch towards the Sinuous Blue that both Lila and Terrence rode. Morax was young, very young in fact – but her sharp temperament (and even sharper nips that she gave with her teeth) had seemed to match with Lila Penna's prickly nature. It was a blessing in some ways that Morax the Blue was indeed so young, as she would play and roughhouse with Lila and Terence, but did not react with outright aggression or fear at the idea of being ridden by a human.

"Socolia is more nervous," Paxala said, indicating the stockier Vicious Green that Sigrid Fenn rode, alone. They, too, had appeared to bond on the small forays that we had made into

the dragon crater, and they (Sigrid and Lila) had been a part of our original mission to try and liberate the dragon eggs from Zaxx. Perhaps it was because of this early goodwill that the other dragons warmed to them, or perhaps it was because they were women for all I knew – as it seemed that the dragons got on better with us women of the monastery than they did the men! *Maybe us women had to listen to our dragons more, as the men always relied on their muscles to yank at the reins, or shouting to get their dragons to hear them...*

"Ha!" Paxala returned into my mind to laugh at my suggestion, but I didn't know if that was because it was true, or not.

Behind Morax and Socolia came two more dragons, another green which was always trying to fly next to Socolia, and another Blue on the far side. I did not know their names, and neither did I ask Paxala for them, as it seemed to me that the dragons were very private creatures when it came to their names, and it was only after they had started to bond, connect, or otherwise communicate with a human did their name get 'released' into the wild, as it were. What was it Feodor told me, before? I felt a pang of sadness over that brave souls' death at the hands of the Abbot. *Keep your dragon's name a secret, as it may grant power.*

But the sight of those other two dragons following along behind us – and even managing to stay in a sort of V-shaped formation flight despite not having any riders at all, filled me with hope. They will be the next to bond with a human, I thought, feeling, right now, almost happy at what we were doing.

"Char! Smoke!" Paxala invaded my optimistic reverie to inform me, her awareness pushing my mind to the horizon.

"There's nothing there," I said in confusion. All I could see instead were the hazes and smudges of the horizon where the land and woods turned into brown, orange, and green watercolors.

"Wait for it," the lizard beneath me counselled. *"I forget that you humans don't have noses. Or eyes."*

"I do!" I contested. "They're just a bit *smaller* than yours, that's all."

A moment or so later, though, and I could see just how right that she was. The horizon's colors deepened slightly, and out of the haze came a smudge of something darker, and then darker still – a small blot of dark black and grey, that rose into the air before being tugged apart by higher winds.

"Neill!" I shouted, pointing to the rising column of smoke that rose below and ahead of us.

I saw Neill nod, and then make a gesture with a hand, sweeping around the smoke and coming across low, like a fish eagle might do. I gave him a thumbs-up sign, and conveyed our intentions to Paxala.

"Easy!" she reassured me, and then I felt that strange moment of twittering tension in my mind, like hearing a conversation just out of reach, or of suddenly finding yourself walking through pre-storm clouds; a pressure and a heaviness to the air that meant Paxala was talking to the other dragons in whatever strange mental language they shared. I wondered if this was what it was like for Neill all those seasons, hanging around me. Did he 'almost' hear my conversations with Paxala, the way that I could

'almost' overhear the conversations Paxala was having in her dragon tongue?

Whichever, there was little time for speculation as I nodded to Neill, who held up one finger, and then made a big show of pointing at his eyes.

"He just wants one pass, to look at everything," I reiterated for the benefit of Paxala, who again relayed those instructions through the tension-language I felt in the space between my ears.

"Grakkle," Sigrid's Green, Socolia, answered aloud with a whistling chatter.

"Skrey-eww-char-eww!" Paxala said, her tail lashing back and forth in the air as she started to beat her wings, and climbing to prepare for her swooping fly-by.

"What was that?" I asked, able to sense the humor emanating from the dragon beneath me.

"Socolia just wanted to ask what good allowing the human to look at things will do, when he can't even see his own tail!" Paxala said with another chirrup of laughter.

"But humans don't have tails," I pointed out.

A moment's silence from the dragon below me, and then, *"Char shouldn't worry about it, it's dragon humor,"* she said wryly, before, with a final flap, she filled her wings like a sail, hung almost motionless for just a moment, and then started to drop forward.

My stomach lurched, as the world tilted towards me, and the horizon swung upwards. Everything was so delicate and graceful for just one pure second, and then—

"SKREYAAR!"

We roared downwards towards the column of smoke, accelerating with every heartbeat. What was the cause of that smoke? My heart was in my mouth. Are we flying into battle? But already we were moving faster than a hunting hawk, or a killing arrow. We were speed incarnate.

CHAPTER 5
NEILL, DRAGON RIDER

The black smudge became smoke, rising from a settlement, rising from the flames that engulfed a wooden tower that had once sat proud beside a long, thin lake. *Sheerlake.* My heart lurched, recognizing what I saw in front of me. One of the settlements of the Eastern Marches, almost all the way out on the edges of the Clan Torvald land. I was surprised at how quickly we had flown, and once again marveled at a dragon's way to use the different air currents to speed across the face of the world. Farther ahead of us in the west rose the Gorstan Heights, a range of hills that turned wild and cracked, treacherous and heavy with woods and waterfalls. This was the extremes of the Middle Kingdom, where the laws and the dictates of Prince Vincent were seldom even heard, let alone obeyed.

And it was also the hunting place of bandit kings and renegade lords. Like the Blood Baron, I thought with a snarl as the world rushed up to greet me.

In just the fraction of time it had taken to register all of this, the tower had grown tall in my vision, and I realized that we were now flying lower than the smoke, in an arrow-sharp flight that would send us screaming low over the waters of Sheerlake, and right beside the wharfs and rickety piers of these lake people.

It wasn't just the tower that was burning, however, it was the village itself. The houses were mostly wooden log cabins and halls (like many of the settlements in clan land), and the palisade walls had been breached – a large section near the wooden gates had been burst apart as if by a giant hand, and the ground was churned and blackened with mud and fighting.

And now there were small shapes amidst the wreckage. Bodies on the ground, most wearing the simple tunics and furs of Torvald clansmen and women.

"Char!" I called out from my seat behind her between the shoulder spines, in our makeshift saddle. I saw her worried expression and pale face nodding that she had seen it, but she also pointed to the collection of ferries and small fishing boats that clustered the tiny fishing port.

There was movement there. People still alive!

"Skreayar!" Paxala bellowed as she flew, although whether in fierce joy at her speed or in challenge I didn't know. There was an answering shriek and echoing boom from behind us as the blue and green dragons kept their formation, and flew in our slip-stream towards the wharfs.

The clanspeople of Sheerlake were engaged in a desperate rearguard action as they fought their way to the small flotilla of fishing vessels and boats; already there was a ragged line of boats and rafts making their way out into the center of the lake, away from the fire. Coming behind them, releasing a hail of arrows, came the bandits of the Blood Baron. As I watched, help-lessly, the burly fur-clad warriors brandished their axes, mallets, and swords, preparing to cleave the last of the defenders of the ferries, as the Blood Baron's soldiers sought to finish off their murderous campaign against the fleeing refugees. In one of those awful, perfect moments of stop-motion time that happens when flying at such speeds, I saw a black arrow skipping the water below the dragon's belly as we flew over, churning the water in our wake, and zipping under the tower and out across the ends of the lake as Paxala shot back up into the sky.

"Neill!?" Char was shouting just behind me. "What do we do?"

"Skrech!" Paxala rumbled, and, as she did so I saw the blue and green carrying Sigrid, and Terrence and Lila shoot past the tower just as we had done, and then rise in the air to follow our trajectory. The final two dragons – the riderless blue and the green had been following our flight formation, but broke off before they swept under the tower smoke, seemingly alarmed by the fires and the shouts and screams to break up their sharp swoop: they flapped and turned, seeking higher and cleaner airs.

Pheet! Pheet! More of the nasty black arrows soared up into the heavens – this time at the riderless dragons as the Blood Baron's men changed their target to what was clearly a much more pressing threat.

"No!" Char shouted, as the offending barbs struck at the slowly moving, lumbering forms of the riderless blue and green dragons – but no harm appeared to have been done, as the dragons merely shuddered, shaking their scales in a rattling storm of noise as they flew higher.

"Dragon! Dragon attack!" the Baron's fighters shouted as we circled the burning remains of Sheerlake. I didn't have long, and so I tried to think. What should I do? What would a Son of Torvald do?

Trap them by the water's edge, my father's words rose unbidden into my mind, almost as if he were standing there right at my shoulder. I had spent years listening to his councils – whether as a child I would play on the bearskin rug as he conducted his meetings and strategies, or when I had been older, and actually allowed out onto the training fields along with my brothers.

That was what I would do if I had a force of warriors, I thought. I would use their own devastation and wanton destruction against them, turning the burning village into a trap which *they* had to defend if they wanted to live.

I was shocked at how coldly I was thinking. It had been a long time since I had thought like a 'proper' Son of Torvald; one who could make those sorts of life and death decisions with such casual ease. It was like listening to the dramatic boasts and exploits of my brothers Rubin and Rik. The long last month that I had spent in the Dragon Monastery had been a time of challenges and stresses, of course, but also of waking up every morning knowing that I was surrounded by allies and friends. I hadn't been thinking with the language of blood and terror for a long time, and now I wondered if I had even missed it at all.

But I had to answer my father's call. I gestured to Char that we should circle around to the other side of the tower, the land side, so that we could trap them there—

"Oh no." I saw Char's words as she mouthed them rather than heard them, and saw, over her shoulder, that the two rider-less dragons were already coming to much the same conclusion that I had. The Sinuous Blue had snaked over the wreckage of the town to land in the smoke-free churned areas beyond, whilst the riderless stocky Green, still getting peppered with arrows from the marauders below, was coming down hard and fast in a fury of wings and claws.

"They're going to attack!" Char shouted – and this time I did hear her over the roar of the wind as Paxala flew. She was right. Without any clear orders or direction, the two crater dragons were doing what their instincts dictated to them: eliminate the threat.

It must be the long years of living under Zaxx the Golden's terrible rule, I thought. They have learnt how to be cruel, and to defend themselves, and now that they have all of this giddy freedom of flying far beyond the crater without Zaxx bellowing at them, they were doing just what Zaxx would do.

But was it so bad? Wasn't it exactly what I had intended to ask of them? I wondered as Char wheeled Paxala around to the far side of the village. It was, after all, just what a Son of Torvald would do…

WHOOOSH! The Blue, already landed, managed to roar a jet

of dragon flame at the offending town that had challenged it.

Oh no.

Dragon fire isn't the same as ordinary fire, it is not fragile and blown away with the wind or extinguished so easily with water and rain. I knew that they made it in their necks somehow, the sides of their lower necks swelling and becoming hot as they shot out a bolt of ferocious energy at their target. The fire could stick to buildings and people, before burning itself (and its target) away to nothing more than melt, slag, and ash. If the village of Sheerlake wasn't already destroyed, then it would be in a matter of minutes.

As I watched, the stocky Green dragon landed, crashing into one section of the still-standing palisade wall with its back claws, ripping the wooden stakes and beams apart as easily as if it were kindling for a hearth fire. Now on the ground, the Green roared its challenge into the sky, and its neck started to swell.

Your father had wanted aid in defeating the Blood Baron, that small, cold and cruel part of me that had been raised by Rubin's and Rik's beatings advised. What could be a more surer destruction of that hated figure, than turning the captured village he cowered in, into a towering inferno?

"No," I said, as much to the memory of my brothers as to what I saw was about to happen. "Char — we can't let them do this!" I shouted, and I saw that she understood, nodding. The wails of the last survivors of Sheerlake out on the lake rose to my ears, and it sounded like a plea for help.

This destruction is not how I wanted the Dragon Monastery to operate, I thought. I wanted the people of the Middle Kingdom, of all of the Three Kingdoms, of the entire world to look upon dragons as I knew that Char and the other students and I did: warily, but with respect and wonder, even with friendship.

What are the survivors of Sheerlake going to say now about what happened here? That the dragons of the Draconis Order were flown here, and that they destroyed the village and everyone in it? The hope that Rudie's arrival had brought for our future would be dashed before it had even begun.

But Char, it seems, had already communicated with Paxala, as I felt a pressure against my mind as I always did as they talked, and Paxala made a whistling, shrieking noise as she dove down towards the riderless Green and Blue.

"Screch-ip! Ip-ach-ech! Skree-Skree!" She whistled and shrieked as she swooped to an elegant landing beside the Blue. The riderless Blue flinched and lowered his head, backing away from the much larger Crimson Red.

"Vsss!" The Blue hissed at Paxala, but Paxala just snarled and stamp-scratched at the floor, causing the Sinuous Blue to lash its tail as it took a few more steps back.

"I'm telling Paxala to call off the others," Char was saying ahead of me, and I could already see that it was working. Far above us, the other two dragons (Terence and Lila, and then Sigrid on her Green) circled the tower, unsure what to do. As Char and Paxala negotiated, I waved to the higher-up dragons, indicating that they had to go to the *far* side of the town, the lake side, to try and help the refugees, as well as to block any escape for the Blood Baron's soldiers. We could arrest the Blood Baron's warriors when they realize that they are surrounded, I thought. No more have to die this day, if they recognize the strength that we have…

It was frustrating, waving and signaling to them from on the ground as Paxala was already busy arguing with the hissing and stamping riderless green. There has to be an easier way to do this, I reasoned, until eventually I saw the Sinuous Blue bearing Lila and Terence take the hint, and the team darted down to the other side of the lake, and Sigrid on her Vicious Green wobbled a little unsteadily after them.

Phew! This dragon-wrangling was proving *a lot* harder than I had originally thought.

Pheet! Pheet! More small arrows shot out from the burning remains of Sheerlake, as some of the warriors, seeing the dragons descending to the water line there decided to try and escape in *our* direction. I watched as one of the arrows splintered on stone, and another landed in a still-standing section of palisade wood with a loud *thock!*

"Hsssss!" The Vicious Green lashed its tail once more in fury at the challenge, dismantling a hovel as it did so.

"Easy!" Char shouted across to it, raising her hands in that universal calming gesture. Below her, Paxala was also making a lowing, gentler noise at the Green, who raised her snout defiantly, but did not fire on our attackers.

Pheet! Another arrow skittered across the rocks.

"Really!?" I shouted into the ruins at wherever our attackers were crouching and hiding in the ruins of Sheerlake. "We're on *dragons*. You can't scare these dragons off. You cannot drive them away."

The arrows stopped coming at us, but there was no answering call.

"Char...?" I muttered under my breath to my friend ahead of me. "Can you stop these dragons from killing the next humans they see, just for a moment?"

"I have no idea," my friend answered. "But Paxala is threatening all sorts of things if they do not listen up and start thinking."

Good. It'll have to do, I thought, as I turned to address the burning ruins of Sheerlake beyond us.

"We are the *new* Dragon Order, and these dragons have come to the aid of the people of Sheerlake. Lay down your weapons and come out, and I promise you that you won't be harmed." *I hope.*

Still, no sound from the ruins. I would just have to try again.

"Blood Baron! You are responsible for crimes against the Eastern Marches, against the Torvald Clan, against the Middle Kingdom *and* the people of Sheerlake here. Do not add a whole brood of angry dragons to your list of enemies!" I demanded, half rising from my seat to shout at him. "Now come out, hands up, weapons down, and I promise that you will get a free and fair trial. I will give you to the count of three to respond to my offer — we *can* go in after you on the back of these dragons, but I think that you will find that you are surrounded, and none of you wants to fight an already angry dragon, do you?"

Silence, save for the burning of wood and the collapse of weakened timber.

Oh hell, I thought. This was also not what I wanted to happen. I wanted the dragons to be a force for good in the world, not always to be doing the bloody and terrible work that would make them feared.

"One," I shouted, my eyes scanning the wreckage for any sign that they were about to follow my demands. Nothing.

"Two…" I called again, starting to sweat as Paxala tensed beneath me, anticipating violence.

I raised my hands to my mouth to shout the final number, when suddenly there was movement from the smoke-filled wreckage. A clang as a shield and an ax hit the floor, and out came running a large warrior, his beard and face blackened with soot.

Damn, I need some ground soldiers to be able to round up the prisoners, I was thinking as the man ran out, terrified, and immediately started to edge away from the dragons to run into the wilds. Before I could say anything, the riderless Blue a little behind us growled and half-pounced, landing with a thump a few meters in front of the warrior, snarling.

"Aii!" the warrior wailed in fear, falling to his knees with his hands still above his head. "Don't let it eat me – please! Don't let the thing cook me or eat me!"

"Thing…?" Char snorted in indignation, but before I could smooth over the situation, there were already other soldiers running out of the fog of war and burning Sheerlake. They, too, dropped their weapons as they ran, first in any direction at all (away from the fire) until they saw the fury of the Vicious Green, her head low and her tail slapping the ground behind her, raising up clods of dirt with every swipe. With low groans and fearful moans, they backed towards where their friend was already shuddering on the floor.

It's working, sorta! A glimmer of hope sparked in my heart as the warriors knelt on the floor, their arms in the air.

"Where's the Blood Baron?" I asked them. The men glanced among themselves but none answered. In frustration, I slid from Paxala's back to the ground below, striding towards them.

"Neill – be careful," Char said, but I was angry. I was angry at these warriors for choosing to protect their murderous lord, and I was angry at myself for having to act like this. I didn't want this for myself, I kept thinking, as my frustration and anger mounted. I don't want the Draconis Order to be the arbiters of justice. I just wanted us to round up the monsters and the bandits and hand them over to my father for judgment.

Now, it felt like these Blood Baron men, in their unthinking loyalty to their lord, would force me to act to try and threaten and intimidate them. *Is this what a lord has to do? A 'master'?*

"Where is the Blood Baron!" I demanded again, now that I stood under the snarling snout of the riderless Blue. I knew the Blue could sense my own anger, and was only adding to it with his own snarling rage. I wonder if I felt then an echo of that dragon's rage as well, making me want to teach all of these stupid bandits, thugs, and killers a lesson that they could never forget...

"Here," growled a voice, as one of the warriors who had fled with the others stood up slowly. I was shocked at how old he was. He looked not a little like my own father, but with fiery red and sunburst hair and beard (now laced with white), one eye gone milky, and a barrel of a chest that came from decades of fighting and harsh living. He leered at me with blackened and broken teeth. "I am the Blood Baron. What are *you* going to do, little boy?"

It was true that he must have been almost four times my age, but I had something that he didn't. I had the friendship of dragons.

"Blood Baron, you are charged with treason, murder, looting, robbery, theft, and taking up arms against your sworn lord," I said.

The Blood Baron spat on the floor. "Treason? Taking up arms?" he said with a stubborn snarl. "Against whom? We all here can see what is going to happen next. The Middle Kingdom has become a battlefield with Prince Vincent too busy fighting his northern border war with his own brother, and with Warden of the Eastern Marches dying in his sickbed not a day from here. It's every village for itself, now, kid. You think that the Prince Vincent cares about this place? About what happens out here?"

The horrible man was right, of course, only he wasn't right about one thing. He'd forgotten that I was the one standing before him, with a collection of very large, and very angry dragons at his throat.

"*I* care," I said, finding what I said to be true. "I care what happens to this place, and these dragons care. So, Baron, you are going to subject yourself to justice."

"Under whose authority?" the Baron snarled back. I'll say this about him—he was certainly brave (if perhaps more than a little stubborn and foolhardy at the same time).

It was Char who answered him, calling out over my head. "Under the authority of the Dragon Order."

The Blood Baron blinked, then his face collapsed into a scowl once more. Even he could not deny the obvious authority that we had, I saw as his eyes flickered from the snarling dragons to the woman behind me sitting up on the saddle on Paxala's neck. Grumbling, he sat back down, and I felt a surge of savage joy.

～

"Neill!" It was Lila, waving her arm at me from where the two dragons stood, half in the waters of the lake. I had just left Char and Paxala in charge of the warrior and made my way around the edge of the ruined town to check on the others. They were helping out the survivors, the dragons using their tails or paws to create waves to lap their boats easily ashore, farther away from their smoking homes.

Lila and Terence's Sinuous Blue dragon, Morax, was even wading out to gently grasp one of the largest of the Sheerlake refugee rafts with the tip of its teeth, pulling it gently back into land under the terrified, awe-struck eyes of the refugees within. From where they sat atop Morax's back, both Lila and Terence were grinning wildly– they were just as smitten with their dragon as the refugees seemed to be.

Sigrid, on her Vicious Green Socolia, however, appeared to be having problems. She was now clambering half up the neck of the Green as it decided to wallow in the cooling waters of the lake, and the human girl was angrily pulling at Socolia's horns to try and turn her back towards shore.

I started to laugh, but Sigrid shot me a murderous look.

"It's not funny!" she called out. "She never listens to me! Ever!"

"Maybe you're not asking the right questions!" I called back, before she glared at me. Socolia, the Green, was stocky and was definitely going to do her own thing it seemed, as she settled into the mud of the lake's edge and kept only her head, back ridge and wings above the waters. Sigrid Fenn was stuck, at least until the Green had cooled down. It was hilarious, of course, watching Sigrid huff and plead with her dragon before sitting back down on top of the dragon's head, her arms crossed petulantly over her chest.

But it was still going to be annoying, though. If Sigrid and Socolia cannot perform the tasks that we need them to, then they might have to fly on different, less urgent missions? I sighed, as I walked over to welcome the first of the refugees to shore.

Still too many questions, I thought. Too many questions about what out 'new' Dragon Order could do, and what the dragons would do, and whether any of it would work at all!

"You – you're the boy who rides dragons?" said an elder

40

woman, her hair black but not streaked with grey, and her skin smeared and dusted with soot and ash from her burning home.

"I am," I nodded, as I helped a woman carrying a baby from the raft and up onto the shore. There were more survivors than I had first thought—thankfully— as it seems that the people of Sheerlake had a solid tactic of fleeing out to the center of the lake when threatened, and so a sizeable community of boats, rafts, and platforms had managed to get away before the Blood Baron had set their tower ablaze.

"I am sorry for all that you have lost," I said sincerely, "and I only wish that I could have gotten here sooner." And I'm glad that our dragons didn't finish off the job of destroying your village, I mentally added.

"No, I am only pleased that you got here at all," the elder woman said, encouraging agreement from the others around here. "Sheerlake is ruined, but we can rebuild, and we have each other," she said with a grim smile, before turning her attention to the dragons above us. "They are..." she searched for the words to describe Morax. I saw a handful of expressions flicker across the old woman's face; from surprise to fear, caution, anxiety, joy.

"I had never thought to see one this close," the woman whispered, and all I could think to do was to nod. I didn't want to steal this moment from her and the rest of the refugees by talking. This is their first encounter up close with a dragon, I thought with a sense of pride at how the elder woman stepped towards Morax and gently patted her large scales on her blue legs.

"*Reeyar.*" Morax bent her head down very gently, making a purring growl in her throat as she snuffed at the elder woman, before blinking her eyes and carrying on her way. Although, I knew that to the dragon it was little more than a 'hello, what are you?' to the elder woman it appeared to be like having a spiritual encounter.

"They are so gentle!" the elder woman said in shock.

"When they want to be," I said wryly. *Thank goodness she didn't see what the riderless Green was doing to her village walls before!*

"And they are strong. Yes." The elder woman nodded, before frowning as she looked at me. "But you are not wearing the black. None of you are. You do not seem like Draconis Order monks."

"We're not," I said, feeling oddly fluttery in my chest, as if I were about to lie – but I could find no falsehood in what I was saying. *It's because this is new. You don't know what you are yet, either.* "We're new." I confided in her. "The Draconis Order, as was, has fallen. The old Abbot has gone, but all of us here have had training at the monastery…"

I saw a shadow cross the woman's face; a look of calculation, and worry. The Draconis Order had never really had the best of reputations, and even despite the many of us noble's children who were sent there to train, I rather fear that it had just widened the gulf between the Order and the common folk of the Three Kingdoms. A place full of haughty, arrogant monks who sucked taxes out of the Middle Kingdom treasury for no good reason. The healers and the scribes that it supplied the country were just as corrupt and as self-serving as the Order itself seemed to be, demanding money from their lords for their supplies and their upkeep, and all in the name of 'tradition.'

"But we're not like them," I said quickly. "We…" I searched for a description of what it was that we did. "We are finding ways to work *with* the dragons," I added lamely.

"Hm." The elder woman nodded slowly, frowning a bit at me, before looking up at the bulk of Morax as she ambled up the beach. This time, her look was one of barely-constrained wonder.

"Well, thank you all the same, Master Monk," the elder said.

"Oh, I am no Master Monk at all!" I said quickly, a blush rising to my cheeks. "I am just Neill, Neill of Torvald," I said, before a second later, the woman's face fell.

"Oh, I am so sorry for your loss," she said to me. "None of this would have happened in *his* day, of course…" she added, although I didn't know precisely how that was meant to be congratulatory.

His day? I wondered. *My loss.* "I'm sorry, I don't quite know that I follow you. Whose loss?" I asked with a distracted, bemused grin on my face.

"Your father, of course," the elder woman said. "You're Neill of Torvald, you said, so I suppose that you must be the same Neill Torvald who was sent off to train at the Draconis Order, right?" Sheerlake was, still, technically under my father's protection and counted among the lands of Clan Torvald. Many people here would know the story of the mighty Malos Torvald, Clan Chief and Chief Warden, and his three sons Rubin, Rik, and Neill.

"I am," I said a little uneasily.

"Then I am sorry for the loss of your father," the elder woman intoned sadly. "A messenger reached us just last night, a few hours before the attack by the Blood Baron himself. Your father was a good man."

Was he? I thought, reeling. My father was dead, I kept on thinking, the words rolling around and around in my head in an endless loop. My father was dead.

CHAPTER 6
NEILL, MOURNING

"My father is dead." It was strange, to think those words, and even stranger to say them out loud. I stood in front of the small camp we had set up (with the help of the people of Sheerlake), as the sun started to set, casting the water into a sea of burnt rose and bronze.

"Oh Neill," Char said, standing up from the fire to rush over to me, flinging her arms around my shoulders and hugging me. I didn't move. I didn't know what to do in response to that.

I felt weird. Hollow, in a way. Like this was news that had happened to someone else, not me, and not my father. *How distant had I grown from him over the last few years?* He was a man who I respected, I admired, and yes, and I had to admit that I loved him – but he was always a distant figure. Someone at the far end of a council hall, someone stalking away from me and calling for his spurs and his shield, someone at the other end of a letter.

"It's going to be okay…" Char said as she pulled away from me, but I could see she didn't believe it any more than I did. Char's own relationship with her father was complicated as well. Just a few months ago he had tried to marry her off to secure a coveted tribal alliance with the mountain people of her Northern Kingdom, and from what she had told me, her father, the Prince Lander, had done little more than regard her as an asset for his royal strategies.

Malos Torvald wasn't as bad as all that, of course. I knew he had thought well of me, at least, but just like Prince Lander, he had been too involved in his strategies, tactics, skirmishes, and politics to ever give me anything greater than essential training.

So, why was I upset? I thought, before realizing, with the next breath, I wasn't. I felt numb and oddly floating in mid-air, like the world beneath me had grown insubstantial.

"I've already tasked Lila and Terence with watching over the prisoners, and a team from the Sheerlake refugees are going to be leading them to your father's fort," Char said. "We don't have to get back too early to the monastery, do we? We have time…"

"Time for what?" I asked, confused.

"Time to fly to your father's fort!" Char looked surprised. "To bury your father, of course."

"Oh," I nodded. The idea hadn't even occurred to me that it was something that I should be doing at all. Ever since my brothers had attacked the Dragon Monastery last year (or tried to, anyway, before being repelled by the Abbot Ansall's dark magics, and indeed by me on Paxala's back), I had thought less and less of myself even as a Torvald at all. I had switched allegiances to the dragons of the crater, to my friends Dorf, and Maxal, Sigrid, Jodreth—and of course Char.

I sat by the fire, dumbly accepting the pot of fish stew that was pushed into my hands. It was garlicky and rich, tangy with pepper, salty-creamy with the fish, and filled with delicate new potatoes. It was simple fare, and it should have been delicious. *Then why couldn't I eat it?* I thought, taking a few slurps before putting the cup of stew down by the fire. Char sighed from beside me.

"You have to go, Neill. He was your father, after all," she said.

"I know. It's just…. We were so different. And my brothers declared me a traitor, and my father did nothing to stop them…" All of a sudden, my hot anger returned at the betrayal I felt from my family. Rubin and Rik had hated me all of my life, for being born of a Gypsy mother after my father's first wife (their mother) had died. We were all motherless sons, but it seemed that Rubin and Rik deemed that I was less of a 'true Torvald' than they obviously were. "My brothers, Rubin and Rik, had beaten me on regular occasions when they had thought that father wasn't looking. But surely father must have known…" I tried to explain some of my complicated thoughts and feelings to Char. "He must have seen what was going on," I said, as the same old knot of ugly thoughts that I always had whenever I thought of my family welled up inside of me.

"Could he have stopped them, though?" Char said at my side as she sat on the rock beside me. "You told me yourself he had been shot in some skirmish or another. That he was ill."

"And poisoned," I added. Clan Torvald's Healer Garrett had been one of Abbot Ansall's spies. The Abbot himself had told me that I had to work for him or else the healer wouldn't reverse whatever horrible poison he was giving him. I shuddered. "I think that my brothers killed Garrett in the end." I remember Rubin saying something about it, but even back then I had blanked out the grisly details.

"So, there you go…" Char tried to reassure me, setting the delicious and bland cup of fish stew back into my hands. "Your father might even have been too ill to understand what was going on. Certainly, he wasn't well enough to stop them when they rode to attack the monastery."

"Great," I said, but now there was a terrible image in my head of my father wasting away on his sickbed, whilst I ignored him. My anger at my family turned into the hot shame and guilt of being a terrible son.

There is no way that I could lead the Dragon Order, not now, I thought to myself. I cannot. I can't even look after my own father – how can I have Char and Paxala and the others relying on me to make the right decision?

"Neill," Char said sharply, once again putting the cup of fish stew in my hands after I had unconsciously set it on the floor just a moment ago. "Listen to me, Neill. You are my friend, and I know you. You are a good man, Neill, son of Torvald, and I am willing to bet that your father saw that in you as well. You have saved *my* life more than once, as well as Paxala's, our friends'… You are not defined by whatever madness your brothers decided to commit."

"Yeah." I nodded wearily. I knew that, I had to admit. I knew that there was so much more to me now than just being a 'son of Malos Torvald' – but what I was having trouble asking myself was what I *should* be, and what I *could* be. Before I could even pursue that line of thought, however, Char stood up and tapped the top of the cup of fish stew, still warm in my hands.

"Now, eat that, or I swear to the stars I will force it down your throat. And tomorrow, we are going to get up bright and early, and you are going to take me and Paxala to the Fort of Torvald, where we will pay our last respects. Understood?"

"Uh, yeah." I nodded, not really sure what I was agreeing to – but right now it just seemed easier to take orders than to give them.

CHAPTER 7
NEILL, RETURNING

The Fort, as we still called my family's ancestral home and town, stood on a broad hill overlooking a wide valley. It was a good, strong, defensible position, as apparently my great-grandfather had said when he'd raised the Fort's walls. It was dominated by a broad, sprawling hall that had reinforced ramparts, which were really wooden balconies underneath the broad eaves. Over the years, adjoining halls had been added to form wings – each with their own collection of hearths, sleeping quarters, and training areas.

It rose on the horizon in dawn's grey light, looking not so much as the expansive *home* that I had once imagined it to be, but instead like a slouching, snarling dog.

It's so small, I thought as we flew down towards it, raising up flocks of crows and magpies from the nearby coppices of the valley, and warning bleats of the flocks of the sheep and goats that the Torvald clanspeople kept. And so...simple, I couldn't help seeing. The outer walls were still the same old tree-trunk palisades, sharpened to spikes, with internal balcony walkways from which the guards were gesturing and shouting at us. The Fort had very few stone buildings like the sort that Prince Lander had in his town, or that I had seen elsewhere on our aerial journeys.

The Fort's wooden walls contained open pens for the animals and about the thatched roofs hung a haze of rising smokes from morning cook fires, smokehouses, and the baths. The purple and green pennants and banners of Torvald colors fluttered in the morning light, but they looked tired, tattered, washed and re-dyed, patched and re-sown with care but without access to the fine silks and rare dying powders that the monastery had. Our Torvald austerity was self-imposed, I knew. Even though we were one of the most powerful clans in all of the Middle Kingdom, my father was adamant that the money returned to the defenses of the Eastern Marches, to building wells and maintaining bridges, for raising work teams to build more walls, more guard towers. Few if any luxuries were permitted inside the Fort. It was one of the many reasons why my father hated – *had* hated, I corrected myself – Prince Vincent with all of his love for spending the people's taxes on lavish parties, balls, and architectural wonders.

I didn't want to admit it, but I felt a little disappointed as we flew towards home. Its spartan demeanor, its overt militarism made me feel more than I ever had like the Torvald Clan was mean and small-minded. Could they not raise a few more statues, or even parks, for the good of the people?

"Neill?" Char was asking me worriedly as we flew closer, and I nodded that I saw the guards already rushing to the gates. Big, strong Torvald men and women with long spears and short bows, readied to fire on the offending dragon that dared to approach their heartland.

I unfurled in my hand the purple and green banner that Rudie had brought with him, signaling to us that he was an emissary from my family. I held it out, letting it flutter and crack in the wind as Char directed Paxala to circle the great fort once, twice, before descending to a flapping, furious wing beats in the central space that made up our main training ground.

"Dragon! The Dragon Rider has come!" people shouted, although it wasn't in awe or joy, but in fear.

"The Order! The Order is here!" Clansmen and women rushed to shutter their windows and doors, as guards ran to seize weapons and edge to the entrances of the central training ground. In front of us stood the strong wooden gatehouse of the Fort, usually kept open as every Torvald clan member was free to wander in and out of the central hall to seek audience with the Chief.

Or so it had been, once. Now I saw that the gates were closed, and piles of purple-headed thistles with their dark green stems and spikes had been laid in front of the door.

Oh yeah. The Fort is in mourning. Mourning for my father.

"What is the meaning of this?" shouted one of the head guards there, a clan's warrior that I recognized with his long wild brown hair and brown beard, limping towards us.

"Captain Garf the Lame," I recognized and called out to him, waving the flag of Torvald. "Do you not recognize me, Garf?" I asked. Garf had been the wall captain here for as long as I could remember, a close bond-warrior and blood brother to my father. Garf had fought at my father's side on many campaigns, and now had been given the 'reward' of maintaining the gatehouse, the walls, and the front gates of the Fort. He had never had much time for me, but he had taught me and my brothers in wall defenses on several bruising occasions.

"Neill? Is that you?" Garf said, a look of suspicion and surprise mingling on his scarred and ruddy features. "I had heard the stories that it was you who had become the Dragon Rider of the Order, but I never believed it..." Garf thumped his chest, a sign of honor. "Now look at you – little Neill, riding a dragon!"

"Thank you, Garf," I said, not really knowing what I was thanking him for, as our roles felt strange now. He was always the grumpy, older soldier to me, and now he was looking at me as if I were a captain in my own right, and not the bastard half-Gypsy child of his liege lord.

Char coughed beside me.

"Oh yes, this is the Princess Char Nefrette of the North, and this," I inclined my head to where the Crimson Red beneath us was looking at Garf inquisitively, delicately sniffing the air in his direction. "Is the red dragon, our friend," I said.

"Ski-rip!" Paxala chirruped her assent at me, blowing a small puff of sooty smoke, causing a ripple of exclamations from the watching Torvald Clan.

"We have come to pay our respects to the passing of my father, captain," I announced as I rolled up the Torvald flag, set it in my pack and eased myself out of the saddle. "When is the ceremony? Where are my brothers?"

"Your brothers…?" Garf said awkwardly, looking worriedly from me to the dragon.

"Yes, Garf – where are they?" I asked again, a tremor of agitation rising in me. The last time that I had met with my brothers, the whole exchange had ended with them declaring me a traitor to Torvald, and then putting a bag over my head and knocking me unconscious. It was not the sort of thing that I would forget in a hurry, but I reminded myself that I did not come here for them. I came here for my father.

Too little too late, a dark, cynical part of me reminded myself, and once again my heart lurched into darkness.

"Easy, Neill." Char laid a hand on my shoulder, and I turned to her. Could she read me so well, as to know even when I was upset?

"It's okay," I said under my breath, turning back to Garf, who was looking at the dragon warily.

"All she needs is some fish and an undisturbed space," Char advised, before stopping suddenly and inclining her head towards where Paxala was looking at her. "Anyway, she says that she will be happy in the valley, by the river. As long as none of your warriors seek to approach her…" Char suddenly smirked as I felt that buzzing sound between her and the dragon again. "And, if they do," she repeated Paxala's threat, "she'll have to consider her lunch to be some of those fat little sheep you have around here."

"She won't be disturbed!" Garf said quickly, still looking

confused between me, Char, and the dragon behind us. "I'll send word to all of the warriors now, and she'll have free rein of the rivers..."

You couldn't stop her even if you wanted to, I thought, as Garf hurriedly gave the orders to the other guards as Char patted Paxala's nose, shared some more thoughts, and stepped back to let her reptilian friend leap into the air, and dart as fast as an arrow towards the river. Even though she was not at our side anymore, I did not feel threatened by being surrounded by the guards of my brother's forces. The dragon could be here in a heartbeat if we were threatened, and I knew that Char would be in constant contact with her.

"Now, Garf, as you were saying about my brothers?" I said with a smile that I did not feel. The old gate captain indicated for us to walk with him as he led the way around the front gatehouse to one of the side entrances into the main Fort. I could feel the people watching our backs as we walked, but they could not overhear our discussions.

"Your brothers, sire," Garf demurred, looking uncomfortable. I kept silent, waiting for him to fill in the blanks. "They are taking your father's death very hard."

"Of course." I nodded. They had been closer to him than me. They were the big and strong, true-born, fighting Sons of Torvald who had accompanied him on campaigns and trained with him when I had been too young to do anything but stay at home and look after the horses.

"They... they blame the Draconis Order," Garf said, with a look of skepticism and doubt.

"As well they should," I growled.

"Oh." Garf frowned. "But you... you are now the Dragon Rider of the Order, are you not, Neill?"

Did he think that I had come to inflict the Draconis Order 'justice' on them for daring to attack the monastery last year? That I had come as a messenger? I sighed, feeling the weight of the wall I would have to cross to get my family and clan to ever see dragons in the same way that I did.

"That Draconis Order is dead and gone, Garf," I murmured. "The old Abbot has been exiled, and we have a new Order now..."

"Yes, but..." Garf made to say, before shaking his head.

"You think that we're going to be just as bad as before?" I spoke what the old warrior must be thinking.

"Of course not, sire," Garf lied as we approached one of the side doors and he unhooked the heavy iron keys from his belt to unlock it.

"We're different, Garf. We ride dragons, as you yourself said. But we have excommunicated all of those monks who had anything to do with the ways of the old Abbot," I explained, feeling tired.

"I see, sire. But these are dark times..." Garf said as he swung open the door to the sound of lyre music and the smell of wood smoke and cooking meat. "Your brothers have declared themselves at war with everyone. With the Order that killed their father, with anyone who would seek to threaten their land..." Garf shook his head. "No clan warriors have been allowed to leave Fort on the patrols that we used to."

That is why Sheerlake fell, I thought, feeling a surge of anger. "What?"

But before I could take out my astonishment and outrage on poor old Garf, my frustration was redirected by a rising shout from inside.

"Just *what* is the meaning of this?" It was my brash and heavily built brother Rik – rising from the oaken Chief's chair that dominated the hall, surrounded by lounging warriors and attendants, all of them clearly having drunk and feasted their way through the night. Rik was the middle Torvald son, and my most vociferous accuser all through my childhood.

The main hall, however, looked different from how I remembered it. It was smaller, to start with, and it was messy. This place had never been messy in my father's time, I thought with a rising sense of indignation. There were stools and benches upturned, there were tables still laden with the remains of last night's feast, there were warriors lying on rugs in front of hearths, still snoring. Someone had taken down the banners and the display weapons that had hung at intervals along the ways and clearly used them in some mock tournament, leaving them on the floor or tables where they had discarded them.

"What is the meaning of *this?*" I counter-demanded of Rik. I no longer feared of my larger, meaner, baleful big brother. Somewhere along the way I had lost all of that fear over what he might do to me or how he might look at me. "Look at yourself, Rik. Would Father be proud of the way that you use his hall?"

"My father," Rik spat, stumbling down the dais that held the Chief's chair and pointing at me as the other groggy warriors started to scramble for their weapons. "*My* father would want me to run a sword through the heart of the treacherous little worm who killed him!" he shouted. "Someone! Give me a sword! Now!"

"So that's how it is, is it?" I growled.

"Neill didn't kill your father," Char called urgently, and a bolt of annoyance zagged through me that she sought to stop the bloodshed I was more than ready for. The months and years of riding dragons and training to be a dragon protector had readied me for this, and my hand slipped to the scabbard at my waist, while a warrior fumbled, unbuckling his own sword to give to my brother. He was still drunk. This would be an easy kill.

"*Skreyaarch!*" A muffled, distant sound from Paxala came from far above the walls, making my brother blink in confusion.

"Yes, sire," Garf said from where he stood at my side. "They came on the back of a red dragon. The Crimson Red that drove away our soldiers before…"

"Ach!" That only infuriated Rik the more. "You see? He's come to finish the job, clearly…" He snatched the scabbard and belt from the inebriated warrior, before himself dropping it onto the floor and cursing at his own irate clumsiness.

"We haven't come to attack Torvald land!" Char tried again. "And no one here is responsible for your father's death! We threw out those who were! The Draconis Order is no more…"

"I'd shut her up, if I were you, Neill…" Rik slurred his words.

That was it. I took a step forward and punched Rik as hard as I could across the jaw. I had been in a lot of fights with my brothers before – but my relative size compared to them had always meant that it ended up being little more than an effort to stop them from beating me to a bloody pulp. Now, my rage and anger and training combined to deliver my indignation and hurt in one blow.

"Ooof!" my brother exclaimed, though he still stood, swaying slightly on his feet. He looked at me thoughtfully as his tongue moved against his cheek, until he finally spat out a bloodied tooth, and then sat down in a thump on his rump, looking confused. "You learned a thing or two, then..." he said groggily.

"You'll apologize to the *lady* and my friend," I demanded of him.

"Neill... It's all right. The guy is drunk," Char was saying.

"No. It's not all right," I said, a hot, black rage descending over me. Is this what it had come to? Did I have to teach my brothers some manners now? The knuckles on my fist hurt, but my hand itched to move to the pommel of my short sword. *All those years of beatings. Of pinches, of slaps, of sly remarks and curses.*

"Rik?" Another shape appeared behind my brother, and my rage-filled senses revealed that it was Rubin, the biggest and oldest brother of all of us. He was no better than Rik in many ways, but at least he had performed the 'punishments' with a practical emotionlessness. He didn't revel in the cruelty and power that he could have over his weaker victims like Rik did. Instead, my eldest brother Rubin just believed fully, and totally, in the Torvald way. That you only learned by getting the facts beaten into you, and the mistakes beaten out. Courage was born through strife and struggle, and the fact that I was the smallest and weaker brother – taking after my thin-limbed Gypsy family rather than my stocky Middle Kingdom Torvald one – was a sign of my unwillingness to try harder.

Rubin was a brute, whereas Rik was a shark.

"Brother," I greeted him, still in my warrior's crouch.

"Come on, Rik." Rubin seized my brother under the arms and hauled him to his feet, before setting him down on one of the nearest benches with a heavy thud. "He's sorry. We're sorry for any offence caused," Rubin said. He wasn't drunk like my other brother was, but his eyes still glared at me in suspicion. "I heard that there was a battle up there at your monastery," he said stiffly. "So, I'm willing to give you the benefit of the doubt, at least for now."

Oh thank you, most-gracious Rubin, I thought sarcastically, before biting down on that criticism. He was trying to be like Father. Strategic. Tactical. Intelligent, I saw.

"But what's more important, Neill…. Is that, despite your treachery to us, despite the fact that you worked for the Order, that you rode that dragon against *us,* your own clan…" Rubin's voice grew heavy with accusation and hurt. "Despite all of that, Father still spoke highly of you, right up until the end."

I felt my throat tighten suddenly.

"Father never believed us and we told him that you were a traitor, but I suppose that isn't important now," Rubin muttered. "And in honor of our father's memory, you will get one day of mourning, with us, as a Son of Torvald." His voice turned to a growl. "And then we're done. After today, I don't ever want to see you on Torvald land again."

"But Rubin – he wasn't responsible!" Char burst out, frustrated by my brothers' clear truculence to believe anything but their own views. "How many times do we have to tell you...? It was the old Abbot who poisoned your father, who sought to undermine all of the clans in favor of his own power. We drove the old Abbot off. We drove the old monks out!"

"Maybe so," Rubin said. "But Neill should have flown that dragon out there straight to *us*, for the good of the clan. Not kept it up there for himself."

"You sound just like my father," Char muttered, shaking her head. "The dragons cannot be commanded, not by you, by me, or by anyone. If you want to ally yourself with the dragons, you have to meet with them."

"Enough." Rubin shook his head, a gesture that I knew meant that he was already tired of this talk. "One day, Neill. You have one day. Garf can take you to the tomb, but after that I want you and your dragon gone."

～

"I can't believe that brother of yours!" Char said indignantly, as we strode through the halls of Fort, following the lurching limp of Captain Garf.

"Rik?" I said wearily over my shoulder, my feelings having changed from pure rage to sad resignation. *Why had I expected anything different from them?*

"Rubin," Char said, shaking her head. "I mean, he *knows* that you weren't responsible for Healer Garrett's actions, he has even heard of the battle that we had in the monastery, but still he regards you as an enemy."

"You're either with us or against us." I quoted some oft-repeated choice lines of Torvald history. Of course, it had been because there had been *no one* 'with us' for so long out here in the Western Marches. The entire region was more or less abandoned by Prince Vincent, leaving just us to fight the armies of bandits and outlaws. That self-sufficiency had gradually turned to self-reliance, and eventually it seems, to paranoia.

This is not what I would have wanted for my clan, I thought, not knowing quite how I would be able to change course. Not that Torvald was really my clan in the same way that it was for Rubin and Rik. They saw me as just a bastard, a by-blow of my father's. Not someone to uphold the family name.

"They were probably glad for a reason to cast me out anyway," I said with a wry smile, seeing Chars look of aghast hurt, but curiously not feeling that bad about it. "It's okay, really – it's okay," I said with a hollow laugh. It was odd to finally admit it out loud. But as hard as I tried to always please my father, and as much as I looked up to him - it was always to my Gypsy Uncle Lett Anar that I looked forward to seeing. He regarded me with joy and pride every time. Unconditional acceptance, just for the sake of the blood of his sister and my mother that ran through my veins.

Ahead of us, Garf's footsteps slowed, stumbled, then halted.

"Captain? Are you okay?" I asked him.

"No, I'm not, young sir..." Garf replied sadly.

We had stopped down one of the long halls that formed the 'wings' and adjoining annexes and segments of the Fort. On the wooden board walls hung the pelts of giant black bears and the ancient spears that killed them. All relics of our ancient clan past.

"I've tried to do my duty, Neill, to keep silent and to not make trouble for the clan – but I also can't help overhearing what it is you and the lady Nefrette there are saying..." Garf muttered into his beard. "And I think that you need to see something. Whatever it is that your brothers say – you're still a son to your father, and his blood still runs through your veins," Garf said slowly, clearly reasoning it out at the same time as he told us. I could almost sense him asking himself '*is this treason?*' in the back of his mind.

Garf nodded to himself, before looking at me with his brown, strong eyes. "As you know, sire – I knew your father well. I fought at his side more times that I can recall. We shared blood together. He saved my life, and I daresay that I saved his on more than one occasion. We spent a lot of time campaigning, far from the Fort, holed up in yurts or in muddy fields, and in those times a man learns to trust and talk to his comrades-in-arms," Garf said.

I felt a flutter in my chest, it was almost fear – I wasn't sure that I wanted to know just what this old war dog was going to tell me about my father. *Don't make my heart hurt again,* I begged him silently.

Captain Garf ignored my silent plea. "Your father loved you, Neill," he said, and my heart broke.

"I know that," I said, although I didn't.

"No, Neill, you couldn't," Garf said as tenderly as the large warrior could. "You couldn't know it, because he had to keep you at arm's length all your life. You were not his first-born son, or his second. Your mother was a Gypsy. He had to make sure that the Torvald clanspeople would follow his decisions and his family explicitly, all the time – and he didn't want to cause a rift within his own clan at such a dangerous time by asking them to follow you – his last son, not even his first."

I felt as if he ground was shifting under my feet. "What are you trying to tell me here, Captain Garf?" I asked unsteadily.

Garf frowned, but I could see that it wasn't unkind. "Your father had many faults, don't get me wrong, but he always put the people first. That was *why* he sent you off to that Dragon Monastery in the first place…"

"I know that, Garf," I said, remembering the council that my father had given me and me alone. "He wanted me to steal the secrets of the Draconis Order, for the good of Torvald." *And I hadn't done it. I had tried, but when I had found out that the dragons themselves were the source of the magic of the Abbot, how could I give up these noble and intelligent creatures? How could I try to persuade the dragons to just become servants and war machines of another clan?*

"Yes, but you only got the half of it, Master Torvald," Garf replied irritably. "I know, because he told me. He told me alone of his plans a long time ago, when we were camped out in some scrap of bog waiting for reinforcements. He knew even back then that the Prince Vincent was no leader for the people. He knew that the entire eastern half of the Middle Kingdom would fall if it wasn't for your father's sword arm and Torvald land, and Vincent has never cared about anything other than taxes, tithes, and lining his own vaults!" Garf declared hotly.

Wow, I thought. Things must really have changed out here if Garf and the other Torvald clansmen and women feel so comfortable talking open sedition against Prince Vincent. The prince, as the overall head of the Middle Kingdom was still nominally our liege lord, despite his laxity.

"Your father was preparing for the time when Vincent would push the people too far, or he would start a war with his own brothers," Garf flickered a glance at Char, "and that it would be us clans who had to do all the dirty work of fighting for him, and then having to rebuild the Middle Kingdom after him." Garf shook his head at the madness.

"And your father wanted the power of the Draconis Order on *his* side when that happened..." Char said, reaching the conclusion before I did. I saw a look of awe on her face as she looked hopefully at me. "Don't you see, Neill – he wasn't sending you to the monastery as a punishment, or just to further Torvald aims – he wanted to make sure that the people of the Middle Kingdom were going to be looked after. He wanted *you* to help him do that."

"You mean..." I said, "he wanted to *save* the Middle Kingdom from Vincent?" The horror and the hope of what I was being told combined in me, strong enough to make me shake. *Why hadn't my father just told me?* I thought in anguish. *Because I had been young. Too young to hear such things, maybe?* And my father didn't know what I had eventually found out: That the Abbot had allied himself to Prince Vincent, in return for money and power and the freedom to continue his vile experiments on the dragons. Maybe it had always been like that, because we had discovered at Char's father's fort that even the Old Queen Delia had turned to the Draconis Order to unnaturally prolong her life. *My father had been an optimist, of sorts – he had wanted the dragons to defend the normal people of the Three Kingdoms, he hadn't known that the dragons themselves had been prisoners under Zaxx, the Abbot, and even Vincent.*

Garf nodded. "So, you didn't fail your father's wishes at all. You were doing everything that he could possibly dream of, and more, even though he couldn't tell you himself – because that would mean that he had to challenge Prince Vincent outright."

"He was a clever man, your father," Char said. "He must have been very proud of you, Neill, when you were the first to ride a dragon."

I didn't know what to say to that. Maybe he had been proud, maybe he hadn't. I just wish that he could have said it to me in person. Damn all these politics and damn Prince Vincent! All this silence and sneaking around and decades-long plots had stolen any relationship that I was to have with my father away from me.

"So, you see, you shouldn't be so down on your father, and you shouldn't throw away your Torvald heritage just yet." Garf gave me a sad smile, before turning back down the long hallway that led out past the kitchens and storerooms, and to the rear of the town of the Fort beyond.

"No," I agreed, saying quietly under my breath. "Not just

yet." I thought of my brothers, and their decision to blame me for everything. I could try to make them see reason – but I realized that I didn't even want to. They had spent their lives tormenting me in some fashion or another, and I didn't want to play a supporting role to *their* rule of the Torvald Clan.

"Here we are." Garf trudged out past the cold mews of small buildings that housed pigs, ducks, and sheep at the back of the Fort. It was noisy with the sounds of the animals, and butting up against the rear palisade wall was the storehouses and the great outer gate: a giant set of wooden doors with two smaller doors set in the middle of them, through which a steady stream of people was passing. I knew where this led, and I didn't need to Garf to lead me anymore.

The Burial Mounds of Torvald, I thought.

Out from the far side of the Fort, where the ground became rougher, with short, much-cropped grasses and bright heathers, sat the ancient burial mounds of our people. Not everyone got to have an elaborate burial mound, and there were still many who preferred their relatives to be burned in a pyre rather than interred forever into the dark earth. However, it was tradition for great heroes, ladies, and chieftains to be given their own tombs or enclosed in the tombs of their own ancestors.

They rose like semi-circular tumps, overgrown with grass and scattered with wild flowers that wavered in the stiff breeze of the day. The mightiest of them all, the one to which a steady line of mourners snaked fore and back, was almost the size of a house in itself, but low and set into the earth. Its walls were still bare stone, but its top was a curving dome of grass and flowers. The Tomb of Torvald, home to the dead of my forebears for nearly seven generations.

"Neill? Are you okay?" I heard Char whisper at my side, and I nodded. Strangely, now that I was here, and now that I had the stiff breeze blasting the tears from my eyes, and was surrounded by others mourning my father, I knew that I would be okay. It felt peaceful in a way, sad, but peaceful.

There was a slight murmur from the assembled ragged line of clansmen and women as they saw me, but none of the murmurs sounded aggressive or as if I wasn't welcome here. I started to trudge up the hill towards the large tomb where my father lay, and along the way I started to hear voices murmur at me.

"Sorry,"

"He was a great man,"

"A great chief,"

"We're so sorry,"

It was like walking through a rainfall of voices, even though none of them ever got louder than a whisper. It made me feel supported, and held as I trudged. Along the way I took out my belt knife and cut from the slopes of the hill one of the many giant thistles that sprang up all over this area, just as everyone else had done before me and were doing behind me, carrying the thistle up to the top of the hill, to lay at the foot of the giant cap stone that stood over the entrance alcove.

I knelt and said a few words under my breath – wondering

what a strange thing this was, to be here at the end of an era and at the start of a new, as far above my head, a Crimson Red dragon soared and whirled, shrieking her defiance and challenge to the world itself, and her lust for life.

I would never see my father again, I thought, looking at the tomb. But, in a strange way that I couldn't quite explain – my sadness was mingled with hope. Thanks to Garf's words I had seen a side of my father that I hadn't before. *He had trusted me. He had faith in me.* Again, that belly full of regret and sadness threatened to overturn me as I cursed the fate that had driven us apart. I knew that I would carry that sadness for a long time, perhaps forever, and I felt as if I were growing older by the second.

When I came down from the tomb, I felt as if something had lifted from my shoulders – although I couldn't quite put a name on what it might be. *Fear? Worry? Guilt? Shame?* I didn't hate my brothers anymore – not even Rik. They were just idiots, doing what they thought that they had to do. I wasn't going to be the one to convince them that they are wrong – the good people of Torvald would do that, but, I thought as I set my eyes back to the western horizon – *they had better not stand in my way, either.*

It was, I surprised myself by thinking, quite a Torvald thought to have.

PART II
NEW TROUBLES

CHAPTER 8
CHAR, TROUBLES & TIDINGS

We left the Fort, the center of the Torvald Clan lands before evening – we hadn't even stayed a whole day, but we had made sure that at least Garf knew of the coming refugees from Sheer-lake. He had promised us solemnly that they would be looked after, and that it would give the Sons of Torvald a mission to learn some of the ways of chieftainship.

But I was glad to be flying westwards again, returning to the Dragon Monastery, and I could tell that Neill was happy too.

"There – down there!" He pointed at the glint of large shapes, blue and green against the darker sprawl of the forest. It was the dragons of our flight that had come to help defeat the Blood Baron, and, somewhere down there also would be our friends Sigrid on Socolia, Terence and Lila on Morax, and the crowd of prisoners and refugees.

Neill seemed fresher and brighter after having been home, I realized as I watched his face darting at the signs of our friends below. I didn't think that it was having seen home that had made him more assured and confident, and neither was it merely fact that we were now flying towards *our* home as well. I remembered how I had felt at being back at my father's fortress; even in my old chambers once again with their cutesy-princess decoration.

It had made me realize who I was now. That I wasn't who I had been, and that I had already outgrown the worries and fears of my youth. My father, the Prince Lander's fortress, had seemed small to me, and confining, and that had only increased my desire to be a Dragon Rider – whatever that would mean! And so, it seemed to me that Neill must have had the same experience as well. He now flew more confidently, he moved more confidently, he was no longer so deeply troubled by the ugly feelings as he had been before going to honor his father's passing.

But we would still have a lot to do, I was thinking, before Neill poked me in the back. "Ow!" I said.

"Haven't you been listening to a word that I've been saying?" Neill said in exasperation. The wind was low, and Paxala beneath us wasn't particularly flying very fast so I couldn't pretend that I just couldn't hear him. "There's something wrong down there!" He pointed once more down at the crowd of prisoners, refugees, and dragons.

"Is there?" I looked. The central gaggle of prisoners was trudging alone, the two groups of refugees in front and behind, as well as walking alongside the gaggle. Flying in a circling pattern were the riderless Green and Blue, and, farther away I could see the quick movements of the Sinuous Blue that must be Morax.

"I can't see what's wrong..." I began, before I registered what it had to be. *Three dragons. There were only three dragons down there.* "Where's Sigrid and Socolia?" I asked.

"I know, right?" Neill was already scanning the horizon and land I joined him in looking for the telltale silhouette of dragon wings against the sky, or the flash of green that could be Socolia... Nothing.

"Pax?" I reached out to Paxala with both my voice and mind, my sudden nervousness giving speed to my thoughts. "Can you sense where Socolia is?"

"Of course. To the west, and south, following the hot currents there," Paxala said to me, a pleasing feeling accompanying the thought of warmer winds. From my long time spent with Paxala, I knew that the dragons often thought of the airs of the world in *currents*; rivers of warmer, colder, sharp or slow airs that blew across the world, bringing with them all of the scents and noises of the lands that they crossed.

"What is she doing there?" Neill asked when I told him, as we sped down towards where the Blue Morax was circling. Morax's flight was erratic, flapping his great wings quickly and awkwardly as he attempted to hover and make turns quickly.

"Socolia is upset," Paxala said to me, a note of urgency in her voice. *"She is unsure of what her rider wants, she is struggling against the girl who rides her, and that is causing more anguish for Morax and his riders."*

Oh no. This was what I had feared could happen. The dragons had only been bonded to their riders (if bonded was even the right word for the tentative friendship that they had with their riders) for such a short time – had Sigrid done something to upset the dragon?

"Can you reach her – Socolia, I mean? Can you talk to her?" I said.

"Dragons can speak with tongues that humans cannot, it is true," Paxala informed me, and I nodded. This was what I would call speaking with our minds, telepathy, but Paxala thought of it much differently. *"But we cannot talk to every dragon, everywhere. It is stronger if we are closer, physically, and closer, by friendship."* Paxala grumbled, making a worried clicking noise in her long throat. *"I can sense that Socolia is upset, but her confusion and struggle with her rider makes it difficult for me to reach her…"*

"We have to get to her," I told Paxala, as Neill was waving in alarm to Terence and Lila.

"We heard a roar from this direction, a dragon's roar – and then Socolia and Sigrid just took off! As fast as an arrow – and we're trying to find out the reason why!" Terence hollered across the slow-moving winds as we hovered near them. He was pointing southwards, and I saw him trying once again to shift his weight on the neck of the Blue Morax, using his knees and hips to try and encourage the Blue to follow the Green Socolia. But Morax couldn't – or wouldn't follow, caught in a moment of indecision, the Blue dragon was turning in circles towards the south, then seemingly getting fritted, and turning back once more.

"What is wrong?" Neill shouted, looking devastated at the haphazard riding and flying of the dragons with whom he wanted to change the world. I knew what he must be thinking: if we cannot even work with the younger dragons effectively – then how could we ever become what we needed to be?

"It's Socolia, she's worried about something – and Sigrid cannot control her, I think," I relayed to him, before it suddenly became abundantly clear what had upset the green dragon so much.

I felt it through my connection to Paxala underneath me: a sudden shake and tenseness in her muscles as the scent of a large, powerful, and terrible dragon hit her.

"Skreayar! Skreyar!" Paxala suddenly bellowed, losing a few feet as she beat her wings quickly in startled fright.

"What is it? What is wrong?" Neill shouted, as I reached towards that place in my mind that connected to Paxala, to feel the shape of the mightiest dragon to fly the skies of the Middle Kingdom heavy in her mind.

"Zaxx the terrible," Paxala roared again, and I felt an icicle of fear drop down my spine as I shouted it to Neill.

"Where?" both me and Neill behind me were calling, looking this way and that, down below and above us. The thought of encountering the mighty Golden Bull dragon, once the tyrant of the dragon crater itself, out here and with just our four dragons here was too terrible to contemplate. We had only managed to defeat him and drive him out when *all* of the dragons of the crater had risen up, flying behind Paxala's lead to announce their willingness to do battle.

Zaxx the Golden was huge; many times the size of even Paxala here, and he was ancient as well. Some say he was one of the oldest dragons alive – and I knew that he had certainly been ruling the dragon crater for as long as the Draconis Order had been in existence. He was old, canny, and cruel, and was able to perform many strange things that I had no name for.

He was also Paxala's father.

"I should have killed him," the Crimson Red beneath me said savagely, in a tone of such animal intensity that it made me shiver. I knew that the enmity Paxala felt for Zaxx wasn't just due to the many years of abuse, of bullying, attacks, and preferential treatment the Golden Dragon had dispensed in his time as bull of the crater. For Paxala, it was personal. Zaxx had threatened me, and Zaxx had killed her mother when she had sought to hide her eggs from him; for that was the terrible secret at the heart of Zaxx's bloody reign of terror over the dragons of the crater. He had been helping the Abbot Ansall to cull and select the dragons that the Abbot used for his magics, and Zaxx had used it as an opportunity to do away with any challengers to his authority, such as young males or the eggs of powerful females.

"Yes, you probably should have," I said, feeling scared at my own echoing ferocity. The world would never be safe with Zaxx in the skies. A monster that ancient and that evil would surely not rest quietly in the hidden places he had wormed his way to. He would be back to wreak vengeance on the dragons and the humans who had dared to defy him.

But then, where was he? I thought in alarm.

"My father is not here," Paxala said in disgust. *"But he has been. What we can sense, what is upsetting Morax, and what is driving Socolia so far away is the scent trail the brute left in*

78

his wake." I suddenly understood. Dragons think as much in terms of sounds and smells as they did in visions, words, and feelings. For them, the world was a vibrant, living place where the recent past and the far away were all just as vivid and present as the ground below them or the trees over which they flew.

And because Sigrid, Terence, and Lila, cannot talk to the dragons as I can – their dragons could not communicate with them about what has upset them so greatly. I saw what was going wrong now. The dragons Morax and Socolia wanted to warn their human riders of the danger; and when the human riders did nothing or could not respond to their fears, both dragons are trying to find a way to save them and their riders from it.

I told Neill what was going on, who looked aghast at the trouble that this could cause for all of us.

"Sigrid is on her own," he said. "She won't be able to guide Socolia as Terence and Lila can."

I nodded. "But we can try to calm their dragons… Pax?" I spoke out loud.

"I will try…" The Crimson Red beneath me growled, before sending a stream of cooing, wittering sounds in the direction of Morax. I once again felt the pressure-filled buzz of invisible communication as Paxala talked to Morax, and, I saw in front of me the Blue start to slow his rapid wing beats, and squawk in nervousness and agitation – but at least he wasn't threatening to fly off, away from Zaxx's scent as before.

"I have done what I can, but Morax will want to return home," Paxala growled. *"And we are only lucky that the other*

riderless dragons are upwind of Zaxx's scent at the moment. When they catch it, they are sure to scatter."

"The refugees of Sheerlake will have to guard the Blood Baron prisoners on their own. They are not far from Fort now, anyway," I said, quickly conversing with Neill behind me, who saw that it was a good plan.

"Let Morax, Terence and Lila return to the crater and get some rest," Neill said. "We will go after Socolia and try to calm her down."

And, with an encouraging and bloodthirsty challenge from Paxala into the bright airs, we flew south.

~

The ground beneath us moved from speckled rivers, woodlands, hills and meadows to the wider fields and plains of the southern half of the Middle Kingdom. There was no fear of losing Socolia's scent, as a hunting dragon can scent a fish in the waters of a lake although many hundreds of feet above – but that consolation still did nothing for our nerves.

What if she gets attacked? What if Zaxx is close by? I thought, again and again as we raced over greener and golden lands.

Zaxx's scent was still strong, but it was starting to fade just a little as we flew, and with it, I could feel the anxiety and pent-up aggression of the dragon beneath me subside as well.

"Do you think that he did it on purpose?" Neill was asking.

"Zaxx, I mean – laying tracks that he knew would scare up the dragons. But why would he do that? Just to upset our work?"

"I wouldn't put it past him," I muttered darkly. "Terence said that they heard a roar – that had to be Zaxx nearby, right?" What game is that old toad playing, I thought, as we passed over lands that were soft and gentle, and with high currents of warmer air. We can't be far from the southern border with the Southern Kingdom of Prince Griffith, Terence's father, I thought, wondering if I could see an orange haze start to appear on the far southern horizon. The lands of the Southern Kingdom, my father had told me, were characterized by steaming, hot oases, and forests as well as broad empty lands where nothing but rock and sand could grow. I had never been there (nor this far south, at all), and I had no intention of my first visit to those far lands to be under such a dark cloud!

But Zaxx could be anywhere, my heart hammered.

"Not anywhere. I would sense him, wouldn't I?" Paxala consoled me.

"Yes, of course." But still, the sudden incursion of that monster into our lives made me feel edgy and panicked. Like all that we were accomplishing was for naught, if he could just fly by and kick over our carefully laid plans like a giant child.

As the sky started to darken on our right, and the stars pricked the scattering clouds, Paxala informed me that she had tracked Socolia and Sigrid down. They were still flying, heading south, although Socolia was tired. I was sure that Paxala underneath me must also be tired by now, although she said nothing about it if she were.

Before long, Paxala called out a note of warning, and finally, looming in the twilight, I saw a dark shadow moving through the sky. The stocky green dragon, wavered in her flight and answered with a hooting call. Socolia's wings drooped, as even she had to accept that she was tired, and the relief of having another friendly dragon nearby clearly made her feel all of the air leagues that she had flown.

Beneath me, Paxala wittered, clicked, and whistled at the Green, and from the shapes of the thoughts I could sense through our connection, I knew that my dragon sister was consoling and calming her, although I could not make out what she actually said.

Eventually, once we'd flown close enough to see the form of Sigrid atop her, waving back at us, the Green slowed and turned back in a lazy circle towards us, and the northwest direction of home.

"I don't know what happened!" Sigrid wailed from the back of the tired green dragon. She looked awfully ashamed, as if she had done something wrong. "We were flying just as you had directed, keeping watch over the prisoners and the refugees of Sheerlake, and then all of a sudden we heard a distant bellowing roar, and Socolia startled and panicked."

"It wasn't your fault," Neill said. "It was Zaxx. We think he's trying to disrupt the crater dragons, prevent them from doing what they want to." Neill glowered, and I saw the look of apprehensive fear on Sigrid's face. No one had any answers to what to do about Zaxx– not yet.

"We have to find a way to counter him," I announced,

causing emphatic nods of agreement from both Sigrid and Neill as we flew in tandem back home, sharing each other's slipstream in turns.

"And we have to find a way to communicate better," Neill said. "With the dragons in the sky, and between riders. The battle at Sheerlake had me thinking, and now this…" He fell silent, a look of intense concentration on his face. "The riders need to be more in tune with their dragons, and the dragons need better training if this is going to work."

"But it's not all bad," I reminded myself. "Zaxx isn't here, and we solved the problem – *or rather,*" I admitted, "Paxala has done it – she found and returned Socolia and Sigrid, when you and me, Neill, would have been totally lost."

"Thank you," I felt a brush of the dragon's mind against mine, and a sense of pride at what she had achieved. It was a pride that I shared in her, as it seemed to me that she was on the verge of becoming a real leader to her comrades, and maybe one day, even a matriarch.

"Matriarch – what is that word?" Paxala asked me, purring in my mind at the adoration and praise that I was heaping on her.

"It's like a mother, but a mother who is in charge of everything, not just her children," I said. I knew all about this, as half of the wild mountain clans of my own family operated by a system of wise woman matriarchs, and not the large and loud, generally bearded male chiefs.

"Pfft! Dragons have brood mothers, who would make excellent queens if we can get rid of the bulls!" Paxala growled at the thought of any bull telling her what to do. *"And I have yet*

to find another dragon whom I would even consider for a mate!"

That was an entirely other complication that I hadn't even thought about yet: what would happen when the crater started to produce more broods, hatchlings, and newts? How would they manage their mating rights without the presence of the bull? Would Paxala get to choose whom she wanted? I couldn't force her to choose a mate – I wouldn't, I thought with conviction. Not after what my father had tried to do, to marry me off to the Tar Clan in return for their mountain warriors. As it was, Tobin Tar had been a good man, and hadn't wanted to marry an unwilling wife anyway – all that would have come of my father's plans would have been two unhappy people. Was it much different with dragons? Or was it all about just securing the next generation of newts? *Isn't that what any clans lord wants as well, though?*

"I WILL get to choose, thank you very much!" Paxala said with a snort of indignation, making me smile, but still the questions lingered at the back of my mind.

"Of course you will, Pax, I couldn't dream of anything else for you." I knew well what it was like to have your society order an arranged marriage for you, as I had only narrowly escaped one myself!

But I hadn't thought of what would happen the day that Paxala chose to raise a brood. Was it even safe to raise a brood at the moment, the way that we were threatened by Zaxx's presence out there in the world? I felt a small spike of jealousy, too, at the idea of *not* being the center of the Crimson Red's attention. *Is that what will happen? Will I become just a friend from Paxala's childhood?*

"*Silly Char,*" Paxala enfolded me with her feelings of warm rebuke. "*Char will always be my sister, and human-aunt to any eggs I decide to hatch.*" I felt honored, and, despite all of the worries and the terrible threat of Zaxx somewhere nearby, I even felt hopeful as we finally saw Mount Hammal, the Dragon Mountain rising over the horizon to the north. But that was before we learned of the strange tiding awaiting us at the monastery.

CHAPTER 9
NEILL, JODRETH, & DARKER NEWS

We arrived at Mount Hammal just as the night was starting to lighten towards dawn, and all five of us were exhausted. By my reckoning, we had flown nonstop for an entire day, and covered a massive area of land. I was saddle sore and weary, but I was also faring better than Sigrid and Char were, as my experience with riding ponies and horses paid off, it seems, when dragon riding.

"Neill? Char?" It was Dorf, clearly worried as he came down the wall steps towards the still-as-yet unfixed ruins of the rear wall. He held a wavering, guttering torch that highlighted the broken bits of masonry like broken teeth. We had landed just beyond it, with Char taking her leave of Paxala and Socolia who had gratefully flown back to the crater, where, even now I could hear squawking and calls as the other dragons either greeted or challenged the Green who would disturb their rest.

"What now?" Sigrid said at our side, stumbling on weary feet and rubbing her eyes.

"Don't worry," I told the tall and thin girl, her blonde hair disheveled from all the flying she'd done. "Get to bed, Sigrid, I'll see to this," I said – although, given the look of alarm on Dorf's face, I wasn't entirely sure that I would be able to.

But this was what my father would have done, I found myself thinking as I trudged towards the well, beckoning Dorf to talk to me there as I doused my head in cold and fresh mountain water. The shock to my system made me feel more awake, though the fatigue and tiredness wasn't lifted from my bones.

I guess something happened to me after Sheerlake and my father's tomb, I thought as I stripped off my greaves and gauntlets and stretched. It was strange to be thinking of my father now, in the past tense, and strange to think that he had wanted me to do this, and that he was now even *more* of a role model to me than he had been before. I felt like I could see my father's decisions compared to how my brothers were running Torvald lands, and I could begin to see why my father acted as stern as he did, and how dedicated he was.

He always put the people first, I thought tiredly, starting to feel very small indeed under such a heavy, heavy burden.

"It's Jodreth," Dorf said.

Oh by the stars, what's happened now? I thought in alarm as Char joined us, yawning. "Is he all right?"

"Oh yes, well, if you count a broken heart all right. He's had a row with Nan Barrow, the cook, over the fact that he's leaving."

"Leaving?" I said, startled. "You don't mean…*actually* leaving, do you?"

Dorf shrugged, his eyes cautious. "I couldn't say. He started packing up things earlier this afternoon, scavenging bits of tack, a pony, extra feed, rope, all the sorts of things you'd need if you were going on a long expedition, and he told Maxal Ganna to look after the student Mages now, as Jodreth wouldn't be around, and that he didn't know if he was going to come back."

"Has he left?" I asked, frustration clutching at me as Char groaned. "Char – get some rest, please," I asked her.

"Why? If you're not going to sleep – then why should I?" Char pointed out, grumpy and indignant.

Fair enough, I suppose, I thought. I was just so tired. I shook my head that it was no matter, and sent Dorf back to his wall duty. Then, with Char following close behind, I started off in the direction of the Kitchen Gardens, where I knew that Nan would usually already be up, baking the day's bread. Char following close behind.

Next to the old stables was the small door that led to the Kitchen Garden, a place enclosed in thick brick walls and warmed by the underground vents and steam of the mountain itself. The plants were already growing strong here, just as they did every year thanks to Nan and the kitchen staff's consistent care.

But the kitchen itself seemed to be in a state of chaos, as pots were being clattered, and angry words exchanged behind the frosted-glass windows.

"No, *that* is the ladle, and *that* is the soup spoon!" Nan said tersely as we rounded the kitchen. That wasn't like Nan, I thought in alarm. She was one of the first people that I had met coming to this place, and one of the only adults to always show me some kindness, no matter the color of my skin or the circumstances of my birth.

The broad kitchen was in a state. Half of the hearth fires were still unlit, the tables were piled with pots that needed sorting and washing, and half-unfinished projects were scattered all over the tables.

"This isn't like Nan," Char said at my side.

"Well, these *times* aren't the same either, are they?" The plump and usually smiling form of Nan appeared, but now she looked miserable. "And unless the pair of you have come to help wash up, then I really don't have time…"

"Of course." Char and I moved to the counters, rolled up our sleeves, and started to stoke fires, draw water, and ferry the pots back and forth to be plunged into the hot water and scrubbed. Even though we were both exhausted, it felt good to be doing routine, monotonous tasks after all of the war-like battle planning and worrying about the imminent threat of Zaxx.

"Nan?" I heard Char ask as she worked. "What is this we hear about you and Jodreth?"

"Oh, that idiot has got one of his hare-brained schemes in his head again, and now he's told me that he might never see me again!" Nan said with real vehemence in her voice. "I mean, how could he? After all that we've been through? And here's me with my arms up to my elbows in work as half of the staff have run off after Abbot left."

"Really?" My ears shot up. "Do the staff have that much loyalty for the old Abbot?" I asked.

"No, of course not." Nan shook her head as she started to pound dough. "Once again, it's Jodreth's fault. He told them the news that this monastery was going to be very important to a lot of people, even *more* people, and that the Prince Vincent was even starting to mobilize his forces to come here. Jodreth had meant it as a warning, and I guess, in his addle-minded way a sort of rallying cry, but instead all it did was scare off half of the best workers I have – not that I can blame them."

"Nan!" Char said in alarm as the sun started clipping the horizon, and warm, golden light was flooding in from the east. "You're not thinking of leaving us, are you?"

"Oh, of course not," the woman sighed, her anger and temper draining out of her in one long, slow groan. "Although the heavens search me why not, with all of this work on my shoulders! No, I would never leave all of you to fend for yourselves, and the dragons to whatever schemes Vincent has in mind. But the staff aren't Dragon Mages, or Protectors, or Scribes, or whatever else you have going on up there in the stone halls. They are just simple folk from the village below, who have a passing respect for the dragons, and who want to do some good in the world. They don't want to be frightened, beaten, imprisoned, or at war for the sake of washing a few pots," Nan said.

I could have groaned. How could I have been so blind? Why hadn't I thought about them as well? What with trying to placate the older Draconis Order monks that, if they loved dragons they should stay, and trying to find ways to keep the walls guarded, and getting the students to interact more with the dragons, I had completely ignored that the monastery wasn't just a building of stone and books. It was a community. It *needed* a community to make it work.

"I'm so sorry, Nan. I'll see if I can get some of the students down here to help..." I said, as I worried about Nan's next words.

"And Jodreth has taken it upon himself to ride off, just when we need all hands on deck, everyone pulling in the same direction, to try and track down where the Abbot Ansall has vanished to!" Nan said, her stern exasperation dissolving into what had been at the heart of her temper: worry.

"He's going to try and bring the Abbot to justice. He says that we cannot rest with Ansall out there..."

"Or Zaxx," I added as Nan continued.

"And now my Jodreth says that *he* is the only Dragon Mage strong enough to do it, despite getting half killed the last time that he tried to fight the Abbot Ansall!" Nan said. "He thinks that the Abbot is up to something, and so he is going to search him out and try to confront him." The cook of the monastery shook her head. "It's madness. I forbade him from going, and from breaking my heart – and then he got angry, telling me that he had to." Nan was still upset, looking at me in despair. "Neill? He always said that you were his closest friend here. Can you speak to him? Stop him from going?"

"I can try? Where is he? When did he say he was leaving?" I asked, quickly drying my arms and hands as Char nodded, saying that she would go and organize some students to start helping the monastery staff as well.

"He told me the Main Gate, and that he was going to leave at first light." Nan frowned at the first sliver of orange glow that had reached the top walls of the garden. "You might just catch him on the road."

I hastily grabbed my cloak and ran to the stables, where feisty little Stamper was still happily making a living. After a not-so-short wrangle with harnesses (in which he had to be bribed with quite a few dried apples), I was once again astride the tough little pony that had carried me here, and we cantered through the open gates and down the road.

The sun was already brightening the world as I rode down the wide but steep tracks of the mountainside, and, although cold, it looked to be a beautiful morning. The heathers and the gorse were coming out in full force, but I could take no pleasure in the naturally wild beauties around me. My heart sank as I rode, my body so tired that even the colors appeared wan and drained around me.

But down there, right at the edge of the forests and woods that skirted the mountain I saw a shape walking beside one of the monastery's ponies. Stamper underneath me gave an excited little whiny as he saw one of its stablemates, and I waved to the figure.

"Jodreth! Jodreth – wait, it's me – Neill!" I called, and, to my relief the black-clad figure slowed, turned, and then stopped at the entrance to the forest.

By the time I had reached him, he was sitting on the broad way-marker rock that sat at the entrance of the path, chewing a piece of bread as he considered the dawn.

"I knew that it would be you, you know," Jodreth said, his tone neither cynical, sad, or even apologetic.

"Jodreth, my friend – what are you doing?" I slid from Stamper's back and gasped at him, as the horse gratefully started to nuzzle at the short mountain grass. "You can't leave us now, please," I said, looking at the packs on the side of his own pony, and how they were laden with supplies and belongings.

"I'm not *leaving,* Neill," Jodreth said kindly, "I'm just doing what has to be done." His dark eyes flickered up to the monastery above us. "What you have started here is incredible, but we are beset by dangers, and our academy of dragons needs to be defended," he said.

"Academy?" I said, startled by his choice of words.

"It's a word I've been playing with, ever since the wall came down. The monastery, the Draconis Order, those are the places that *I* grew up in, and I can see its mark still carved into the hearts of the older monks. It was a cruel, austere place, full of control. But what *you* and the other students are trying to do here, Neill…" I could see Jodreth searching for the right words. "It's more about *learning* new things, new skills. 'The Dragon School' seemed a little trite, so I thought maybe 'academy' had a better ring to it…"

The Dragon Academy. It *did* have a nice ring to it, but

Jodreth's good idea also annoyed me. "Then come back and help defend this new academy!" I said in exasperation, my fatigue getting the better of me, I feared.

"No, Neill – it needs defending *out there.*" Jodreth jerked his head to indicate the wide sweep of the Middle Kingdom outside. "Up in the old monastery you need to start re-training the students, you need to find a program that will allow them to work with the dragons, you need to rebuild..." Jodreth ticked off all of the duties that I knew that we were already far behind on. At every task he mentioned, my heart sank just a little deeper and deeper. There was just so much, and I was just one young man.

"You need to find out which of the remaining Draconis Order monks can be trusted, you need to find out what hidden tunnels that Zaxx had wormed through the mountain..." the list went on and on, as Jodreth turned his attention to the world outside of us. "And all the while, our enemies are amassing. You have heard the news, of course, that the war between North and Middle Kingdoms is on hold, as the princes decide what it means that the Draconis Order and their crater full of dragons has fallen." Jodreth raised his eyebrows at how the everyday folk described what had happened here.

"...And my allies in the village below have let me know that Prince Vincent is already calling up more troops, more militia, and more warlords like your own family to come here with him en masse."

Oh no, I thought, remembering how hard it was just for us to drive away the Sons of Torvald, let alone the rest of the Middle

Kingdom forces. "We will be overrun. Everything that we have achieved..."

"Lost," Jodreth agreed. "Now you see the dangers that you face, and you know why it is I have to go. Sometimes, Neill," he looked at me sharply in the eye, "sometimes you have to put the needs of others ahead of your own, and that is why I have decided to leave and find out what is happening out there, and to act as an advocate for the *new* Dragon Academy if I can, and to track down the Abbot Ansall as well," Jodreth said with a growl. "We can't let him roam free. There's news that the other monks out there – the old ones from the Draconis Order – have fled their posts stationed at the various warlord's great houses and halls. I have to ask, where have they gone? What evils are they plotting? Is the Abbot behind all of this?"

I felt honored and grateful for his dedication of service to the new academy – one that hadn't even come into being yet. Jodreth must have sensed some of my guilt and shame, as he said in a slightly gentler tone, "We do this, Neill, because we are committed to the future, to *tomorrow*, to having a better future than we did the past. That is the burden we all have to face, and we all have to live up to, in our own way."

But if Jodreth had meant for his words to sound inspiring to me, then he was badly mistaken. Instead, his words sounded like a dire warning, not unlike his warning had sounded to the kitchen staff. My entire life had to be given in service of an idea so fragile it might not even work. Why couldn't we just fly away on the dragons to somewhere new? I didn't want to be this impor-tant leader of the monastery, and I didn't want all of these lives depending on me and my actions. I had never expected to lead anything in my life, being the third son, and the one that my father spent the least amount of time with. Always it was Rubin or Rik who had been at my father's side and discussing important decisions – but with Garf the Lame's revelations about my father's *real* reason for sending me here ringing in my head, I now had to at least admit the possibility that my father had wanted me to lead *something* all along. He had wanted me to guide the Draconis Monastery away from Prince Vincent. He had wanted me to stand at his side, with the Draconis Order behind me.

I couldn't do it. I wasn't trained. I knew nothing of how to get people to like me.

"I, I understand why you feel like you have to go," I said awkwardly. "But still, I would rather that you stay. To help us. To advise us." *To help me*, I didn't add.

Jodreth barked a self-deprecating laugh. "I don't think that you need my counsel, young Master Torvald. You seem to be doing a pretty good job all by yourself."

"But what of all of those tasks and duties that you said I have to complete?" I burst out, hating myself for sounding childish, but unable to stop it. *My father was dead, and I had no one who could tell me what to do.* "I know nothing about wall building, about training, about leadership!"

"Take heart, Master Torvald," Jodreth said, in that almost mystical way that he had. He must have sensed some of my reticence about what I had to do next. "Maybe it's no mistake that you caught up with me here. Don't you remember this place?"

He pointed to the way stone, and the path that led back down to the forest behind us, or widened up to the slate and broad avenue that crossed the heath and rock mountain above.

I did, of course. "This is where you saved me."

"No, this is where we talked," Jodreth corrected me. "I saved you down there, in the Claw Gully. Did you know that it was called that? Because it's so steep, and that it was supposedly made when the first dragon itself clambered up this hill. I saved you from the assassins down there in the gully, but here is where you first told me your name, and I told you mine."

I didn't see what he was getting at.

"The point is, Master Torvald, is that this is a place of beginnings. The beginnings of dragons living here at Mount Hammal, however many thousands of years ago, and the beginnings of your journey here as well. Just as what you are doing up there is also a beginning; a new chapter in the ancient story of the Dragon Mountain."

"Okay…" I said, still not quite being able to crack the meaning of the wisdom that he was trying to reveal to me.

"And do you remember what I said to you, back then when we first met?" Jodreth asked.

I shook my head. I remembered thanking him for saving my life, and offering to be considered in his debt.

"I told you that you were more than just a warlord's son. That you had a good heart, and that you were your own man, Neill," Jodreth said. "You will *know* what the right thing to do is, *when* it is time." He smiled, before nodding and turning. Feeling more than a little dumbfounded, I watched as my friend walked down the path, away from where we had met, and vanished into the darkness.

I couldn't stop myself from thinking that if I had such a good heart, and if I was more than what everyone thought I was – then why did I feel so helplessly out of my depth, then?

CHAPTER 10
CHAR, CONCERNED

"Neill?" I called out to my friend, standing just a little way away from me on the still-intact ramparts of the Dragon Monastery. It was midmorning, and the air was cold and the clouds thin and high, but the sun was shining and we had a slew of students and monks standing below us, waiting for our decision.

"Neill, everyone is waiting!" I hissed again, making him startle and shake his head, dragging his attention away from the south where he had been gazing.

"Oh yeah, right." He blinked, nodding distractedly as if he had forgotten what it was he had been about to say.

"The *training,* Neill?" I whispered out of the side of my mouth up at him, reminding him of what we had been talking about just last night, when we had decided to call this general meeting of all the remaining Draconis Order and students. Really, I thought, what the hell happens to boys when they are two steps away from adulthood? I remembered Wurgan becoming an idiot, although, in his case, he had *remained* an idiot ever since.

"Er... friends..." Neill called out, in a voice I was sure wasn't loud enough to carry across the main courtyard.

"*Speak. Up,*" I mouthed at him, to which he stuttered, nodded, and started again, this time in a marginally louder voice.

"Friends!" he called again. "Thank you for coming here this morning at my request. I realize that this may be new for you..." he said, his brow suddenly furrowing as he looked at his hands and sighed, before carrying on again. Neill is looking anxious, fretful even, I thought. *He's changed since hearing about the death of his father...* "Anyway. This is new for all of us. A lot of you might be asking just what is going to happen next, what we are going to do now that the Abbot is gone, and now that we have a crater full of dragons to tend to..."

I heard a ripple of muttered voices from the crowd below us, the audience filled with tonsured monks and bald-headed elders dressed in black, as well as the ragtag sea of younger faces, only a few of whom wore the traditional black robes of the old Order. The assembled throng was only a fraction of the size of some of the gatherings the old Abbot Ansall had regularly convened in the Great Hall, and now it seemed that the students made up at least half of those assembled. We'd lost a lot of the old Draconis Monks when Ansall fled, I thought darkly. Where were they now? What were they plotting?

"We've been doing some thinking..." Neill began.

"*Who* has?" A voice I didn't recognize rose from the group...

I was sure it must have been one of the older monks, as I knew all of the students.

"Who?" Neill looked a little discombobulated by the question. "We, me, Char Nefrette here, Maxal Ganna, Sigrid Fenn..."

"No one asked us!" the voice shouted up, and I scowled at the crowd. Who was it, causing problems? I wondered, before biting my lip in confusion. *Wait. Don't they have a right to ask these questions? Why should they follow us?* I had hated being given orders by the Abbot, Monk Olan, and the others, especially because the orders had always seemed so cruel, like Master Greer commanding women could not be Protectors, just because of our sex. But I also knew that the hopes of whatever we were going to build here hung in the balance. At any moment we could lose the rest of the older monks or the staff could flee, or the dragons could decide to fly and nest somewhere else, especially now they were without a bull.

"Silly Char." Paxala's warm reptilian purr rumbled through my mind. *"Dragons will never leave the sacred mountain."*

"At least you'll still be here then," I whispered under my breath, more to myself than to Paxala, but felt her swift rebuke at my sarcasm. It was just all of this talking and negotiating. It was so difficult – why didn't the older monks down there just see things as we did? Why was it so hard to believe that the dragons were noble and great creatures, and that it would be a pleasure to work and learn with them?

As I bit my lip in my own worries and anxieties, Neill's voice rang out above me.

"Well, we're asking you now!" he said, sounding like he was

arguing with his brothers. "We've got an idea. As well as rebuilding the monastery, we also need to start again with the training. No more Scribes, Protectors, and Mages," Neill called, and I nodded.

I had been adamant that we *not* continue with the Mage lessons as the Abbot had taught me, Maxal, and a few others. His methods had created suspicion and jealousy in the monastery, and the magic lessons themselves, with their regime of half starving ourselves and sitting in uncomfortable 'control postures' for hours at a time had been torturous. No, even if there were *anyone* who knew anything about magic enough to teach it (which would be a no, in my opinion), then as sure as the stars I wouldn't be going to those classes ever again! I had ended up hypnotized, an unwilling puppet commanded by the Abbot's whims.

"That's right. No more of the three-part system!" Neill raised his voice over the rising tide of grumbles coming up from below, mostly coming from the older monks, it seemed.

"And we are going to reinstate the dragon training," Neill shouted. "Although, I am sure that everyone here misses Monk Feodor." I saw Neill's hand shake just slightly as he mentioned the older dragon trainer and Advanced Protection trainer who had died trying to thwart the Abbot.

"But how? Those dragons are wild! Feral!" An accusative voice, the same one from before, I thought, rose up from the morass below.

I couldn't hold my tongue any longer, "Yes, the dragons of the crater are wild. But they are not vicious, as the old bull Zaxx the Golden was." I hope they aren't, anyway... "They are wild, and we are *not* going to tame them!" I said, which, this time at least, garnered a few cheers and claps from the younger students– particularly Lila and Terrence, who were starting to build an actual relationship with their Green dragon Morax.

"We are going to *befriend* them," I called, seeing Neill shuffling nervously beside me as I nodded to him. "Go on, Neill!" I hissed.

"Oh yeah, right…. So, our new training isn't going to be trying to command the dragons to do anything. Instead, it's going to be teaching you–us–to be better Dragon Riders." Neill's voice became a little calmer and clearer as he enthused on the subject that he had been thinking deeply about. "From our studies and experience, we think that riding a dragon is easier with two people, and we already have been trained as Scribes and Protectors in the past, but now we're going to figure out if we can have a... a *fighter* maybe? And a scout?" he called. "The *fighters* will be led by Lila Penn, the best fighter amongst us, and the *scouts* will be led by Dorf Lesser, the best map-reader!"

"What about the Mages?" A voice shouted.

"Anyone who wants to try and study magic can do so," Neill said firmly, repeating almost exactly what I had suggested last night. "And you work together, in groups, helping each other. It doesn't matter if anyone has told you that you can or cannot do it. From now on, anyone who wants to give the meditations a try can form a group and go to the Dragon Library to read the scrolls there. All that we ask is that no scroll leaves the library."

Yes. Maxal Ganna, the most skilled of all of the magical

recruits would be in charge of overseeing the study groups, and I knew that he was sensible enough to manage it well. And he was kind, which made all of the difference. But from now on, our focus would be on the dragons, not making glowing balls of light with our minds!

"And *everyone* here," Neill said that last part of the proclamation, "Whether you were a Scribe, a Protector, older or younger, even if you are one of the staff…"

A sudden angry hiss from the crowd, as many of the older monks still cleaved to the old notion that the 'servants' and 'staff' should best be not seen or not even heard, just able to produce clean linen, good food, and tidy up their messes whenever expected. It made me angry, thinking of poor Nan Barrow in the kitchens, surrounded by her dwindling supplies of both food and workers.

"*Everyone,*" Neill insisted, "has to be given the chance to learn dragon training. That is going to be the only daily lesson, every day. Now, if you'll all wait here for a moment, we'll get you all organized into different groups and each group will have a time that they are to approach the crater, in order to get to know the dragons."

"It's madness!" someone shouted from below, and I heard mumbles and disagreements break out. "We'll get eaten!"

Well, with an attitude like that you will, I thought grimly, before clearing my throat. "No, you won't," I said.

"*Oh, go on. Just one,*" Paxala intruded upon my thoughts with a gleeful snicker.

"*You're not helping,*" I told her with my thoughts, before

continuing to speak. "You won't get eaten with me and my Crimson Red watching over you, and the other Dragon Riders here to help you..."

"No! We refuse!" someone shouted from below, and I could see that there were now more grumbles from below. The crowd was clearly splitting into the older monks and the younger students. I looked up at Neill, desperate for him to say something that might bring some order to this mess. Sometimes, I think, we really need someone to just be able to bark at the crowd and make them see sense! But Neill was once again looking far to the southern distance, distracted and anxious himself, as if maybe the monks below *would* get eaten.

"...Council?" someone was saying, and I looked around to see that it was Dorf, climbing the stone steps up the side of the wall to where Neill and I were. He waved at me once again in that worried and over-excited way that he always seemed to have.

"What did you say, Dorf?" I said hurriedly.

"A council," he said again, his words only reaching us here on the wall. "Why not have a council? Like, where people can air their disagreements."

That was it! I thought. "Dorf, you're a genius." I congratulated him.

"Er... I am?" he said, flushing pink.

"Yes!" I turned to the crowd. "We're also going to organize a council," I shouted, raising my voice in order to be heard over the general grumbling and mumbling from below.

"What? We are?" I could hear the assembled throng saying below me.

"Yes! A council for people to air their concerns. Like this, but where we can organize how to conduct the trainings, and how to run the monastery. Every dorm room could send someone..." I said, looking over at Dorf, who nodded.

"I'll organize it," he said, looking almost ecstatic at the prospect of all that paperwork.

They can come up with a new set of laws, as well, I thought gratefully, turning to see if Neill agreed.

But once again, Neill was just biting his nails, nodding and waving his hands that this was all a good idea, but nothing that he wanted to add to. I could have groaned.

"Okay, everyone. That's it! Stay around to get organized into dragon training classes, and to sort out your representatives for the council," I shouted, clapping my hands to signal that the meeting was over. Below us, the crowd started to mumble and move. Dorf raced back down the steps, and joined Sigrid and Terrence as they moved around the crowd, taking names and organizing groups.

Phew. At least that is over, I thought with a heavy sigh, as Neill brushed past me. "Neill! Wait – we should talk about this," I said. *Where was he going now?* "You know, work out the training regime and all of that..."

Neill paused, looking at me with shadowed eyes. "You can do that, can't you? I mean, you know more about dragons than anyone here, right? You're the one who befriended Paxala in the first place, after all. And Dorf is great at all of that paperwork and scrolls stuff, and Lila spent her childhood learning how to fight..." He shrugged. "I just need to get some air, just to think..."

But we need you, I thought, but my surprise stopped the words from reaching my mouth. He was the first rider. He had been the first human to actually ride a dragon. He had changed the way the others looked at dragons. They respected him. *Well, I* corrected myself, *the older monks might not actually respect him, as they don't seem to respect anyone, but still... Neill is the one who made the change happen.*

But somehow, I found myself watching my friend's disappearing back as he hurried the opposite way from the assembled throng down there, head hunched. Neill hadn't been the same since his conversation with Jodreth, just yesterday. Something had happened, but he wouldn't tell me what.

Well, the guy has just lost his father, I thought with a twinge of sympathy. That is bound to mess you up, isn't it? How would I feel if I had lost *my* father?

A knot of awkward emotions welled up in my heart. Hurt. Anger. Shame. My father had tried to poison Paxala, and then tried to enslave her so that he could make his own rival Dragon Monastery in my home, the Northern Kingdom. I didn't think that I could ever forget that or forgive him for it. But that didn't mean that I wanted him to die, just, sorta – be sorry. Beg my forgiveness. Tell me that he had been wrong all along and that he knew that I was his little princess! *But I still had a chance with my father, a chance that Neill will never have.*

Oh nuts, I thought, as my ugly emotions turned into misery,

and a tear crept down over my cheek. That was never going to happen now, and my father wasn't the sort of man to beg forgiveness from anyone. He was as good as dead, for all the chance that we'd ever be reconciled to each other.

We were on our own up here. Me and Neill and all of the others. We'd all had to break our ties with the past to build something new.

"You are not alone." Paxala's voice rose in my mind, wrapping me with the fiery warmth of her heart.

"I know," I whispered to her where I stood, feeling better that in my heart of hearts, I still had a dragon there, waiting for me and looking out for me. Who did Neill have?

CHAPTER 11
NEILL, HOPELESS

I managed to avoid the throngs in the main courtyard, threading my way past several of the older monks who scowled at me, as though they wanted to further elaborate on how much of a failure I was. Then I headed through the servants' corridor back to the boys' dormitory tower, and up to the same old room that I shared with Dorf.

I didn't really want to bump into anyone at the moment, I just wanted space to think. By myself. Not have people asking me questions about this, that, and everything else. It just seemed that the whole business of 'leading' - if that's what you could even call what I was doing—was really just arguing with people. No matter what great idea you had, or heard, there was always going to be someone who disagreed with it. It was infuriating, and I had no idea how my father had put up with it.

My father. The thought added to the weight that I was already feeling in my stomach. He would have known what to do. And even if he didn't, everyone would still have listened to him anyway, just out of respect.

Luckily for me, my guess that mostly everyone would be outside at the general meeting had been correct, and the dormitory was pretty deserted as I clambered the steps wearily.

My father knew how to lead, I didn't, my thoughts circled. My father knew exactly how to address a crowd, and how to organize people so that they weren't always at each other's throats. What did *I* know? I emerged into my room, and my eyes slid naturally to the one thing that I didn't even know that I had been looking for.

The single splash of color in the whole room. Back under the old regime of Abbot Ansall, such things as luxuries and decorations had been forbidden as distractions from studying, but I had managed to bring one brightly-woven red and blue blanket, inlaid with fabulous cross-hatching designs of my mother's people, the Gypsies. To be honest, I didn't have to argue to have it, nor fight to keep it during the old Order, as I had hidden the blanket when Quartermaster Greer and Monk Olan had been running the day-to-day training of us students. I hadn't even brought the blanket, but had been given it one freezing night by my Uncle Lett and Jodreth, after suffering a particularly cruel punishment at the hands of the Abbot.

I hadn't known that this simple homespun cloth had been what my heart needed, but I knew that it was as I sat down heavily on the bed, kicked off my boots and pulled the blanket around me. My Uncle Lett had always told me that I was a Gypsy, no matter what, and that he was proud of me – that all of my mothers' people were proud of me. I didn't have to be able to unseat a horseman with a spear, or be able to fight off two attackers at once, or to defeat an enemy in battle in order to win their respect.

Just by virtue of being my mother's son, my Uncle Lett had bound his life to mine, I thought, as I breathed in the warm dark under the blanket, the delicate hints of cinnamon, patchouli, and cardamom still detectable.

What would my mother think of me now? I wondered as I allowed myself to fall into a fitful and restless sleep. *In charge of a monastery. Exiled from Clan Torvald lands. Half the world wanting to either destroy us or was jealous of us.*

My dark dreams of warfare, fighting, and of my dead father didn't provide me with any answers.

~

"Here he is!"

I awoke at some point in what must have been the late afternoon to the sound of voices at my door. Instantly, I tensed, for some reason my mind replaying that horrible image of Monk Feodor, my friend, engulfed in a ball of flame as I struggled out from under the scratchy red blanket.

"Dorf," I muttered, rubbing my eyes to see that it was indeed Dorf and Terrence coming to get me. Both looked tired, and were wearing the heavy, padded leather suits that the Protector students had worn for their training.

"Morning." Terrence rolled his eyes at my apparent sluggishness. "Come on, group one is approaching the crater, and we might just be able to meet them there, if we're quick."

"Group one?" I echoed, swinging my legs from the bed. In actual fact, I didn't feel rested at all.

"Dragon training. You announced it just this morning, remember?" Terrence almost snapped at me.

"Are you sure that you're feeling all right, Neill?" Dorf's quieter voice said at my side, already offering me the padded leather overalls. The question made me stop and think. *Was* I feeling all right? What was wrong with me? I just felt so very heavy and slow, as if I were about to catch a cold.

"Maybe I'm coming down with something," I muttered, shaking my head at Dorf's worried looks.

"Put these on," Dorf said, holding out a leather training vest and greaves.

"I'm sure I won't need them," I said, loathe to expend any more energy, but Dorf and Terence gave me looks that said they weren't going to back down.

"It's not like dragons are fire-breathing lizards or anything," I said with a wry smile and acquiesced, following my friends out of the dorm room with just one longing look back at my warm bed and the red Gypsy blanket.

The first dragon training lesson had been devised by Char, and she looked nervous as we hurried along the path out of the collapsed wreckage that was the rear of the monastery, and climbed the stone trail that curled up to the crater.

"Where have you been?" Char said at me in a sharp tone. "What if I'd needed you this afternoon?"

"I, uh…" I didn't have an excuse or an answer. "I guess I've failed the monastery again," I muttered.

"Neill!" Char looked at me strangely, like I'd just insulted her or something. But, before she could say anything else, we had arrived and there were students and monks looking at us expectantly.

There, at the edge of the crater in the fading afternoon, Char, Dorf, Terrence, and I stood, along with about a dozen assorted older monks and students. It was clear to me that the group was divided into two camps: those who were terrified of what was to happen next, and those who were excited, and it was no surprise that the older monks were the terrified ones.

"Voices down, please," Char said distractedly. "Dragons have very sensitive hearing."

The idea, I remembered, for the first few training sessions was only to 'meet' the dragons, and hopefully, perhaps encourage a choosing between a human and a dragon. Previously, the monks had come up here to throw meat down to the dragons, in order to placate them (and to placate Zaxx the Gold, no less). Char had decided that we should continue that tradition, but only when we wanted to meet them – she wanted the monastery to abandon having set feeding times.

"Are you sure that this is a good idea – they might be hungry?" one of the older monks asked nervously.

Char snorted her disdain for the question. "Dragons can hunt. They need to hunt for themselves, and anyway, I am reliably informed that humans don't taste that great anyway, compared to fish and deer."

"Wonderful," the nervous monk said dryly, taking a step back from the edge.

"Okay." Char nodded at me, and I raised the short red hand flag I had brought with me, holding it in the air and signaling to what remained of the Astrographer's Tower.

A moment of silence. I wondered if the monks inside had seen my signal, even though they should have been waiting for it – and then it came, a pleasingly deep, sonorous *BWAAARM, BWAARM,* that was nothing like the raucous shrieking of the old dragon pipes.

"Char?" I looked at her in worry. We still didn't know how the dragons would react to this new dragon horn, but both Dorf and Maxal had spent the last few days studying the books to try and create a sound that would mimic a den mother's encouraging rumble. The old dragon pipes had been used as a weapon of torture, high-pitched and sharp enough to damage tender dragon ears, but this one we wanted to use as a signal *for* the dragons, not *against* them.

BWAARM, BWAARM....

"It's working." Char was grinning breathlessly, cocking her head as if listening to the updrafts of wind that came up the side of the steep crater. Her pale hair streamed out beside her. She was a vision, as wild as the rocks and the beasts below. "Paxala is telling me that she isn't in pain. That the dragons are alarmed and surprised, but not in pain..."

"Great," the nervous monk said sarcastically.

Down below us, the foliage of the ever-warm dragon crater was swathed in mists from the hot pools and springs that bubbled up through the rocks. Something made me raise my head just a moment before the mists parted, and there, flaring towards us with a joyful cry was Paxala the Crimson Red.

"Skreeyar!"

"Duck!" one of the other monks said, throwing themselves to the rocky floor as a few students and some of the more skittish adults scattered, but Char laughed where she stood, just a few meters beneath the passing body of the Red. I joined her in grinning at the sight. How could anyone not look at the creature and feel awe and wonder? Her body was a tight suit of gleaming red, orange, and blood scales. Her wings made a *thrumming* noise as they passed by. The fact that she could fly at all when she was so large and had such thick slabs of muscle was astonishing. She was a beauty—and she wasn't alone.

"Srech, Srrekh!" Out of the disturbance of mists below also came the young Sinuous Blue Morax, following the larger Crimson Red as if trying to chase her. Morax was Terrence and Lila's dragon, I knew, and Terrence raised a joyous fist at the sight of her.

The two dragons flew high over the slopes of the mountain, darting and turning their wings to perform sudden and fast movements, before sweeping back around to the crater.

"You shouldn't be afraid," Char was saying to those who were still huddled at the crater (all younger students like us, I saw, as well as a few of the older monks who had some grit about them), before I saw her consider with a smile, "well, maybe you *should* be a little afraid – but you have to learn how to control your fear around them. Look!" Char reached down to the sackcloth bag that she had brought, which was layered with cured lake fish – each one silver and as long as her forearm. I watched as she seized one up and held it aloft in the air, and, even though the dragons were now on the other side of the crater and looking no bigger than herons, Paxala suddenly turned on a wing tip and flashed towards us.

"Their sense of smell is even better than their hearing, you see," Char said. "Which is something you can use when you're flying, isn't that right, Neill?" She looked at me encouragingly as she threw the cured fish high into the air above her, and, with a wooosh, Paxala flickered her wings and caught the treat with an audible snap in the air above our heads. I thought that I heard a low groan from the more nervy-looking monk.

"Neill?" Char prodded. "Trusting your dragon's senses?"

"Oh yeah." I cleared my throat. "Well, it's more those who are lucky enough to hear the dragons' thoughts who can take advantage of them, but for the rest of us, we have to learn how to rely on the dragons' responses. When they suddenly don't want to go somewhere, or are seeming alarmed, then that usually means that they've caught wind of something that they don't like..."

Char was looking at me a little oddly, like I had failed once again. How do I know how to train a dragon? My father never even let me train clansmen warriors! My heart lurched once again at the thought of my father. I had lost so much now that he was gone, and I hadn't even realized what the loss of my father might mean until it was too late.

All of those lessons. All of that wisdom. All of those hours he spent with my brothers, and not with me... The dark thoughts whirled, as Char continued her lesson in the background.

"Well, who wants to meet a dragon then?" she asked the other students, who were all eager and excited to get their hands on the fish and do the same as Char had.

As I stood there, feeling awkward, Char showed the students how to offer the fish to the dragons without making sudden movements, helping the humans to get over their fears and anxieties around the larger beasts more than allaying any qualms that the dragons might have. A few students threw the food just as skillfully as Char had, before Paxala, and then Morax alighted on the crater's edge (their claws dislodging rocks and gravel the size of cart wheels). She then encouraged the students to approach Paxala, and the much younger Blue (with Terrence standing protectively close by, like a young father hovering near his child).

"There now, who's a brave dragon?" Terrence cooed at Morax, and I found myself pleasantly surprised at just how protective he was. Terrence Griffith, the youngest son of the Southern Prince had gone from a stuck-up princeling to a slightly-less stuck up princeling, who was in love with a dragon.

"This is going well." Char was beside me. "If this lot take to it, then we can start with trying to get them down into the crater and see if any of the younger dragons wants to bond with them."

"Yeah, sounds like a good idea," I said. "We should try to encourage the other dragons to take saddles, the ones without riders," I suggested absentmindedly. "That way they can get used to them if they ever choose a human rider…"

"No!" Char stiffened. "Don't you remember when Monk Feodor tried to do that? It was a disaster, and Paxala will never allow it!"

"That was different! Monk Feodor had brought chains and goads with him…" I remembered well the old regime's attempt to replicate what I and Char did so naturally. Feodor had balked at the suggestion, but he had been commanded by the Abbot to try to force the younger dragons to take harnesses, before they had even bonded with a human. *How could Char think that I meant to do the same as that? Had we really grown that far apart in the short time that we had been in charge?* I guessed that she must be as stressed as I was about what we were doing, and I tried to allay her concerns. "I just meant taking the saddles, bit, and tack down to the crater floor, and getting the dragons to investigate them, not forcing them to wear them," I said. *Which reminded me. We needed to find a good leather worker and smith to work on the designs that Char and I had come up with… Always more problems to solve!*

"Oh, I'm sorry," Char said (in a not-very-sorry tone of voice, I noted), "but Paxala tells me that she wants to be the ones to train the dragons, not us. She's close to becoming one of the den

118

mothers now, and the other dragons respect her for helping them to drive away Zaxx."

Pax might train the dragons of the crater? I thought in wonder. I had never dreamed that one of the dragons themselves would help to train the others, and now it seemed such an obvious move. Why hadn't I thought of that before? *Another way that I am unsuited to leadership,* that small, snide part of me said in the back of my mind. *A true leader would have already worked that out by now...*

"Neill," Char huffed at me. "What is wrong with you? You just don't seem to be taking an interest in any of..."

Before she could finish her statement, there was a sudden hissing noise from Morax, and we turned to see her lashing her tail and growling at the students and monks in front of her.

"I knew it! I knew it wouldn't last..." the nervous monk cried, backing down the path back to the monastery.

"What's wrong?" Char called out, and then I saw that Paxala raised her long neck, bared her fangs and raised her wings in a warning flap. "Oh no..." Char said a moment later, before even us humans could tell what it was.

"Ruauarggh...." A roaring sound was whistling towards us on the winds. It was fierce and terrible, growing louder and louder and full of spite. My heart hammered. It wasn't the same screeches and calls of the younger dragons, but a guttural threat of violence and destruction, and it was heading towards the mountain.

Zaxx.

"Where is he? Can you see him?" Char was shouting as I was already running towards Paxala. The Crimson Red was flapping her wings aggressively, starting to hiss and snap at the air as she turned her head, first this way and then that. The old golden bull dragon was wily it seemed, he knew how to use the air currents and the deep ravines around Mount Hammal to mask his approach.

Not wily enough, however, as Paxala fixed her head in one direction alone, southwest, where the ground grew hillier and wilder, and her eyes flared as smoke wisped from her nostrils.

"Char!" I called, discarding the cumbersome leather jacket that was only making my movements slower as I raced to the Red's foot. *Why hadn't I thought that this might happen? Why don't we keep the dragon saddles nearby?* I cursed my own stupidity, as Char leapt onto Pax's other front foot, and started climbing the young Red's scales and tines to our positions.

"Get the others back to the monastery, now!" I shouted at Dorf, as Terrence also tried to board Morax, who was hissing and twisting on her perch, too agitated to let him up. "Get the dragon horn primed, get archers to the walls!" Paxala jumped into the air above the dragon crater, opening her wide wings to catch the updrafts and soar into the air.

"Skrech! Sreee, Sreeee!" But the Crimson Red underneath us wasn't the only dragon I saw. There, emerging from the disturbed mists came the Vicious Green Socolia, who had almost fled all the way to the Southern Kingdom just a few days before at her first whiff of Zaxx's presence. Now, however, she was angry and hissing. At her back came other dragons, disturbed into the air by the approach of the tyrannical bull dragon that had made all of their existences a misery. As I held onto Paxala's shoulder plates, I could see the older Vicious Greens, more of the long-tailed Sinuous Blue, hissing and alarmed, and around them exploded a storm of the smaller Messenger dragons, swooping everywhere in their shock.

"Char!" I shouted, as Paxala suddenly dove to avoid slamming into one of the immense Giant Whites, a den mother, whose eyes flashed and was growling a challenge at the offending bull.

Was this it? I wondered. *Was this going to be the moment when Zaxx would wrestle back control over the crater again?*

"No," a voice said, but it didn't come from Char. She was too busy biting her lips, holding onto the tines and scales, and trying with her hands and knees to warn the dragon underneath us of colliding dragons. The voice felt warm, female, and reptilian—it had to be Paxala! She rarely shared her thoughts with me and Char said it was because I wasn't as strong in whatever skill or secret power that allowed Char and Paxala to communicate telepathically. But I heard it as clear as day, and I knew that Paxala was telling me that there was no way that she would let the bull back in charge here, even if it killed her.

"Pheet! Pheeet"! Messenger dragons careened and darted past us as fast as arrows. It was hard to see where to fly, or whether to raise or dive to avoid the storm of reptilian bodies all around us.

And I didn't have any weapons on me. Why didn't I have any weapons! Once again, I cursed my stupidity. I was sure my father always carried weapons on him. What sort of warrior's son was I?

"Neill, up ahead!" Char shouted, as Paxala roared.

"Skreyaarckh!"

The tempest of dragon shapes had cleared momentarily, and we could see down the southern slopes of the mountain, to where the canyons were cut wide and deep and jagged runnels ran through the earth, and there, swooping down one of them, was the immense shape of the golden bull dragon.

Even from this distance, Zaxx was immense. He almost filled the ravine that he flew down, and was many times larger than the trees he flew past. A quick calculation compared to the trees made me think that he must be easily four or five times the size of Paxala – and Crimson Reds were themselves large dragons!

He'll kill us, I thought, as Paxala bellowed her challenge, and flung herself down the southern side of the crater and toward her own father.

Some of the dragons decided to follow us, but only a couple, as it seemed the others were too upset and agitated to focus their hatred. A quick look over my shoulder showed more of the great beasts boiling out of the dragon crater, the skies about Mount Hammal now a storm of winged and hissing shapes. But the dragons were too disorganized to act as one, leaving just us on Paxala, Terence of Morax, and one of the Great Whites actually chasing the old dragon—the one who mattered.

"Can we lure him back to the crater?" I shouted at Char as we flew.

"Back? Why?" Char threw me a pale-faced, worried look. "We spent almost a year trying to get rid of him!"

"The other crater dragons might fight if he's right there in front of him," I shouted. It was a bad idea to force the crater dragons to fight Zaxx, but it might be our only way to finally put an end to the monster.

We dropped into the canyon where I had just seen the golden bull. A thin stream flowed in the center of the canyon floor below, and the high walls on either side of us reflected orange and grey. *Where was the bull?* I grimaced. There was only one way to go; to follow the canyon as it curled and curved crazily around. Our trio flew in tight formation, as fast as we could. I saw the Sinuous Blue Morax landing to catch some of the rocks of the walls, before launching off in our newest direction.

The roar from below was loud and bellowing, as it echoed along the canyon walls, first this way and then that. We couldn't know if we were getting closer or further away from the beast.

"We need height!" Char said, leaning forward and closing her eyes to concentrate on communicating with the dragon who carried us.

I shouted my agreement and, with a screech, we were half-scrambling and climbing out of the canyon and launching ourselves higher into the air, with Morax following us a moment later, and the Great White continuing for a few moments before doing the same.

"Higher!" Char said, breathless either through excitement or terror, I didn't know which. Probably both. At her request, the Crimson Red flapped her large wings harder. We circled higher over the landscape, looking down into the canyons as if they had become one of Dorf's cherished maps.

But there was no Zaxx.

"It, it doesn't make sense..." Char was shaking her head. "Pax?" I heard her say. "Can you track him?"

But to me, it all made perfect sense. Zaxx had done the same thing earlier, when he had 'spooked' Socolia on our journey to my father's Fort. This was a new tactic that the golden bull was displaying; to upset, frighten, and vanish, destroying the good work that we were doing up at the monastery. "We won't find him," I said heavily. "He's trying to disturb us, to show us he's still in charge."

"Well, he's not," Char said begrudgingly. "The crater doesn't have any bulls in charge any more. It has den mothers ruling the roost."

"But Zaxx can come and disrupt us whenever he likes," I pointed out. "He's got the upper hand."

At that, Char fell into a silent scowl – but it wasn't until we got back to Mount Hammal and the dragon crater that we could assess the real damage of Zaxx's actions.

~

When we arrived back at the monastery, the recalcitrant monk from the training was now rabble-rousing from atop a pile of rubble that had been the rear wall, surrounded by a band of other black-clad monks.

"It's no good! It's hopeless!" the nervy-looking monk shouted, pointing to where both Paxala and Morax had alighted on the slopes of the mountain, eager to dislodge their human charges in order to return to the community of dragons in the crater.

"Good heavens, what now!?" I demanded, as beside me both Terrence and Char glowered at him.

"You should have seen them. Fierce, they were!" the monk's voice rang out. "Those dragons are almost wild, I'm telling you – and any day now we'll have just the same troubles as they do up in the northlander kingdom…"

What is his name?" I hissed at the others with me.

"Don't know, Berlip, I think?" Char said.

"Berlip!" I shouted up at him as we climbed the other side of the stone blocks.

"O-ho, so here he comes, our great and fearless leader!" Berlip said in a snide voice. Just something that Rik would say, I thought as I balled my fists at my side.

"Neill…" Char said urgently to me. "Don't fight him. We talk through problems now…"

Talk through problems? It would have been a whole lot better if I could simply punch him, or throw Berlip out of the monastery entirely, but Char was right. Rik and Rubin might have resorted to cuffs, slaps, and kicks to get their orders done, but it didn't mean that I should.

"Well, you have an *awful* lot of talking to do, then!" Berlip said sarcastically, eliciting a ripple of amusement from the older monks assembled below. "Because we have *many* problems. The dragons won't obey you. Zaxx the Great has returned, and will bring doom to us all any day now. *And there's nothing that you can do about it,* Torvald!" He pointed a finger straight at me.

Nothing that I can do about it. He was right, there was, indeed, nothing that I could do about it. A real leader would know what to do, when, and how…

"Go on, admit it, Torvald!" Berlip was seizing on my moment of indecision to press his case home. It was all play acting for the crowd, I knew, but it still made me feel stupid. "Admit that you have no idea what you are doing!"

"I don't," I said, my words sounding heavy and thick even to my ears. "But that doesn't mean that I'm not trying to…"

"*Trying?*" Berlip looked incandescent with rage. "What good is *trying* if we all get eaten? We helped you overthrow the old Abbot, helped you start rebuilding this place, and now you think we're all going to live in la-la land with the feral dragons up there?" He shook his head. "It is *you* who doesn't understand, Torvald. Dragons are gods, and all gods are terrible, as well as glorious. We were better when we offered tribute…."

A mixed chorus of "yay" and a few, very outnumbered "nays" from the crowd. More than a few students had emerged from the practice courts or the buildings to see what all the hubbub was about. It was hard to miss the cloud of dragons that still whirled and raged over the crater, their grumbles and screeching cries finally dying down, though they still flew about wildly instead of roosting. Even to me, it looked like the entire community of dragons that we had been so hell-bent on saving were on the verge of fleeing, or going on a rampage.

"Neill, I'm here with you." Char stood at my side. But I could see that she was looking at *me* to come up with something clever and wise, strong and authoritative to put Berlip down. I didn't know what to say to him. Sometimes arguments had to be messy, I think…

"Berlip," I cleared my throat. "This is not the way that we do this. Dorf has set up a council, and there…"

"Dorf? Council?" Berlip made a dramatic sigh, before raising a finger and impersonating a weak and ineffectual Scribe. "'Excuse me, sir, but shall we vote *before* or *after* the dragon has eaten us?'"

"You demean yourself, Berlip." I said in a growl, once again feeling my chest tighten, and my fists start to clench. He could make fun out of me all he wanted, but if he thought that he could make my friends feel stupid or silly, then he had another thing coming.

"Do I? And how will our great Torvald deal with those who argue against his rule, hmmm?" Berlip said, his self-righteousness forcing him to be brave. "Will you beat me? Throw me in jail for voicing my opinion? Exile me?"

I didn't know what I should do, but I knew what I *wanted* to do. Imagine my surprise when my desires were voiced not from my own mouth, but from someone else's entirely. A brightly-clad figure stepped from the throng below and shouted up.

"I don't know what a Son of Torvald would do, but a rover of the Shaar Anar would have knocked you onto your rump by now, little man!" The figure laughed, tall and good looking, with skin that was warm and tawny, a luxuriant black curly beard and hair and darting eyes. It was my mother's brother Lett, of the Gypsies of Shaar. "Neill, can I have the pleasure?" The man grinned at me.

"Who are you? What right do you have to be here?" Berlip said, looking suddenly unsure next to the much broader, taller, and completely unfazed man. Uncle Lett was a man of the outdoors. He and all of his family spent their lives traveling the Three Kingdoms, sleeping in their finely-wrought caravans, training the wild ponies that they bred along the way, hunting and poaching where they wanted, and never having to be beholden to anyone but each other.

"This man has as much right as you, Berlip," I growled, adding, "At least he *wants* to be here!" I offered my uncle both forearms in the traditional greeting of the Gypsies, which he clasped, our hands to each other's elbows.

"Look at you, Neill – what sour company you are keeping these days!" Lett laughed, guiding me down from the rubble. Around us I could see the other monks muttering amongst themselves, the moment of tension and crisis starting to dissolve under my uncle's booming laugh.

"We'll call a council meeting!" Char said from behind us. "We'll discuss your issues there…"

Another meeting, I groaned internally, pausing beside of Uncle Lett as I knew that Char's words had also included me. But what could I do that Char couldn't? I was tired and weary, and I was failing this place. I'd probably only make the meeting worse, somehow.

But I was just nodding, too happily distracted by my uncle and his bright caravan of people who were even now parking in the central courtyard. After our panicked hunt for Zaxx, and the disastrous dragon training, the sight of these wild and unfettered people felt like home to my tired eyes. And besides, Char was handling everything just as well if not better than I was.

CHAPTER 12
NEILL SHAAR-TORVALD

"This is a fine place you have made here," my Uncle Lett Shaar Anar lied, as I led him around the grounds of the Dragon Monastery on a small tour. I had showed him the practice yards as we stopped at the stables to get my still-irritable pony Stamper, the grand architecture of the stone-built main hall, the impossibly tall Astrographer's Tower, and the outer walls each stone several feet thick—not that it had stopped the dragons tearing them from their mortar beds when they settled on the ramparts.

I could tell that my Uncle Lett was lying because of the way that the words never reached his eyes or his lips. Like all of my mother's people, Uncle Lett was a very expressive man. His voice boomed when he was happy, or thundered when he was not. His eyes sparkled when he talked to you, and only now, when his voice was deadpan and disinterested could I be certain that he was lying.

"Yeah, it's...*grand*," I added, looking out over the collapsed pile of rubble and up to the slopes of the mountain and the crater beyond. I *wasn't* lying, but then why did I feel so out of place here?

"Show me this lake then, where you first met that big red," Lett said, nodding up the hillside in the direction that I was peering. He could always read my thoughts, even though I only saw him occasionally, usually in the summers when his family moved north to bring rare southern silks and spices to trade with us Middle Kingdomers. I was only too happy to agree, fetching my cloak as Lett called up one of his horses and a couple of his traveling troupe to come with us.

"You remember my wife Maya, of course." Lett leapt onto the back of the horse already occupied by his small and dark-haired wife. "And Daros, Sami, they are your second cousins, or was it third?" He laughed as the two young men shrugged. Each had the same dark hair and tawny skin of the Shaar, although Sami kept his cut short as I did. They were about my age, perhaps a little older, but their dress and manner couldn't be more different from my restrained and somber monastery black. Daros wore a white linen shirt, embroidered with red and purple swirling lines, while Sami wore a sleeveless leather jerkin, heavily beaded, and a crimson sash belt. I greeted them all as I tried to encourage Stamper to take a walk with us.

Stamper was eager to be moving, but as soon as we had got out from under the shadows of the monastery stones, he started throwing his head and chomping at the bit.

"*Pshaw!* Neill, have you forgotten everything I taught you?" Lett nudged his own horse aside mine, and leant over to loosen

Stamper's bit, all the while murmuring whispered words to him at the same time, rubbing his nose and neck. To my surprise, my recalcitrant little pony swiveled his ears and *huffed* at him, and was rewarded with some mysterious treat from a hidden pocket.

"He doesn't like the bit, and he doesn't think he needs it," Lett said by way of answer, and I duly unfastened the bridle with a jangle of steel and leather, as Lett pulled from his saddle bags the wide padded leather halter to reattach the reins to, and for a wonder Stamper was remarkably easier to handle from then on, and that gave me a thought.

If Stamper here doesn't like a bit between her teeth, then maybe the dragons won't want one either? We didn't have a bit for Paxala, because, well, Char and Paxala had almost grown up together, and most of the time that Paxala had offered to take me on her back, we had been in the throes of battle or urgent missions when I had no time to set up the complicated arrangement of leather straps and metal buckles and bits.

But it was something I would have to raise with Char, when I got the chance, or—now that Paxala is helping to train the dragons –with the Crimson Red herself!

Uncle Lett had always tried to teach me such small little things when he passed by. How to ride a horse, how to palm a coin, how to speak a few words in the Shaar Gypsy tongue. How could I have forgotten so much? I thought, my heart feeling heavy.

"Ah Neill, you look like your father did at that age," Lett advised me sagely as we climbed up onto the ridge, and back down the other side.

"My father who is dead," I said, suddenly sunk into that cold and grey silence whenever I thought about him.

"Neill, I know." Uncle Lett reached over to place a comforting hand on my shoulder. "I have heard the news of your father's passing, even on the southern roads. That, and stranger tidings besides…"

I struggled to swim out of my grey blanket of mourning, coughing as I managed to ask, "You knew my father when he was young?"

"Of course! He was the first man to throw me in chains when we traveled through Torvald lands. He looked like you did now, young, worried, with too much on his shoulders and his mind." Lett laughed. "Until he met my sister, of course, and the rest is history. *Your* history," he said with a scandalous grin towards me.

That was my uncle all over. No care that couldn't be overcome, and no troubles that couldn't be left behind. It was a balm being in his company, and he and the others soon had me laughing as they recounted their exploits up and down the Three Kingdoms.

"Your father hated me, of course, and I disliked the Midlander who would make a settled woman out of my sister…" My uncle laughed. "But when the Gypsies came under the curse of that old Sorcerer Thrangor, well, it was your father who rode with me to hunt him down," Uncle Lett said.

"The Sorcerer Thrangor?" I asked. I'd never heard any of this.

"Oh, it was a long time ago, and far away. An evil sorcerer who tried to enslave the Gypsies. Just let me say this: Never, *ever* offer a sorcerer cake. That is my sage advice on the ways of magic, young Neill." Uncle made me laugh as he always did, but as we neared the secluded lake, all of our thoughts naturally turned to the dragons.

"Everywhere, everyone is talking about the boy who rode a dragon," Lett confided in me as we slid from our steeds, and Maya and the boys started gathering dried wood for the fire.

"Really? Even down in the south?" I asked, looking out at the lake that was burning with the lowering sun.

"*Especially* in Prince Griffith's realm, young Neill." Lett nodded emphatically. "They have their own wild dragons down there you know – I've seen them! Orange and yellow and as vicious as a snake."

I listened, enraptured. Despite all of my dark feelings around my own capabilities as a leader, the very thought of the dragons was usually enough to lift my spirits a little. My uncle told me how they lived in outcrops and towers of rock that stuck out from the desert floor, surrounded by verdant green oases, and how they terrorized the local tribes and occasional merchant travelers who passed by those routes.

"That is why the south are in awe of you, Neill, of managing to ride a dragon, and overthrow the Draconis Order." Lett gave me an elaborate clap with his hands, as if this were a show and I was performing.

But that's half the problem, isn't it? If this were one of my uncle's plays, I would know what my role was. I would have learnt my lines…Whatever confidence I might've had seemed to have vanished along with my father.

I am not half the man that my father was, I reminded myself. He was always so big and gruff-voiced and strong. I had seen all my life how the others responded to him. I could never do that – I could never *be* that!

"Well, maybe they shouldn't be so easily impressed," I grumbled, knowing that I sounded churlish, but unable to stop myself.

"Neill! What is the meaning of this?" Lett frowned at me in the deepening night. "The last time that I came here, you were being punished by that old Abbot and the Prince Vincent, that monk friend of yours helped me to find you – but all of that is over now, isn't it? You are your own man again!"

"It's just..." I started, unsure of what I was going to say even, but the look of kindliness in my uncle's eyes – the complete lack of judgment or expectation poured the words out of me. "It's just that I don't feel like my own man. I feel like I belong to everyone else. The students want me lead them, the monks want me to make them safe. My brothers want me to disappear forever, and who knows what Prince Vincent wants of me..." I said.

Uncle Lett didn't say anything, just nodded, and started to pile the wood for Maya to set sparks to the kindling. In a strange way, his silence helped me to speak *more*, not less.

"And it's not as if *I* know how to give anyone what they want, anyway..." I said. "If I did, if I knew what words to say and how to act around people so that they would respect me and believe me, I would! But I don't! I have no idea what it is that I am doing...." I ended on a plaintive note, and Maya made a sympathetic, hushing noise as she patted my shoulder.

"I see your problem, Neill, and I will think on it – but first, we eat! No problem is helped by an empty stomach!" Uncle Lett said, waving over to Daros and Sami as they came wading back from the shallows of the cold lake, and dangling from the short lines in their hands a brace of long, silver-scaled fish. In no time at all we all pitched in to have the fish cleaned, skinned, and were cooking them over the embers of the fire.

"You are a young man, Neill Shaar-Torvald," my Uncle Lett said, and his words made me sit up. He had never called me by my mother's heritage before. Shaar was a distant, distant land, so far away as to only be guessed at on the maps, and all of the southern Gypsies claimed to have come from it, although none could remember the way back. *What was my uncle trying to tell me, by calling me by my mother's and his heritage name?* The question flashed through my mind, before I shook my head at my own twisted thoughts. *Why was I second-guessing my own uncle? That was what I ought to do with Berlip and the other monks back there, not my own blood!* It saddened me that the politics of being a leader had changed me so much, even the way that I thought about things. *When could I just be riding the Crimson Red, free and wild?*

"Like your father," Lett continued, "you have had a lot of responsibility thrust on your shoulders at a young age. Did you know that was how he began, as well? That his father before him died in battle, and so Malos, *your* father, had to unify his clan quickly, and fight off the raiders when he was barely a handful of years older than yourself?"

"Oh," I said. No, I didn't know that. It made me feel strange towards my father, as if knowing more about him made me resent the memories that I *did* have of him, like they were fake, and this man that Lett was talking about was the 'real' Malos Torvald. "I wish he had left some diaries or something of how he did it, then," I said, making Lett laugh.

"Ah, Neill, you sound either very wise, or very old. Too wise and too old for such young shoulders! You should be thinking about music, and dragons, and food, and *girls,* if that is your fancy!" Lett nudged me in the ribs, almost making me choke on my piece of cooked fish.

"Hey! Uh – what?" I said, covering my sudden blush as I coughed and patted my chest. Daros and Sami laughed at my discomfort, but I also noted that it wasn't a nasty or a cruel laugh like the ones that the old Monk Olan, or even Berlip had sounded.

"Oh, and what do you two know about girls or boys, huh?" Maya scolded the two. "What happened back in that port town we passed by this spring? I was sure I saw you, Daros, get slapped at least twice, and you, Sami, get a bucket of horse-water tipped over your head!" She cackled, making the two younger boys and the rest of us guffaw as it was their turn to plead, argue, and blush that it wasn't what anyone thought. When we had wiped away our tears of merriment, it was Lett who cleared his throat and turned back to me, however.

"But that girl. The fair-haired Northlander. She likes you, I can tell," Lett said with that same old twinkle in his eye.

"You mean Char?" I asked, my cheeks burning. I was suddenly quite thankful it was nighttime, so at least no one would see my embarrassment. Char was a princess, and I am a warlord's son. Even to think of such things was madness, surely?

"Oh-ho! So you know which one I was referring to then, huh?" Lett offered with a wink.

"No, I mean – she's the only Northlander I know here…" I said, which was technically true, as the other Northlander monks and students I didn't know by name. Anyway, what did my uncle mean that Char 'liked' me?

"Of course, young Neill, I believe you – but it is not my intention to make fun of you, just to point out that other young men your age have different preoccupations. Some which don't leave them walking around with a heavy frown on their faces! You do not have to always walk in your father's footsteps, Neill, my lad," Lett said, and I knew then that must be one of the reasons why he had brought Daros and Sami with us. It wasn't just that they had never visited the great and grand Dragon Monastery of the Middle Kingdom, it was because they stood as my peers. Versions of Neill Shaar-Torvald that I *could* be, that my uncle even wanted me to be?

"Yes, thank you, uncle," I said with a sigh, my embarrassment temporarily forgotten. "Really, thank you for this – for this evening away from the monastery, for reminding me of who I am – but I have responsibilities that mean I *don't* have time for music and food and *girls*." –I said the last part a little quickly— "These people here, they are depending on me." I remembered everything I had gone through just to get this far. I had been pushed out of my family home before I was ready to leave. I had been shoved and scolded and harassed, called out for my mixed heritage by Quartermaster Greer. I had been imprisoned by Char's father, Prince Lander of the Northern Realm, I had ridden against Zaxx. How could I throw all of that away to go on dances and enjoy myself, when we were in so much danger? It would be like becoming someone else, I thought.

Someone else. The thought struck in my mind. That was the essence of the problem though, wasn't it? I didn't feel like *me* at the moment at all. I felt like I was trying to be a different person, a leader like my father, and in the process, I was failing to be the friend that I should be, *and* the leader as well. I couldn't be like my father, even though I knew that I had to be—that Char must want me to be a leader like him. That the academy needed me to be a leader like the great Malos Torvald… No, I was just Neill, not anyone else.

I was trying to be someone else. When could I just be myself? The boy who loved dragons. The boy who loved flying dragons? The boy who didn't have to pretend to know what he was doing all of the time?

Neill Shaar-Torvald, my uncle's words came back to me. That sounded like a good person to be. That sounded like a young man who wouldn't have to worry about whether he was in the wrong, constantly. I wouldn't have to be the warlord's son all the time, I wouldn't have to try and be a copy of the great Chosen Warden of the Eastern Marches. The Gypsies were always a free people, they were mistrusted, sure, but looking at Uncle Lett I could see that he didn't care. None of his family cared what the settled Three Kingdomers thought of them. They made their own rules, and made their own names to live up to.

When I looked up from my contemplations of the embers of the fire, I found my Uncle Lett once again waiting patiently, and, at seeing my consternation he gave me an easy smile. "I know that these responsibilities weigh heavily upon your shoulders, Neill. They would on anyone's. You are 'the boy who flew' after all." My Uncle looked sad, as if the legend wasn't a great accolade at all, but a burden. I was starting to think that it was. I had so many questions that I had to consider: How was I going to rebuild the monastery? How was I going to make peace with the older monks? What was I going to do about my brothers? About Prince Vincent? About Prince Lander, Prince Griffith? And *then* there was Zaxx and the Abbot Ansall to consider, somewhere still out there and clearly already plotting our downfall.

"All I am saying, Neill, is that I am an old rover, and a Gypsy Chief, and your uncle." He sighed heavily, patting his belly that was full of fresh fish. "I worry for you, and I want you to be happy. I like to think that I have discovered a thing or two out there in the world…."

"Hah!" Maya rolled her eyes, but despite whatever she thought about her husband's questionable 'wisdom' she didn't go into details then and there.

"…And I have come to learn that whenever great attention is brought to someone, especially to us Gypsies, it usually means that bad will follow. We Gypsies do not have the same types of heroes as the Middle Kingdomers, as you know, young Neill. Our heroes are flesh and blood, real people, they swear and they spit and they pull off great deeds. They are not lofty lords and knights whom we bow and scrape to…" my uncle lectured. "*We* know that heroes have all of the rocks thrown at them. That every time one stands up, there are a ten willing to drag them down. We know that all heroes have flaws and imperfections and make mistakes—that no one can be perfect all the time. There is talk of the Dark Prince, Prince Vincent, rallying his forces, of rumors of war and revolution in the Three Kingdoms, and every time I ask about these rumors, they always come back to this place, this Dragon Monastery, and to the boy who flew.

My uncle's look turned serious, his large mustache dragging downwards into a scowl. "There is talk, abroad, of the Sons of Torvald riding out again. That they have been accepting many strange travelers into their halls, before riding north."

"What do you mean, uncle?" I said.

"The monks. The old ones of this place, those nasty little Scribes with their schemes and plots." My uncle never had time for the monastic traditions.

"The Draconis Order who served the old Abbot?" I said.

"Yes," Uncle Lett nodded. "There are rumors they have been gathering themselves to Torvald land, and it makes me ill to think of it."

"Impossible!" I burst out. My father had mistrusted the Draconis Order completely, and with good reason too, it seemed, as they had poisoned him in the end.

"They may be just the tall tales and rumors of the road, young Neill. You know how it is. The dust gets in one's eyes, but the ears hear all sorts of stories," Uncle Lett said. "Anyway, I know what you are doing here is brave, Neill, but I do not wish this trouble for my sister's son. I would sooner have you happy and safe."

"Believe me, I want to be happy too, uncle..." I said, with tears springing into my eyes. My uncle had come here, bringing his family all the way up to the Dragon Mountain because he was worried about me. He had heard the stories of the overthrow of the old Draconis Order, and perhaps even my rebuff of the Sons of Torvald attack, and he had immediately dropped everything to make sure I was okay. Who else had done that? Who else *would* do that? His compassion and respect for my well-being touched me, and once again I found myself fervently wishing that I had experienced the same from my own, real father.

"Then the way forward is simple, Neill," my uncle said seriously, sitting back up and putting a strong hand on my shoulder. "You are a man now, I see that in you, I see your strength. You must decide if you are going to stand on your own two feet like we Gypsies do, or whether you are going to give your life away to the others. Whether you are going to spend your life forever managing this or that alliance, this contract, that enemy. It is a form of bondage, Master Neill, and that is why we Gypsies of distant Shaar will have none of it. We were an enslaved people once—or so our oldest legends tell us – and we will never be so again!" he said, his eyes flashing with an indignant anger. "Do not be a slave to this monastery, to these people. Give to them only that which you can freely give, and for which you will be rewarded."

"But, but how, uncle?" I was confused.

There was a warning cluck of noise from Maya, and I realized that the two must have discussed all of this conversation intimately before they had arrived. She did not want my Uncle Lett to suggest whatever it was he was going to suggest next, but I pushed him.

"What is it, uncle? I think that you are perhaps the only person left I can trust to give me advice!" I implored.

I watched as my uncle glowered at the fire, before my words made up his mind. He nodded to himself with a grunt, cleared his throat, and then said in his loud and clear voice, "I had counselled myself not to say this to you, Neill, for fear of influencing your decision. And your Aunt Maya advised the same. But you are a young man, and you must make your own path in this life. But my heart could not leave you to these dangers that I see mounting around you on all sides, so I will give you the counsel of Family Chief Lett Shaar-Anar," he flourished his hands formally, indicating himself. "I think that you could leave this place," he said simply.

What? I almost coughed out loud, but my uncle was being deadly serious.

"They are asking too much of you, too much of any one man perhaps. They want you to be Neill Malos-Torvald, but Malos Torvald spent his life wading knee-deep in blood. The Dark Prince Vincent, and all of his brothers will view you as a threat, and you will have to decide whether to bend your knee to one of them, or to fight all of them – neither are wise choices for either you, for those students up there, or for your dragons," Lett carried on, despite the way that I could see Aunt Maya looking dismayed from her seat.

"You should leave this place, with your girl, and your dragon if it will come, and you should fly. Ride like we do, the traveling Gypsies of your mother's people. Become a dragon-rover, traveler of the world over! You know that you will always have a home with us, and we will never insist that you nor your dragon ever fight wars for us or lead us into battle! Just to work hard and to take what joy out of life as we are allowed before the final days. Leave the Dark Prince to squabble with his brothers over the scraps of ancient times! Come live in the now, with us!"

My uncle finished with another flourish, and Daros and Sami cheered, clearly used to listening to my uncle's dramatic speeches.

But for myself, however, I felt a strange, yawning sensation inside my heart. It trembled with fear, but also with excitement as well. *Was it even possible?* I started to think. *Could I really start afresh, somewhere else? Somewhere new?*

Could I just be myself, with my friends Char and Paxala and any of the others who will come with me? It made me feel fluttery and even hopeful, like there was going to be a way through this mess, if we but walked away from it. But what of the academy? I suddenly thought. What of all of those hours of training that we'd put in? Of all that knowledge held up there... Could I really just walk away from all of that?

Yes, I realized with shock. I really could, if it meant helping the dragons at the same time. As long as I stayed here, as the entire academy stayed here then it would always be in danger. Some lord or abbot or sorcerer would fix their greedy sights on it. Why not encourage the dragons to be wild once again? To freely choose their companions however they wished?

Why should I wait here, getting into arguments and plunging the dragon crater into war, anyway? I reasoned with myself. If the dragons really did return to the wild, then maybe everyone could develop their own relationship with the dragons, and not fight over them all the time?

It was a tenuous and fragile hope, but it was one that I threw my heart at.

I didn't have to be Neill, the Son of Torvald, the Leader of the Dragon Academy, I found myself smiling. I could be Neill Shaar-Torvald, Dragon Rider and dragon-rover, with Char at my side...But as tempting as that dream was, as close at hand that it felt, in some corner of my mind there was still a nagging thought that would not leave me be.

"Enough of this serious talk!" My uncle belched loudly into the night air. "We should tell stories under the night skies, and I want you, Master Neill, to make sure that my beautiful Maya and I don't get eaten by dragons in the middle of the night! We will all sleep out under the stars with our blankets as we used to do in the old times!" My uncle raised a heavy eyebrow at the two second or third cousins, Daros and Sami. "Apart from those two, however – your wyrms can eat them. They're only any good at stealing horses, and that is only when the horses are asleep!"

CHAPTER 13
CHAR, THE PROBLEM OF MAGIC

"Char?" Maxal Ganna said as he peered at me with his wide, perpetually-worried eyes from behind the dark door to the main chamber.

Our first council meeting was over, and it had gone disastrously, all things considered. It was now full-on nighttime and I was exhausted. We had had supper as we argued, and I had missed my usual sunset with Paxala, which was something I looked forward to every night—witnessing the dragons' particular affinity for both sunrise and sunset, expressed in caws and shrieks of approval. I was annoyed, and surrounded by the disheveled tables littered with scrolls upon which everyone had been taking notes.

"Maxal," I smiled wanly, despite the fact that all I could think was *not something else, please!*

The smaller student looked nervously about the room as he entered. He wasn't one for the press and tear of people. Maxal was one of the few students, like me, who had gone through the Abbot's magical training – or torture, as I now thought it to be— and I wondered if it had affected him as much or more than it did me. But Maxal relaxed visibly as he saw that only Dorf, me, and half a dozen of the other students remained in the large hall.

"How did it go?" he asked cautiously as he walked in.

"Berlip's faction is threatening to revolt. Nan's staff is over-worked. Zaxx is out there somewhere. The students are desperate to get more time with the dragons, and Neill is nowhere to be found!" I finished in exasperation. How could Neill do this to me, at this time? I thought. I needed him!

"He went off with his uncle," Dorf said, mumbling under a mountain of scroll work that he was trying to collate. "I think it's good, actually. He hasn't been looking himself recently. Maybe his uncle will help to put him back on track."

"We can only hope," I muttered. I knew that Neill admired his strong Uncle Lett, and the way the Gypsy had diffused the tension with Berlip earlier had been excellent. "Anyway, what is it, Maxal?" I looked over at him. Maxal wasn't one to chat or gossip lightly, and so whatever he must want to talk about had to be important.

"Well, two things," Maxal said. "I was doing as you asked, looking into the Abbot's dragon magic, if you wanted us to train people again..." he said.

"Great, thank you," I congratulated him. In fact, I had been all for stopping the magical training entirely now that I knew that the Abbot's magic came from the powdered remains of baby dragons, but I still didn't know if that meant that *student* magic came from the same source. The Abbot had never offered us students a potion, or any concoction to 'help' our magical abilities, so I was still mystified as to what to think about it all. "I guess it's important that people have the opportunity to find out if they have the skill…" I grumbled.

"Well, I had so many students ask me when the training was going to start after this morning that we would have enough for three or four groups, not that I know if any of them will have any magical ability…" Maxal said thoughtfully.

Three or four more groups of dragon Mages? I had to bite my tongue to stop the dismay from creeping onto my face. From my own experience of the magic, I didn't know if it could ever be redeemed. *But who are you, Char, to make that choice?* I told myself.

"Char? There is also another little problem…" Maxal interrupted my quandary.

Oh great. Of course there was. "A problem?" I asked, rubbing my tired eyes.

Maxal nodded and produced from his over-large black robes a small leather book in one hand, and a green-glass vial in the other with a cork stopper.

"What's that?" I felt a chill go down my spine.

Maxal grimaced as he set the vial onto the table in front of me, and turned to the book instead. "You remember this volume. It's *Versi's Voyage,* the memoirs of the explorer who travelled far to the south?"

I nodded that I did remember it. It was from Explorer Versi that we had first got accounts of natural dragon friends in the southern tribes. Hearing about his exploits in the deserts there had made what I did with Paxala seem a bit more normal, if uncommon.

"Well, later on in this volume he starts talking about dragon magic, the types of strange abilities that some of the older dragons have, as well as the humans that spend time with them." He said the last part heavily.

"What?" I looked at Maxal, who cleared his throat and prepared for his favorite past time besides reading, reading aloud.

"So then, we can assume that the older dragons develop strange powers over the soul of a man, powers such as telepathy, suggestion, hypnotism, and even the ability to influence dreams, feelings, and thoughts," Maxal continued reading the explorer's words.

"There are even tales that the eldest of dragons can 'smell the future' although I have never seen it in practice. But even stranger, too, are the mystics and shamans who spend much time in contact with their befriended dragons. It seems that the closer that the human and the dragon become, and the more that they start to share each other's life, the more that the human and dragon qualities become shared...." Maxal gave me a meaningful look.

"These shamans exhibit the same powers of suggestion and hypnotism as their dragons, and can also summon great and strange elemental powers: sudden fires, violent storms, fearsome winds – and move things with the strength of their prayers and mind alone!"

Maxal closed the book with a 'what do you think of that!'

look upon his face.

I didn't know what I thought of it. I couldn't explain it, but I knew that it was the answer to why I had the magic. "That explains it," I said. "I befriended Paxala, and raised her from hatchling to newt to dragon. Some of her power must have rubbed off on me..." I said.

"That explains *everything*," Maxal corrected. "Why the Abbot started this monastery here, at the natural crater home of the Middle Kingdom dragons. He must have known that this could happen, that humans could start sharing in the dragons' powers." Maxal looked around the walls and floors of the monastery. "But he wanted to control that sharing of power. He didn't want everyone to have it..." Next, Maxal picked up the small green vial and shook it in front of me. It gave off a slight hissing, tinkling noise as it did so.

"I was in the Abbot's old rooms, and I found this," Maxal said darkly. "And so I started searching. I found some more near the library, in a crate in one of the old storage rooms."

My stomach turned over. "Is that... Is that what I think it is?"

I remembered the tiny, crabbed and spider-scrawled hand-writing on the Old Queen Delia's very own journal that I had found at my father's fort. It had been a record of the strange practices and ceremonies that she had performed, in tandem with Abbot Ansall, in order to prolong both of their lives and gain more and more unnatural power. They had killed baby hatchling dragons, and used their remains to imbibe their power.

And the old queen lived to well past a hundred, I thought in horror. She had not lived until my time, but she had given birth to my father, the Northern Prince Lander, well into what must have been her eighties or nineties, although her portraits still painted her as a fulsome woman in her middling years.

Which meant that the Abbot Ansall could be ancient. Two hundred? Three hundred years? I shivered at the thought of his pale, papery skin and his wiry beard like frozen briars. *Just how far back does his evil go?*

"I think that it is," Maxal grimaced. "Powdered remains of dragons. The Abbot..."

"He must have been putting it into the food!" Dorf suddenly gasped, a moment before his careful stack of scrolls that he was holding in his hands slipped from them and fell to the floor in disarray once more. He looked decidedly green, and rushed out of the room to the nearest convenience.

I nodded sourly at Maxal. It was a thought that I had considered before now, but hadn't wanted to believe was true. The Abbot could have been dosing us with his powdered dragon, at the same time he used his own magic to subdue and twist us to his own ends. I felt sick, but both my and Maxal's constitution proved stronger than Dorf's.

"No more training." I said heavily. "And we're going to scatter every vial that you found, back to the crater winds where they belong."

"I agree.... But..." Maxal tapped the table with his delicate, small fingers. "But what if some of the students start developing their powers naturally? Without the powder? Just as Versi talked about?"

"Then..." I started to say, before feeling exasperated. *Then what? What do we do then?*

"I think we should teach the theory of dragon magic," Maxal stated. "But the practice...? That will remain a private thing. If someone shows promise, then they'll have to come to one of us."

"Or their dragon, of course," I said. In fact, in a sick way, it was a relief to come to this decision about the teaching of dragon magic. It felt right to leave its mysteries be; to let people and their own dragons find their own rhythm. Yeah, I thought. The Dragon Academy in the future wouldn't be where you came to study magic; it would be a place where you came to study dragons, and if dragon mages came out of that, then that was just an added bonus.

"We'll get rid of the vials in the morning, at dawn," I said to Maxal, yawning. "But for now, we'll have to hide them. I don't want anyone else finding that..." The thought of the uproar, greed, and scandal it would cause between the older monks (who might even approve of the powder) and the students (who I knew would hate it) would be enough to destroy the fragile alliance that we had worked out this night.

Maxal nodded, picking up the vial and the book and turned to go, before pausing at the door. "You should get some rest, Char," he said. "You look terrible."

"Thanks," I groaned. Coming from him, a boy who was so pale as to be almost see-through, I knew I must really need some sleep. "I can't believe how long this day has been. Just a few hours ago, I thought that we were going to have to fight Zaxx the Golden!" I muttered, easing myself to my feet.

"Oh, I almost forgot!" Maxal stopped completely this time,

his hands rummaging in the deep pockets of his black cloak.

"If you're going to produce something else gross Maxal, then really, right now I don't want to know. Can't it wait until morning?" I said.

"No, it's not gross. Well, not *really* gross, anyway…" Maxal instead brought out a dense handful of something black, blue, and grey, and strangely fibrous.

"What is that?" I asked. It looked *organic,* like it was a plant or something.

"Feather-Sponge, it's a type of moss that grows on some of the trees on Mount Hammal. I read about it in *Versi's Voyage,* that some of the tribes put it in their ears and used it to block out the sounds of dragon calls. I was thinking that maybe…"

"We could give it to the dragons!" I clapped my hands in delight. "It might help protect them from Zaxx!" Of course, I knew that the dragons would still be alarmed by the scent of Zaxx, but they would be much better protected than they had been.

Maxal nodded, giving me a shy grin. A large part of the problem, it seemed, was that the golden bull dragon had spent decades – centuries even, training his clutches and broods to fear his roar, and so, like the dragon pipes of old, he could use his roar to terrify and subdue them. If we could even make it just a little more difficult for Zaxx to intimidate the crater dragons, then it might mean that we had a chance to fight back against them!

"This is brilliant, Maxal," I nodded. "We'll harvest some in the morning, after scattering the powder."

CHAPTER 14
NEILL, AND THE DARK PRINCE

The dragon horn blared its alarm across the mountain, waking me up from quite possibly the soundest sleep I had ever had. Even though I had spent the night wrapped in one of my uncle's brightly-woven blankets on the stone and shingle beach of the lakeside, and my body was now cold and a little stiff, I had slept deeply and well, and woke up feeling refreshed.

Neill Shaar-Torvald, I remembered, my heart hammering as Uncle Lett groaned and grumbled awake. That was who I would be.

"What is that heavens' awful racket?" he said blearily, clearly having imbibed in too much of the berry wine he had produced at some point in the evening. "Does that happen every morning? At this hour? No wonder you're so stressed, Neill!"

Daros and Sami slept on, blissfully unaware, but Maya was groaning, and already shuffling to the cold embers of the fire, tutting and snapping twigs.

The dragon horn sounded again, and I checked the lightening sky once again. The sunrise was imminent, but the problem was, we didn't *use* the dragon horn at sunrise. We had stopped the former practice of the old Draconis order of sounding the old dragon pipes at dawn and sunset immediately. We had no wish, no need, to remind the dragons who was 'really' in charge on this mountain, as the Abbot Ansall had, and now only used our modified, gentler dragon horn as an alarm or a celebration of something.

"No, that sound doesn't happen every morning. Something's wrong!" I said, picking up my cloak and running to Stamper who was placidly nibbling grass on the edge of the trees. I was about to leap upon him bareback and urge him up the track to the ridge, and the monastery beyond, when Uncle Lett shouted at me.

"Wait, Neill! Can't it wait until after breakfast?"

It couldn't, and I knew that my uncle would forgive me for abandoning him there. He was a man of taking quick offense, and offering quicker forgiveness. I had never known Uncle Lett to hold a grudge against anyone or anything, as, in his own words, "life is short and the roads are long." So I continued to click my tongue at the surprisingly obliging bitless Stamper and soon we were trotting up the trail until we neared the top of the ridge, the warm air billowing like smoke from Stamper's nose in the cold morning.

"Screch? Skrar!"

The sound of the waking dragons rose to meet me in the early morning air. They sounded normal, and I realized that perhaps I was on edge, worried after my night away. Perhaps they've found something to celebrate, I thought, as we crested the rise, and held a hand over my eyes to stare into the distant spaces around the mountain. But what if it was Zaxx? Has he been sighted? I suddenly thought in terror, my stomach clenching in fear and worry. Maybe it was too late to enact my plan; to encourage us to disband the monastery entire, and to allow the dragons to be finally, truthfully, free. Maybe Zaxx has come to attack us before we could flee! I thought.

But it wasn't Zaxx, though there was a large shape on the horizon.

It was a dark smudge on the road, still many leagues away in the grey and green of the early morning, but I could tell it would be an impressive size when it finally made its way here. There was already a haze of smoke and dust hanging around it, making it hard for my eyes to pierce the gloom.

They must have marched all night, I thought, realizing that I was looking at a sizeable army, approaching out of the north east, and I knew no matter how much I wanted to be Neill Shaar-Torvald, this morning, today, I had to be Neill Malos-Torvald.

"Who is it?" I called out to the wall scouts as I galloped back into the monastery gates, Stamper whinnying in excitement at the early morning exuberance.

"Neill? Thank the stars that you're back!" Sigrid, who was even now waving her long and slender arms at me from the front wall to get my attention, shouted.

I wasn't particularly gone that long, I thought. Only one night, and last year I traveled with Paxala for weeks at a time to the Northern realm! But I guessed that the differences between the Neill of last year and the Neill that they were trying to turn me into were only too clear. Gone were the times that I could just leave the monastery and trust it would go on fine without me, that decisions could be made in my stead. The thought of that awesome responsibility brought me back to Uncle Lett's advice. Did I even want to stay here? But this was not the time for such questions.

"What's going on?" I said, dismounting and handing Stamper over to one of the stable monks, who immediately and warily fed him some dried apple. I was halfway up the stone stairs towards Sigrid as she beckoned me into the guard house that overlooked the main gates and down the road to the lands below. In this simple stone room, we also stored the spears, short and long bows, old suits of leather armor, flags and pennants, and the ocular devices that the scouts had told me were the wonders of the modern world.

"Here." Sigrid selected one of the ocular devices – long tubes of wood, with glass at either end – and affixed to one of the floor mounted stands. She checked it to make sure it was in position, and then took a step back so I could look through.

The road, hills, ditches and hedges were suddenly clear, though my vision was not so sharp as to make out individual birds, or the types of trees that stood here and there, but clear enough to tell the difference between tree and road, between stone wall and field.

And then I saw it, the dark shape I'd seen from the ridge, now visible as a morass of people marching, carrying long pikes and banners. By carefully moving the stand, I could look up and down the long, tramping column of men and women. There could easily be thousands there, followed by caravans and wagons, carts and even ornate carriages moving near the center and the back of the marching horde. There were mounted knights and horses, as well as line after line of marching people, with smaller runners moving up and down the line with many skins of wine or water. This was a well-organized campaign on the move, and it was coming here.

"It's not the Sons of Torvald," I said as an aside to Sigrid – although I didn't know whether she saw that as a good thing or not. At least my brothers I might have been able to reason with, but these were not them. No, these soldiers wore dark burgundy that indicated that they were of Middle Kingdom allegiance and they were well equipped.

And then, when the middle of the column finally came into focus, I saw what it was that I had been looking for, what some deep part of me had known all along from the moment I spotted the army from the ridge, from the moment I'd heard the dragon horn and my mind had begun shouting, *You're too late! You can't leave now! You'll be trapped here!*

Fluttering over the very center of the column, over an ornate wooden carriage pulled by a team of magnificent stallions was a singular pennant, black and purple, edged in gold.

"It's him. Prince Vincent," I said, my mouth drying up.

The Dark Prince Vincent had come to the center of his kingdom, either to demand that I turn over the Dragon Monastery to him, or to raze it to the ground.

～

"Neill?" said a voice.

I turned from the eye device and felt a wash of conflicting emotions—shame, happiness, excitement and worry—as I looked upon Char's worried face. Your girl, Uncle Lett had called her, and it had seemed right. But there was no time for that now, no time to tell her my plan, to tell her I wanted us to leave this place. No time to apologize for having left her to deal with the council meeting and everything else last night. Would Char ever agree to come with me? Or was she too tied now to these stone halls?

Not when she sees that all this monastery brings is violence and bloodshed! I thought, as Char went on in a careful voice.

"I'm glad you're back. Who's it out there?"

"Prince Vincent," I said quickly. "I thought he was fighting your father to the north, Prince Lander."

"So did I..." Char's brows beetled and she pursed her lips. I knew when she was worried; she became frustrated and angry – and now she looked incandescent. "Oh stars, I hope this doesn't mean that he's won!" I could see the fear in her eyes, no matter how much distance there now was between Char and her father, the mountain princess was still close to her brother, the bear of a young man called Wurgan, and general of their father's forces.

"Both Wurgan and Prince Lander are tough men. I'm certain they yet live," I said, hoping that what I said was true.

"We parlay," Char said immediately, not pausing as she searched for an answer to the situation. "Either Prince Vincent has won the border war and now he wants this place, or he's come asking for help in defeating my father...."

"None of those things are going to happen," I said. I had no intention of staying around long enough to start getting mixed up in other men's wars.

"No, of course not. What does Prince Vincent think, that we're just going to roll over and give him access to the dragons?" Char shook her head. "So, we parlay instead. Negotiate with him."

"Negotiate?" I spluttered. "The guy is a madman. A psychopathic madman!" I felt a thread of panic running through me. The last time that I had any dealings with Prince Vincent, he had encouraged the Abbot to leave me to freeze half to death on the top of Mount Hammal. If it hadn't been for Jodreth and Uncle Lett, I might never have made it down alive at all. Jodreth was gone now, but so was the Abbot, and I had Char, the dragons, and my uncle at my side.

A growl escaped my clenched teeth as I remembered the prince's snide and self-important look of disdain. I wasn't going to bend a knee to him, I thought.

"Get Paxala, Morax, and Socolia on the front walls," I said, decisive.

If I were thinking like my father, I would pull everyone back.

I would make it seem that we were an easy pushover, and then surprise him with dragons.

But I am not my father, am I? I am Neill Shaar-Torvald. And one of a Gypsies' great gifts has always been showmanship. Showmanship and cunning. "If we can show them early on that we have dragons that are willing to fight with us"—even if it were only three dragons— "then the prince might be a lot warier about attacking us." After all, it had only taken one dragon–Paxala–with me on her back to discourage the warbands of my brothers. What could three dragons do?

"I'll *ask* them," Char said pointedly, giving me an annoyed look before turning and leaving.

"I need to go to Socolia," Sigrid said, a little awkwardly. The stocky Green Socolia had only showed an interest in Sigrid so far, and so Sigrid had to fly solo, without a partner – which made it difficult for her to pass on suggestions to her dragon, with only her will working with the much larger instincts of the large Green. It made them a less effective team. *Well, it would just have to do,* I shrugged. These were our best riders. Me and Char on Paxala, and then Terrence and Lila on the Blue Morax, and now Socolia and Sigrid. All of the rest of the students hadn't managed to find their dragons yet, and we were still working out how to get them to bond.

"Go," I nodded, knowing that it would take the armies of the Middle Kingdom more than a few hours to reach the monastery. In the meantime, I would try to make the front gates look as defended as possible.

The dragon horn continuously blared above my head as I

worked, calling up several students to position the old wagons the monks had used to haul hay and provisions, to the rear of the monastery grounds, effectively plugging the gaps made by the tumble-down wall.

I had only just finished explaining when Dorf ran towards me, wearing an oversized leather cap and greaves he had only barely tied together. He looked as confused about what to do as I felt, but in his hands, he held a pile of different materials.

"Neill?" he said. "I've an idea!"

"Flags?" I said, remembering how Monk Feodor had showed them to me before the confrontation with the Sons of Torvald.

"Yes!" Dorf said, showing me the different colors, although the greatest number of them were a deep crimson red. "I don't know if I told you this, but when you went to the Northlands to help Char, Monk Feodor shared with me some of his ideas about flags, and how to use them. I thought that we could hang the red banners from the gate, to make us look more impressive."

"Excellent idea, Dorf!" I said, feeling happy for my friend but also a twinge of sadness at the time that he had shared with Feodor, one of the few monks here who had been nice to me at all. The Monk Feodor had been a soldier before becoming a monk, and, in fact, had only been asked to become a Draconis Monk after the Abbot had seen the man's skill with animals.

"Yes, the flags were an idea he brought with him from his soldiering days. Units and scouts can signal to each other over long distances just by waving the right flag…" Dorf explained. I had to refrain from saying, *I know, Dorf – my dad was a professional soldier!* Dorf's clear enthusiasm for the task was not something that I would wish to diminish. "We have red, yellow, blue, green… I thought that we could use them for the different dragons maybe, when we want them to fly, and where to…"

Why hadn't I thought of that? I wondered, marveling at Dorf's ingenuity. Hadn't my own father used flags with his troops?

"And we can use the terrain, too…" Dorf explained, gesturing to the wide mountain track that turned into a causeway, with deep gullies on either side.

"You're right!" I saw his plan immediately. "The faster dragons can fly down the causeway and harry them if they start attacking, and the larger, slower dragons can fly unseen in the gullies…" Dorf was getting remarkably good at these flying tactics, I thought. "You know what, Dorf," I said to him. "I know that you love books and reading, but you should try your hand at the scouting."

"*Navigating,*" Dorf corrected. "I'm good at navigating, and I love maps anyway… now if only my eyesight were better!"

The ocular devices! I thought, telling him to grab a few of the different ranged telescopes and use them. "You could be like our head navigator," I said, indicating the top of the wall. "Go on, start telling the other students and monks how to use the flags, and when you want them used – this is great!"

Dragon navigators and dragon warriors, I thought, thinking that it had a nice ring to it as I picked up my pace, stopping to help students get their armor and equipment on, and organizing shifts at the wall.

At midday, the dragon horn rang out three times, just as we'd planned, and I nodded to Dorf standing on the far wall, who waved his crimson red 'Academy' flag to signal to the operators in the Astrographer's Tower to cease. The Dark Prince was here, and the message had been sent.

"Are you okay?" I asked Char who sat atop Paxala. It had been her idea to have Paxala right here, perched on top of the gatehouse, and with the Blue Morax further to the northern wall (holding Terence and Lila) and Socolia the stocky Green (bearing Sigrid) on the southern.

"I will be when we find out what they want," Char said, looking pale but determined. Her glare at the mass below softened just a little as she looked down at me. "I'm glad that you're here with us, Neill," she said, and it was like I had been sucker punched.

When have I not been here? I thought. But I knew what she meant. Last night. The council meeting. And even though I'd been physically present during dragon training, my mind had been elsewhere. Since getting back from my father's Fort, in fact, I had been distant from Char and Paxala, and I saw now how much I'd let them down.

"Srech-ech-ech…" The Crimson Red made a soft wittering, almost a purring noise at me as if she could sense my thoughts. Probably she could.

"Char… About what's been happening…" I said uneasily, feeling ashamed. I still hadn't told her about my decision to disband the academy, to leave this place and ask her and Paxala to come with me.

"Not now, Neill," Char muttered to me, but her eyes were kind. "We need to talk, but not now…"

"You're right," I nodded, looking at what we now faced. Down below us, it looked as though the entire eastern flank of the mountain had been flooded by a dark sea and there was the distant roar of hubbub and busyness, even the knocking sounds of people setting up animal pens and fences.

Defenses, I thought. They're building defenses against a counter-attack.

Our little academy of five or six hundred humans had no chance against such a force, even given what my father had always said: "It takes five times attackers to defenders to take a town, ten times attackers to defenders to take a castle." What did this rundown, half destroyed stone monastery count as, I thought? These forward walls that we stood or perched upon were easily as strong as any castle fortification, but the walls at the north and to the west had gaping holes forced through them. And the prince's troops easily numbered a few thousand.

But right now, we didn't have to worry about several thousand attackers, just the ornate black carriage, pulled by a team of four stallions making its way up the mountain road, surrounded by a phalanx of mounted knights, as Prince Vincent himself came to parlay.

～

The carriage pulled to a stop in the wide, stony area outside the front gatehouse, and I watched as the phalanx of knights kept a protective avenue around it as first a servant in black and purple disembarked, and then the Dark Prince himself.

"It's easy to see why they call him the Dark Prince," Char muttered above me, and I agreed. Prince Vincent was tall, even handsome, I guess, with skin that was almost as pale as Char's, but long, straight black hair that he wore loose down his back. His clothes were a velvety darkness: tight-fitting, finely-tailored brocade made up his jerkin, with a collection of gold chains around his throat, and a golden coronet atop his head. He stood on the steps of his carriage as the servant attached to his belt a long-handled sword (its scabbard a gem-encrusted black leather, of course). This was all for show. Prince Vincent was clearly visible to both the guards on the tower, and his own men, and he wore no armor on at all.

He wants to prove he's not afraid of arrows or spears, I realized. But what about dragons?

"There's the scoundrel!" I was startled to hear my Uncle Lett hiss as he mounted the gatehouse landing with long strides. He stayed back from the gates, clearly cautious about being in this environment of generals and armies. I knew that it must be an effort for him to even stay here, as he had already made plain his intention to leave.

"Uncle," I greeted him.

"I swore an oath to avenge myself against that man who insulted you," Lett growled, scowling at the elaborate show that

Vincent was giving, dismissing his servant with the nonchalant wave of a hand.

"You might have time for your vengeance yet, uncle," I said, suddenly worried Lett's famous quick temper would prove the worse for all of us.

Vincent signaled to the man who must be his captain or general; a figure astride the tallest horse, with a high, conical helm and a thick red beard. The mounted figure spurred his horse forward, straight to our gates.

"Dragon Monastery!" the man bellowed, with the loud sort of rough voice that I had heard in the throats of my father's war captains and sergeants. "Open your doors for the ruler of the Middle Kingdom, the Prince Vincent!"

"What do we do?" Char asked, and all eyes on the wall turned to me, standing at the side of the red dragon.

What *do* we do? I thought. My earlier decisiveness was gone. I felt awkward and unsure again, and wished that I had found something a little grander to wear. As it was, I had on my black cloak with the fur stole of my Torvald heritage over my normal, weather-stained jerkin and trousers. Nothing fancy, and only a short sword and knife at my belt. No gold finery, no flags.

"Let him stew out there," Lett said with a chuckle. "I bet his high and mighty doesn't like being kept waiting…"

Although it wasn't a bad idea, and one that would please me immensely considering he had left me to 'wait' in the freezing cold of Mount Hammal, I knew that this was not a time for acts of small vengeance. "Fight angry, but never *think* angry," I said, as much for my benefit as my uncle's. It was another saying of my father's, and I was finally realizing its usefulness. But if any time was apt for thinking, when we were on the verge of being destroyed, it was now.

I cleared my throat, thinking quickly. "The prince is welcome to the Dragon *Academy*, sir," I called down. "But we forbid any armed men or women to enter our walls."

"We do?" Char said through gritted teeth, before nodding. "It's a good rule, so I guess that we do."

The red-bearded knight made a scoffing laugh. "You are young, Lord Torvald, and maybe you don't realize that these knights are sworn to defend their prince with their life. The prince cannot travel without arms, anytime, anywhere!"

Once again, all eyes turned to me to see what I would say in return.

"You can't let those knights in here!" Lett whispered to me. "Fully armored, battle-hardened knights against dawdling monks and children? They could have you all rounded up and in chains in a moment!"

"He's right," Char said from above me. "This could be a ploy. A trick to capture the dragons!"

"Do you dare defy us, Lord Torvald?" the red-bearded knight bellowed.

Why does he keep calling me Lord Torvald? I thought distractedly, biting my lip. Beside me Paxala scraped her claws against the stone, and I could sense her agitation. Then my answer came to me.

"Char? Take flight with Paxala! Show them her might and speed!" I said.

"What? Won't that provoke them?" Char said, although Paxala, able to understand what I had asked, was chirruping excitedly. I waved a hand to Dorf, making the pulling gesture that I wanted him to wave the flags as I called down to the prince's man below.

"But why should the prince need any more protection than what we can already provide?" I shouted, feeling a fierce joy running through my words. "Who would dare to counter the will of the dragons?"

"*Skreayaaar!*" At that moment, Paxala launched into the air directly over the prince and his forces, rippling out her wings in a sudden snap like the clap of thunder. The battle-hardened and oath-sworn knights quailed, and several broke ranks as they must have thought a Crimson Red dragon was about to fall upon them all – but Paxala and Char had already caught the wind, and were swooping low over the causeway, as fast as a speeding falcon.

"Krech! Vreyar!" At her loosing, Dorf waved the blue and the green flags to signal to Terence and Lila on their Blue Morax and Sigrid on her Green Socolia that they could fly—and fly they did. With excited screeches, they leapt into the air, the Sinuous Blue Morax whirling and snapping ahead, faster even than Paxala, and with the stocky Vicious Green Socolia pounding her wings to elevate her large body in wider and wider circles over the monastery.

I swiveled a finger in the air, and watched as Dorf copied my movements, swirling the green flag in a tight circle, and sweeping the blue flag in a wider one. He didn't have a red flag especially for Paxala the Crimson Red, but I trusted that Char and Paxala would still fly to best effect.

"I didn't know you could guide them that well..." Lett said, looking visibly taken aback by what he was watching.

Neither did I, I thought, just giving a tight smile in return. I can only pray to the stars that we can keep this show up long enough to impress the prince before the dragons get bored!

There were muttered arguments and wild gesticulations from below, as the elite knights rallied and collapsed into a mounted circle around the prince and the carriage.

"Come on, give in..." I whispered down to them, before order was restored to their ranks by the red-bearded general.

"It's clear they don't mean us harm or else they would have cooked you all by now!" he shouted, and the prince raised one black-gloved, slender hand. At that, his general and his knights fell silent as the prince himself raised his voice to us.

"You do yourself credit, little Lord Torvald, and fine, mighty beasts that you have here. I would be honored to enter your *Academy* of Dragons, as I have much to discuss with you. It is clear that I will not need my knights inside your walls, and that you can keep my personage perfectly safe. But I have to insist that my general Sir Rathon, and my servants will accompany me," he said, pausing to look over his shoulder at the large, dark sea that was his army below. "Who would dare attack us, indeed, with my army below?"

"It's a threat," Uncle Lett muttered beside me.

"I know," I nodded. It was clear that if any harm came to the prince or any of his retinue then the massed armies of the Middle

Kingdom would ride upon the academy with everything they had. "But it's as good as we can get."

"Neill..." uncle said warningly, "I fear that this will not be a good idea, not for you, or for this place..."

I felt a flash of annoyance at my uncle then. As much as I loved him, and as much as I wanted to leave this place and be free as he was, on the airs and roads of the wide world out there – could he not see that I was trying to do the best that I could? "Uncle, please," I implored, as I waved to Dorf to guide the dragons in and open the gates below.

Uncle Lett looked at me, aghast. In his hands, he even held his small, curved knife that I knew would be wickedly sharp. "I swore an oath, Neill... An oath to avenge the wrong that had been done to my family, through you. You cannot sit down and share a table with this man."

"Uncle, please, I must," I said once more, watching as the prince made his final preparations, dismissing his knights and stepping back into the carriage. "I have to, for the good of these people here." I nodded around the walls at the weary, worried, and clearly scared students and monks.

"You are a rover, one of the Shaar, you do not belong here, in these walls!" Lett said, brandishing the knife at the carriage below.

"No, uncle! I cannot allow you to take your vengeance now. Not with so much at stake," I said, even though it broke my heart to deny him.

"I cannot stay here with that man. He is cruel, and you will regret allowing him to enter, my nephew," Lett said, "Come,

come with me now, leave this place which forces you to break bread with those who have no honor!"

"Uncle…" I said in anguish. Even now, Lett was turning and walking back down the stone steps, and the prince's carriage horses were slowly trotting toward the open gate. I had never seen such a stark and clear choice offered in all of my life. But I couldn't do it. I couldn't just leave right now, and jeopardize the fates of all of these young and old people here in the academy, people that *I* had asked to overthrow the old Abbot.

"I can't come with you now, but after. After this place is safe…" I offered, but Lett was already at the bottom of the walls and signaling to Daros and Sami to start up their caravans.

"I will wait for you along the southern roads!" My uncle called out the traditional Gypsy blessing, "And may fair winds guide your journey!"

No, uncle, don't say that to me. I felt heartbroken, watching as my uncle pointedly mounted his pony, making the carriage of the prince pause and wait at the front gates as he and his family slowly wheeled around the courtyard, and headed west, towards the ruined walls where I knew they would find a way through, and out to the mountain trails beyond. I just hoped with all of my heart that he would forgive me when I really *did* have an opportunity to follow him.

But for now, as the black carriage clattered into the space vacated by my uncle's family, I knew that I had serious work to do. I had to entertain a prince.

CHAPTER 15
NEILL, THE OFFER

"Prince Vincent," I said, standing before the ornate, black-painted carriage. At my side stood a handful of the neatest-looking monks and students I could grab on my hurried steps down to the ground, as my closest confidants Char, Dorf and Sigrid were all occupied with the dragons.

"*Lord* Torvald," Vincent said, standing once more on the top step of the carriage as Sir Rathon, the red-bearded general, wheeled his horse to one side of us. The general's gauntleted hand resting on the pommel of his great-sword, and I didn't doubt for an instant that he wouldn't hesitate to use it if I made any move against the Dark Prince.

The prince himself was looking at me with narrowed eyes, but also a small, secretive half-smile on his face.

What is your game? I was suspicious, but forced a bland smile on my face (although I was sure that he could see through it). He had sharp features, much sharper and finer than Prince

Lander did, but there was something in his bearing that reminded me of the Northern Prince, and even of Char herself, I had to admit. A defiant streak that could stare anyone down, should he need to.

When he spoke, though, it wasn't the brusque and candid tones that I was expecting, but instead that of a charming courtier.

"Thank you for inviting me into your halls, Lord Torvald. I see that there have been many changes in the monastery, but also that you are running a tight ship!"

I am? I thought.

"Thank you, Prince Vincent, we are trying out best…" I said, wondering what etiquette that I was to observe. There was clearly something that either I was or wasn't doing that was sending General Rathon on the verge of boiling point, as he glared at me with fury, and his cheeks had flushed a tight, taut, red.

"Well, your best is already better than the many decades that the old fool Ansall was in charge!" The prince laughed and clapped his hand. His casual disregard for the old Abbot shocked me, I had to admit. I had thought them friends. *But maybe they had just been allies instead.* I remembered the advice of my father—that allies were not the same as sworn friends, as a friend you had to stand by with, through summertime and the winter, through hard times and the good; but with an ally you had to judge your every dealing.

But even so, I silently grumbled. *That 'ally' of the prince had poisoned my father, and Prince Vincent has seemingly done nothing.*

The Dark Prince gestured to the skies above us, where three dragons where now wheeling in to land. "The old Abbot never even managed to get one dragon off the ground in all the time that I have been coming here, and yet you already have three, in what, three months? Two seasons, is it?" The prince stepped down from the carriage, and with one gloved hand waved aside the general's warning growl as he crossed the distance to me, extending a forearm. He appeared casual, relaxed, as if we had been old friends and he was here to congratulate me on me achievements already.

"I, uh…" I felt completely discombobulated by the taller and older man's friendliness, finding it disturbingly natural to grasp his forearm to mine in a traditional warrior's grasp.

What is going on here? Why is he treating me like this? Does he not remember forcing me to be punished? I watched the older man carefully.

"Oh, don't be shy now, Torvald – you have done fantastically well here. Overthrowing the old Abbot? Getting rid of that monster Zaxx? I never liked that dragon, you know – it always seemed a bit creepy to me to be honest, the way that Abbot encouraged his acolytes to worship the bull, and all the while, the dragon was perfectly beastly to his own broods!"

I nodded. It was, after all, true. The golden bull had been a monster, and was, in fact, still a monster.

"We're uh, we're trying to do things differently now," I said, finding it awkward to remain standoffish and removed from him when he was acting so friendly. *Remember what he did to you on the mountain*, I told myself, straightening up a bit. It was this man's idea for me to freeze to death. Remember what Uncle Lett said.

"Yes, I can see... And I, for one, fully support it." Vincent beamed at me. "So, Master Torvald, before I tell you the business that brings me here, I simply *must* ask you one question,"

I gritted my teeth, wondering what it could be.

"What was it like riding a dragon for the first time, a creature so vast, so powerful, and so quick?" Vincent shocked me by asking. He smiled at me as he said so, appearing to be interested in the answer.

"Well, I had only ridden ponies before, your highness," I spluttered, caught off-guard as I remembered the moment that Paxala had stretched her leg and shoulder to me and clearly encouraged me to climb high onto her neck. "Uh, it was...incredible," I ended lamely.

"I am sure it was, Lord Torvald." The prince looked up to the dragons above us, bearing their own student riders as if they had been trained all of their life to do it. "I, too, have only ridden horses before. Stallions, of course, the best that the Royal Stables can provide – but how I have longed to ride a dragon, as soon as I heard of your great achievement! What fire and spirit they must have!"

It was hard to remain stoical before the man's enthusiasm. *Does he really like dragons too?* I found myself thinking. *How can he not?* I argued with myself, before coughing self-consciously.

"Thank you, your highness. Yes, they are marvelous creatures."

"They are." The prince nodded, before his smile faded a little and his eyes grew cold, though he had not moved a muscle.

Here it comes, I thought.

"Actually, that is one of the very reasons why I wanted to visit with you," he said in a slightly lower tone, half turning so that we faced the Great Hall, with the clearly visible remains of the wall on the far side. "You are going to have a lot of enemies at your door, *Lord* Torvald. As much as the old Draconis Order were, and I'm putting this nicely—as I'm sure one of your birth knows— *unpopular* amongst the common folk, the Draconis Order had *great* support from the nobles and the clan chiefs. The Abbot Ansall was very good at negotiating power, and securing protection for himself," the prince said darkly. "The noble families of the Middle Kingdom might not look too kindly on the fact that Ansall was ousted."

"Is that so?" I nodded, a reaction which only infuriated the General Rathon all the more. *Are you about to threaten me, Prince Vincent?* I thought.

"It is so, I am afraid to say." Vincent sighed. "Which is why I have come here to try and help you re-tie those bonds of friendship, as the throne of the Middle Kingdom and Mount Hammal have always stood side by side."

Yeah, no matter who is in charge of the monastery? I wondered skeptically. If the throne of the Middle Kingdom thought so highly of what we were doing here, and of me—*Lord* Torvald as he insists on calling me— then why come here with most of his armies to encamp at the foot of the mountain? Why not just send a messenger, seeking an audience? In the next breath, he told me just why.

"I have news, *Lord* Torvald. News that I think Mount Hammal and your people – and dragons – here will definitely want to hear," the Dark Prince said.

"Oh yes?" I said, catching some of the prince's attitude of dire urgency and secrecy as his eyes searched mine out.

The Dark Prince licked his lips, and then quickly stated, "It is Zaxx, and the old Abbot. I have word of them."

With a sudden screech and a rush of wind, a shadow fell over us as wings as large as sails snapped above the courtyard. It was Paxala, screaming to a halt as the large talons of her back feet gouged into the ground and she sat on her haunches, her great arms and leathery wings still outraised in front of the prince, his general, and the carriage. Anyone could see that she was clearly threatening him, and clearly territorial. On her back sat Char, not making a move to either calm or dissuade the Crimson Red.

"Char!" I said, waving my arms in front of my friend and the Crimson Red, hoping to try and calm them down. "The prince has been telling me that he brings us important news..." I said steadily, catching Char's eye as I said so. *I'm not sure if we can trust him. I don't want to trust him,* I tried to say with that look, although whether Char or the dragon could read my intentions it was impossible to say.

"It had *better* be *very* important," Char's defiant voice rang out, as Paxala's chest puffed out like bellows, preparing fire, I knew. "Because the last time that I checked, there was an entire army, maybe a couple of armies parked outside of our walls!"

She was right, of course. The prince owed her an explanation, as Char had done just as much to make this place as I had, probably more. But could we afford to challenge the prince, like this, and right now with his army sitting below us? I was worried. My father had always lectured long about caution over political and military matters. That it was usually better to take no action than it was to force one. *Choose your battles,* I had often overheard him say to his captains. *Choose when to fight them.* But I also knew that the Dark Prince owed the dragons an explanation, as well. This has always been their home, after all. The Dark Prince has come here with an army, and after having thoroughly supported the cruel Abbot in whatever he wanted to do, and perform whatever crazy experiments with both us students and the dragons... I felt caught between the advice of my father on one hand, and the honor of my friends, the dragons. on the other. *Another reason why I don't want to be a leader!* I thought. I didn't want to choose between them, but knew that I must.

Standing before mighty Paxala and seeing the hurt in Char's eyes, I chose my friends. I looked at the Dark Prince at my side, my face impassive. What happened next shocked me.

"Great Dragon!" The prince said, striding forward to stand beside me, before the front claws of the enraged Crimson Red. He knelt down on one knee and lowered his head, almost to the ground in a deep bow that was almost worthy of a monarch, before raising his gaze once again to speak, but remaining on one knee before Paxala.

"Most fierce Lady Red," I watched him call up to her. "I watched your flight with nothing but awe. How fast are your wings! How great your claws! What strength you have!" Paxala cocked her head to one side, unused to such flattery from anyone save Char or me.

"How could I mean you any harm, great Lady Red? How beautiful are your scales that flash in the sun! Instead, I come to offer my support and *friendship* to your cause, and to your own people." The Dark Prince nodded in the direction of the dragon crater. "It is true, that the old Abbot Ansall was a terrible man, and that what he did to you, to your young hatchlings and the newts, was nothing short of an atrocity – but no more!" the Dark Prince avowed. "No more will dragonkind ever have to fear humans…"

Fear? I thought with a subtle smile, as Paxala coughed a little puff of soot at the suggestion that she could even be afraid of anything at all.

"I swear that your kind will be safe here in the mountain for as long as I can draw breath, and I hope that together, we may be able to start a new chapter in this history of the world," the Prince Vincent called.

"Of course their kind will be safe, uncle," Char's voice called down. Oh yeah, he is her uncle, isn't he? I thought. It was easy to forget they were related, despite the similarities in their bearing and appearance. "They are dragons, and they have no one subjugating them now. They are free dragons, and we are their protectors."

"And what a great and fitting job it is for you, little niece," the Dark Prince congratulated her. "I am glad that it is you, here, Lady Nefrette. You were always strong enough to stand out from the crowd, even to defy your father!" Vincent said. "I have not come here to bargain with you and these noble creatures, but to offer my aid – and look what aid it is!" He stood up in one graceful movement, raising a hand to sweep it over towards the gates, and presumably beyond. We couldn't see his armies now from where we stood, but we could well imagine their might.

"With the Middle Kingdom standing beside you, who could ever threaten you again, Lady Red?" the prince said, holding his two hands in front of him and clasping them together, signifying an alliance. "The dragons of Mount Hammal and the Middle Kingdom are welded together through geography and so much more. Our histories are shared, our strength relies upon each other. I swear that the throne will be friends of the mountain of dragons for as long as my kingdom lasts!"

His words had the quality of a great speech, and I wondered if he had spent days thinking of them, or of how to talk to dragons. I had no doubt though, that his words would be remembered through history.

Isn't this just what I wanted, before leaving to travel with my own uncle? I thought. *Safety for the dragons?* I licked my lips nervously. Was this really what the prince was offering the dragons of the crater? No more wars. No more sacrifices. Being left to live in peace, protected by the throne of the Middle Kingdom forever? If that was true, then there was little need for me here anyway... I felt my heart skip a beat. *Could I finally be free to live my own life, to be a 'dragon rover' as Uncle Lett suggests?*

The hope was almost too delicious to admit, it was everything that I had yearned for, both for myself, Char, Paxala, and the rest of the dragons here at the crater. *But who would they get in charge of the academy after I am gone?* I thought. *Dorf, perhaps, or Lila...* They were both strong-hearted and true, and I knew that they would make fine protectors of the dragons – but there was something that still irked me about Prince Vincent's words. Could I *really* trust him? I suddenly realized that the prince was asking the Dragon Mountain and the Middle Kingdom to be friends, not allies. It was friends who looked after each other, who stood by each other, no matter what.

And how could I be friends with this man, who had been at least partly responsible for so much hurt here at the monastery?

It was Char who had the courage to say it out loud, and, as she did I felt my puny bubble of hope pop. "So, you are suggesting that you came all this way, with thousands of soldiers, and leaving your throne unguarded for the first time in history, just to impress the dragons of Mount Hammal?" She sounded skeptical, and Paxala issued a warning, grumbling hiss, so deep it echoed in my own chest.

"Yes!" Prince Vincent stated unequivocally. He was standing with his back now straight, not backing down or refusing to meet the dragon and rider's eyes. He was fearless, in a way, I thought. The same kind of fearless that Char was. The kind of fearless that made both of them stare straight into the face of danger and say whatever they wanted to say anyway...

"And I came to warn them, and warn all of the inhabitants of Dragon Mountain." The Dark Prince's voice carried clear through the courtyard, as everyone, even the two dragons Socolia and Morax on the walls had fallen silent.

"To *warn* us, uncle?" Char's ire rose, pitching her voice upwards slightly, and the deep grumble in Paxala's throat raised into a higher whine to match.

"Yes. There has been word of the Abbot, and sightings of the Gold dragon Zaxx the Mighty. Zaxx has attacked villages up and down the borders of the Middle Kingdom, and I have it on good authority that the Abbot has been working against us all, undermining the throne and seeking to raise for himself an army to retake the Dragon Monastery!"

"An army? Where is the Abbot going to find an army?" Char called out. "Why should we here be scared of one man?"

"He has the Sons of Torvald at his side," the Prince Vincent said heavily, very pointedly *not* looking at me as he did so.

What? I was aghast. *This could not be. Why would they?* My world rocked where I stood, but I knew too, that this felt all too right as well, because of course, why wouldn't they? My father had been preparing for the day when there would be a civil war against Prince Vincent. If my father's closest sergeants were to be believed, then my father, Malos Torvald, had even been preparing *me* to help the fight against the Dark Prince, and now, why wouldn't my brothers and Malos' 'true-born Torvald sons' as they had always styled themselves, carry out my father's final wishes?

But side with the Abbot Ansall? It made no sense. It made a mockery of Torvald honor.

But what honor do my brothers have? I was caught in an argument with myself. They drove me out from their lands, my childhood home. They attacked the monastery when I was inside it, with no care if whether I lived or died.

But still…. Allying with the one man who had conspired to kill our father, even when I had told them that was the case?

They might not have believed me. My brothers have always thought I was a liar, I thought, feeling Char's eyes rest on me as Paxala lowered herself to the floor.

"Neill?" Char asked. "Could this be true?"

"I don't know," I said honestly. "I don't know, but my Uncle Lett did say that on his travels, he had heard of the Torvalds amassing more troops…"

The prince's face was a mask of grim upset as he urged us, "But my friends, I can assure you that it is true. My scouts have been hearing of the old Draconis Order monks abandoning their posts, taking what funds, goods, and people as will follow them and heading for Torvald lands. There is one place, a town called Rampart which has been one of the few places to have resisted their own monks. They drove the old Draconis Order out when they started preaching rebellion against my throne, and then what happened? Their town has come under attack by soldiers and clansmen, clearly well-trained, and with several of them wearing Torvald furs about their shoulders."

Torvald furs. The words made my heart jolt. *Like clansman furs. Like the ones worn by the bandits who had tried to kill me right here, on the foot of Mount Hammal so many years ago.* I wondered just how long my brothers had been building their own private, loyal warband, even under our father's nose. It felt like the sort of thing that they would do.

But then, so could any soldier with a bit of knowledge of clan styles, I considered. What if this was some ploy on the part of Prince Vincent, an attempt to get us to send our strongest dragons away from the mountain, so he could attempt his attack?

The prince gestured to us. "Lord Torvald, Lady Nefrette, the people of Rampart are engaged in a fight to the death, with the town itself under siege from their attackers. I cannot get to them without splitting my forces more, and it seems that they are surely doomed." The prince shook his head sadly. "This is the news that I have come to give to you, lords and ladies of Dragon Mountain, and these are the dangers that I have come to warn you of. When I understood just what was at stake, I saw that the Sons of Torvald would undoubtedly attack here next, and so I came here, with as much of my armies as I could spare to offer you my friendship."

And to save your own throne, more like, I thought, my unquiet and upset fueling my anger. *The prince never wanted to be our friend, he just wants us to save his skin!*

I have never felt so unsure of my actions as I did then, completely at a loss of whether I was going to say *yes*, we will fight my brothers and save the innocents of Rampart, or *no*, you can take your armies and go to hell. *What should I do?*

There was a thump as Char landed on the ground next to us, and beckoning me to cross the distance to stand at her side under the dragon, where we could talk a little more privately. I was surprised when I felt her slipping her hand into mine. It felt good, to know that I wasn't alone, but once again I wondered if anything as simple as a hand would help to hold me together, as it felt as if my world was collapsing around me.

"We must keep the walls here guarded," Char murmured, and I nodded immediately. Of course.

"But the people of Rampart..." I said in anguish. I had been offered all of my dreams; to fly and be free as a dragon rover if I could but convince Char and Paxala to agree, and now it was dashed once more as I realized that it was my family, my brothers, who would cause so much suffering and disaster for so many.

"Neill, what do you want to do?" Char looked at me in concern. These were *my* brothers. She gave me that much respect to make the decision for myself.

"I don't know..." I said quietly, pitching my words for her ears alone. "*What if it isn't even true?*"

The hand in mine tightened a little. "Whatever you decide that you want to do, I want you to know that I will stand by you." Char suddenly cocked her head to one side and I felt that familiar buzzing pressure in my ears. "And Paxala says that she, too, will ride with you if you choose to fight."

What would my friends do? I wondered, looking at Char as my mind raced. Here, before me was the Mountain Princess who had fled her father's fortress just to look after the young and defenseless dragons. Here was the girl who had decided to raise a weak young dragon from hatchling to newt, to the mighty beast that Paxala was now, all because it was the right thing to do.

And what would my father do? I thought. Strangely, it was the words of Jodreth Draconis which swam to mind. *'You have a good heart, Torvald, and you will know what to do when he time comes.'*

So, what did my heart tell me? I gritted my teeth and balled my fists. Whatever game the Dark Prince might be playing, and however selfish he was really being, there could be the innocent civilians of Rampart to think about. Their lives were being destroyed by my older brothers, and by the fact that I hadn't put an end to the Abbot Ansall and Zaxx before.

If any of these words from the prince are true, of course, I thought darkly. "The Dragon Academy will send a scouting dragon," I said thickly. "I myself will ride the Crimson Red here to the town of Rampart."

"But surely that is not enough to defeat an army and the golden bull dragon, Lord Torvald!" Prince Vincent started to scoff, but something in either my glance or Char's made him purse his lips instead. "As you wish, Lord Torvald, Lady Nefrette," Prince Vincent nodded and said slowly. "I wouldn't dream of telling the Dragon Academy what to do."

Wouldn't you? I thought as I turned to share a worried look with Char. *At least I have my friends standing beside me,* I thought.

PART III
BATTLE FOR THE FUTURE

CHAPTER 16
CHAR, AND RAMPART

We flew northeast, away from the Dragon Monastery and away from the world that I had known. This was Neill's territory, I thought, looking over my shoulder to his worried face, pensive as he stared into the grey murk of the low clouds, as if he could pierce the veils between us and the future.

"Neill is divided." The usually warm voice of Paxala's mind rising against my own was cold and worried. *"He feels for what he flies toward, but he thinks far away,"* the dragon said, in a slightly irritated fashion. I knew well that this was close to a rebuke from the Crimson Red.

I just wish it was that simple, I thought at the dragon as I leant lower against her neck, allowing the warmth of her body to radiate through me and bring me some small comfort. Neill doesn't know whether to trust Prince Vincent. He doesn't know whether to fight his brothers, I tried to explain.

Prince Vincent's request was a big ask for my friend. He had been so torn up by his father's death that he appeared to be pulling in different directions: *not* wanting to help lead the monastery with me, but being really good at it when he was forced to, as he'd proven when he had suggested sending the dragons up in their display flight to awe the prince's forces, and earlier when he'd been the first to react when we thought Zaxx was on the attack

That's what frustrates me so much! I could have cried. Neill was actually really good at leading people! His years of growing up as a Son of Torvald—even a bastard one—had left him with solid skills. *And people listened to him!*

I felt it too, when my friend was consumed in the moment with passion and determination. Neill appeared outwardly calm, strong, and clear; an inspiration to all of those around him. *Even the Dark Prince had seemed to listen to him, when Neill said he was going to scout Rampart, and no more!*

But how am I ever going to get Neill himself to realize the skills he has? Why is it that we can never see our greatest strengths, only our weaknesses? I thought in dismay.

"Neill must fly for himself. No one can teach him how," Paxala wisely advised me, and I remembered those awkward first attempts when I had tried to encourage the Crimson Red to fly, running around in the mountain meadows flapping my arms like a crazed goose. All that had happened was Paxala had chortled at me, before getting annoyed when I tried to tell her what to do.

"Just so. Humans are too slow. Their arms too small."

Paxala nipped at my mind playfully, her worry vanishing in that mercurial way that dragons have. Other humans (*stupid* humans, I reminded myself) might call a dragon fickle, when in fact they were just extremely honest. As far as Paxala was concerned, she had said her piece about what Neill needed to do, and he had better get along and do it! No more prevarication or anxiety was going to change that.

I wished I could feel the same.

"Char? Smoke," Paxala informed me, and I lifted my head to sight along her snout in the direction the dragon's nostrils were flaring. I could see nothing, of course, but that was only because I had to rely upon my poor human eyesight. I waited, and soon, before too long, a slight darker haze appeared on the northeastern horizon, between two outcroppings of hills.

"Neill?" I said, turning to tell him what Paxala had pointed out to me. My friend's demeanor changed immediately, his eyes going from clouded and worried to clear and shrewd as he scouted out the smudge of smoke.

"We're in Rampart lands, for sure," Neill called, frowning. "Can we take Paxala higher? Try to keep hidden in and out of the cloud line?"

I nodded that was a good idea, and, before I could convey the messages to my reins and my knees, the Crimson Red had already heard our conversation and was powering herself upwards on strong wingbeats, steadily climbing into colder, fresher air as Neill and I untied and drew out the thicker cloaks we had designed for just such an ascent.

These cloaks had been my and Neill's idea, a layer of leather waxed and sealed on one side, with an inner layer of shorter, warmer fur; mountain hair or stoat that Nan Barrow had helped put together down in the small village at the foot of Mount Hammal. The cloaks helped insulate the human riders at high altitudes, and just feeling them work made me think at how *successful* we could be, if Neill only believed in himself!

"Rampart was the old Count Pathis's lands," Neill informed me as we climbed, and I watched the patchwork of fields, woods and hills grow ever smaller beneath us. "He was a border count, just above Torvald Clan lands, tasked with protecting the north-east border against your father's realm, while my father was Warden to the East."

"The land becomes wild between the two provinces, and that is where the Blood Duke rose, years ago, to try and steal the east from us Torvalds," Neill explained. "There will be lots of ravines and river valleys to hide in, but the land is often boggy and marshy at the bottom. We'll need to keep our eyes peeled."

"You should guide Paxala in," I encouraged him. "You know the terrain, and you can use your stirrups and foot harnesses to tell Pax." We had affixed an array of different stirrup-like loops to Pax's experimental saddle, which would help the rider signal changes to the dragon's flight pattern. I wanted Neill to know that I trusted him, and that I knew that he could be a good leader.

"Well, okay... But you can speak to her much quicker..." Neill said, sliding his boots into the loops on either side of his saddle.

"But we need to see if this new saddle and harness works, as well," I pointed out, and that, at last, convinced him.

"It would still be quicker for you just to tell me," Paxala said in my mind, only slightly affronted.

Yes, but you said this yourself, didn't you? Only Neill can teach himself to fly... I said to her, and was rewarded with a draconian sigh in the back of my mind before she withdrew.

∼

The flying *was* a little clunkier than if it had just been the quick-silver thoughts of me and Paxala, but I was still amazed at how quickly the Crimson Red adapted and responded to Neill's stir-rup-pushing and knee-leaning. This could actually work, I thought, picturing the other Dragon Riders, those without the luck of having the dragon affinity that I did.

The smell of smoke below me brought me back to my senses though, as I realized that I had probably been trying to forget the danger that we were flying towards. Neill had been right, of course—what if this was a trap? What if Prince Vincent had decided to attack the monastery while we were gone?

"Morax and Socolia are fast and strong. They will protect the monastery. And then there is also young Zenema. She will call the others if need be," Paxala advised me.

"Zenema?" I wondered out loud. I didn't remember Pax ever mentioning that dragon name to me before.

"A young Giant White dragon who already has stopped half of the younger newts from fighting each other. She will make a

good brood mother, one day," Paxala said approvingly and I shrugged. It was good to hear that Paxala's influence on the dragon crater was starting to pay off, and without the tyrannical golden bull, the dragons could in fact live peacefully together. Just as long as it works, I thought.

Yeah, we were doing the right thing for the dragons and the students, I thought as Neill signaled Paxala to lower her flight to skim under the cold grey clouds as we surveyed the terrain.

The smoke was thick and dark, obscuring the village of Rampart at times as the wind whistled and whined its awkward way through the valleys. I could even see the sharper manmade lines of walls and buildings now, and what I saw didn't look good.

Rampart was little more than a thick defensive wall from this high up, a few hundred feet high across two ridges of hills, with the buildings clustered or built directly into the wooden structure. I could see why it had earned its name. Over the peaceful years, however, a larger collection of village huts, storehouses, and small stockyards had extended out along the bottom of the river valley floor in front of the wall, and around *that* was another, much, much smaller palisade.

And it was down. Down and burning, as well as most of the outer valley buildings. Clearly *something* had attacked Rampart, and had flowed through the defenseless town with fury and fire before they had washed up against the high walls of Rampart itself.

"That must be where the townsfolk holed up," Neill shouted, using the stirrup-loops to guide us slowly in a curving arc down lower around the town. "But that is a strong defense, I'm not sure why Prince Vincent would want a phalanx of Dragon Riders here..." he sounded worried, before we flew over the crest of a hill and saw the *other* side of the mighty wall of Rampart.

"Oh no," I managed to gasp, before the first arrows started to fly.

CHAPTER 17
NEILL, AND RAMPART

The narrow lands on the other side of Rampart, hedged by higher hills were a black, teeming sea of fighters. We had thought that they had attacked from the southern side of the strange town, where the river village huts had been destroyed – but that must have only been a diversion, as the main body of their armies sat here, on the northern side.

"There's thousands of them!" Char said, her eyes wide.

I nodded. I didn't even know that my brothers had access to that many soldiers, before I realized that of course they didn't – these weren't just Torvald forces, even though many of the soldiers and clansmen on the other side were undeniably flying banners of the Torvald purple and green, with their individual captaincy flags below. I recognized the Bloodied Bear, Fennec's Dagger— some of the fiercest and strongest of the clans that had once fought under my father.

But there were a lot more warriors there too – many dressed

in black, and a large number who didn't seem to ride under any banner or flag at all. Bandits? Mercenaries? I thought.

"Those are the Northern Lances!" Char cried out in horror, pointing to a large corral of mounted troops on one of the gentler sides of a hill under the banner of a grey lance in front of a blue field. "They Northlanders! Supposed to be loyal to my father..." I saw her frown and clench her teeth.

This wasn't just the Sons of Torvald, then, I thought in grim alarm. We weren't looking at one irritant clan, as large and as martial as us Torvalds were. No, this was some sort of coalition of clans and rebellious lords and who knows who else.

This was a civil war, I thought in horror as the air between us shimmered and grew indistinct, as if from a passing cloud or flock of birds. But no—it was no flock of birds, but rather arrows whistling as they shot toward us.

∼

"Turn, dive!" I shouted at the same time as I kicked out the stirrups, working them to drop Paxala's right shoulder and raise her left so that she turned on a wingtip in a quick half-circle, all the while losing altitude.

No time to think, just act – I slipped a foot out of the lower right stirrup, and pushed down with the other, letting the dragon know that I wanted her to dive and then flip up, to catch the thermals and—

"Skreeayar!" Paxala roared joyously as our quick turn and

dive gave us the speed to shoot up and out of the way of the oncoming projectiles like, well, a speeding arrow ourselves.

"Good flying!" Char shouted at me, and I shared with her a brief, savage grin before concentrating on controlling the dragon. Easing on the reins and leaning to my left caused Paxala to wheel in a large circle around the encamped army. We were moving far too fast now for the archers below to catch us, but they had seen us. I saw smaller, brighter flags being waved in our direction, and brash, angry-sounding war horns calling up to challenge us.

"Sckreach!" The Crimson Red roared her own challenge to the small humans, and trailing from her mouth came wisps of heavy smoke. She was eager to fight those that had dared to attack her, her whole body underneath me thrumming with excitement and energy.

"Not yet, brave Pax, not yet..." I murmured to her, and wondered if her frustrated growl was in response to me or not. Instead, I guided her toward the hills at the southern end of Rampart, hoping to take her out of sight of the army below. "We have to get news back to the academy!" I shouted to Char, the wind whipping my words from me as we flew. I didn't know how long the fortified wall of Rampart would hold out against such a foe, and then the army would be free to march straight down the soft Middle Kingdom lands to the monastery itself.

"Neill! Look – down there," Char was pointing back, over our shoulder towards the vast edifice that was the Rampart wall. Turning my head, I could see a tiny patch of color on the heights flashing and flaring in the daylight.

"What is it?" I asked, trying to make it out.

"It's a flag, a flag from one of the top windows," Char said. "There's still people trapped in there, and we have to help them!"

"But Char, there's a few thousand archers and spear throwers and catapults and sky knows what else down there…" I said, before just one stern look from her made me see that she wouldn't take no for an answer. I kicked down on the stirrup-loops, and Pax was once again wheeling in the sky, heading towards the wall with the clouds of arrow bolts rising towards her.

The other side, I thought, changing foot positions to let the dragon know what I was thinking. She responded immediately, flaring her wings and – with one powerful beat that made my stomach lurch where I sat, we flipped over the high Rampart walls and to the other side, where the burned and unoccupied river-village was. I encouraged her to wheel around the still smoking houses, before bringing her down before one of the many gatehouses that stood at the wall's feet.

Thud. The dragon's feet caught the cobbles and decking of what must have once been a large market square, her claws tearing up earth and stone alike as we made a fast landing.

"I'll get to the doors," Char shouted to me, before pressing her forehead to the dragon's neck below and sharing a brief moment, before unclipping her harness and sliding down the scaled shoulder and leg, to land with a plume of dust onto the floor below. From where I sat, I looked around warily over Pax's shoulders, seeing on either side of us burnt and smoldering thatch, demolished houses, and the rising haze of the fires. This side of Rampart is trashed, I thought. The armies must have attacked here first...

Char hammered on the doors on the other side as I turned to look at the wall of Rampart itself.

It was made of wood, for the most part, with stone foundations and stone fittings for the many windows that spotted its height. Strong built, it must have taken decades to finish.

It doesn't make sense, the warlord's son in me thought. Why on earth would Rubin and Rik attack here? Rampart was about as well-defended as any place in the Middle Kingdom, easily as defensible as Prince Vincent's palace, and more than even Mount Hammal and the monastery itself. Even though the rebel army outside was vast, and would win through sheer numbers eventually, the siege might take weeks or even months.

Why here? Why attack a strong position, when there are so many weaker targets available?

There was the sound of scraping and grating from the door in front of Char, as various internal barricades had to be moved out of the way to free those trapped inside.

"But hang on a minute..." I frowned, rising a little from my seat to peer closer at the boarded windows of Rampart's walls. "If the rebel army moved to attack the other side of the wall, why didn't those inside just flee out this side? I thought. Once again, it didn't make sense.

Paxala clearly sensed my suspicion and started to hiss, lashing her tail so that it demolished what remained of a small wagon on one side of us.

"Char, be careful..." I said, just as the double doors cracked open—

"Thank the heavens you've come!" said a terrified-looking middle-aged woman in a belted dress and head covering. I was already figuring out a way we could get the Rampartians to safety. We couldn't carry all of them on Paxala's back—not if there were any more than a couple–but we might be able to escort them to the river, and maybe there would be a barge or a boat or something that we could get to carry them downstream…

Again, I wondered why those terrified villagers inside hadn't thought of this before. *I mean, look at how much damage there is out here!* I thought, scanning the ruined houses, the gouges in the streets, the great blackened marks up the wall of Rampart itself.

"Come in, we have many inside who need help," the woman said, her voice pleading.

"We don't have any great medicine, but we have a few supplies that might…" my friend was saying.

Actually, that is an awful lot of burning, I thought, inspecting a scorch mark that was taller than three buildings stood piled high, one continuous plume of fire—

Oh no. Fear washed down my spine. There's only one terrible machine in the world that can do that kind of damage, and I'm standing on it.

"Char!" I shouted. "Char, we need to get airborne!" I shouted as Paxala huffed and bristled the scales around her head and neck. She had caught wind of what I had realized, and was clearly upset. *Zaxx had been here. That is the remains of dragon fire – but why couldn't Paxala sense it earlier?*

Thock. The sound that broke through my rising panic was

solid and heavy, but muffled, like what you might imagine a rock dropped onto a bed might make. Only it was no rock that was thrown, and it was no feather duvet that it hit. A taller man stepped out from around the other side of the terrified woman, grabbing her around the neck and pulling her out the way as another stepped out from the shadows inside, and fired the small bow he had in his hands – straight into Char's flinching form.

"Char!" I shouted, terrified and furious, as Paxala reared up on her hind legs and bellowed in shared anguish.

"SKREAYARCH!"

The villager woman was thrust to one side, and I saw that this must have been some kind of a ruse, that the women here was a prisoner in her own home, along with however many others, and that the armies had *already* conquered the walls of Rampart. The man tried to jump forward to seize Char's fallen body by the ankles, but Paxala was faster. All I could do was hang on for dear life as she lunged, her feet splaying to grab her dragon friend and human sister in one claw, as the other scraped across the gate-house, splintering wood and fabric.

"Char? Please be all right, please!" I found myself saying, as Paxala roared once more, turning in a fierce hopping jump to spread her wings, and bounded into the smoke-filled skies over the burned village, bearing both me and Char with her.

I had never felt so absolutely useless in all of my life. Even when I was the youngest and most ignored son of my father, never asked for my advice or opinion, I had never felt like I did now. *How much was she bleeding? Fast or slow?* Some of my father's battle training rattled in my mind as I tried to both fly as fast as I could and see what state my Char was in at the same time. It was impossible to see anything from where I sat apart from blood on Pax's claws, and the ashen-like glimpse of skin...

My Char, I thought again, my heart lurching. *Don't let her die... Don't let her die...*

We flew as fast as Paxala could carrying the injured Char, heading southwest, back to Mount Hammal and the monastery. I tried to aid in the Crimson Red's flight, but every effort I made to control her via the stirrup-loops only made her flying even more erratic and clumsy. After a fourth angered "Skrech!" from the dragon, I relaxed all of my reins and let her have her head, flying whichever way she wanted to – and she flew faster and smoother.

The greens and browns of the ridges and hills below us blurred and changed, but it was still agonizingly slow how the horizon started to change and shift, and distant landmarks come slowly towards us. *Faster, Paxala, please, faster,* I was thinking, sparing a look behind us to the blackened smoke to Rampart, still visible.

There were many terrible mysteries eating at my mind. Why hadn't Paxala been able to sense the recent appearance of Zaxx the Mighty? Or *whatever* dragon had been there (if on the slim chance it *hadn't* been the golden bull). *Had* this been a trap set by Prince Vincent, meaning to kill the two main spokespeople of the Dragon Monastery?

Perhaps not, I shook my head. *He had wanted us all to go, all of the Dragon Riders of the Academy.* He hadn't known that it would have just been me and Char who would take him up on his offer. But that didn't mean that it was impossible – the prince might have been in league with this army perhaps?

Could the Dark Prince be in league with the green and the purple, the Sons of Torvald? I didn't know what was more incredible – the idea that my brothers would ever, *ever* work with Prince Vincent, or that they could decide to ally with the Abbot Ansall and Zaxx.

"They would respect Zaxx's might," I murmured worriedly, biting at one of my nails as I hunched over Paxala's neck, before looking over her shoulder to the arm that the dragon held curled up under her chest, holding the body of Char to the space where one of the dragon's hearts should be. It was hard to make out anything, with the wind whipping at Char's hair and cloak, but I could see red spotting the dragon's claws.

"Pax?" I said desperately, knowing the great beast would be able to hear me, but not sure whether she would want to right now. "Pax, please – we need to land. I need to take a look at Char and see if there is anything I can do."

There was a tense moment as the dragon trembled and shivered within herself, as if she was afraid that this might have to happen, and then, strangely, I felt that pressurized buzzing around my ears once more.

"Neill's no healer. Char goes home." The words were spoken in my head, and undeniably by the Crimson dragon beneath me. It was a feminine voice, although, if pushed I wouldn't be able to

say how I knew. I had heard Pax's voice before, of course, but it was a very, very rare thing for the Crimson Red to ever speak to me. Not that I thought that this was because she didn't want to, but because it seemed difficult for a dragon to share minds with just about any human. This difficulty in communication made her words appear stilted and awkward to me, although I was sure Char had never complained of that.

"You're right, Pax, I am no healer like Dorf, or Maxal can be – but I have battle healing. I know how to stick a wound, how to stop bleeding, how to set a bone." I tried to argue with the dragon. How could I explain to the Crimson Red the dangers of human blood loss, or of falling into shock? "Please, Pax, I have to look at her – she is my friend too..." I ended plaintively, knowing that this was the real reason I wanted Pax to land. I couldn't bear not knowing whether my friend was dead or alive.

My friend...? I had never felt this deeply hurt, even when Monk Feodor had been killed. *But... do I care for Feodor, or Dorf, or Sigrid any the less?*

No – I cared for Char more, I realized. And I was about to lose her.

"Dragon-sister's not dead," Paxala snapped at the wind in rebuke, but amazingly, the Crimson Red shifted her wings and angled them downwards, heading for a sliver of blue that was getting larger and larger before us. A smallish lake stretched out around the bottom of a hill, with arable fields and spotted copses on either side. We were far from the more northerly edges of the Middle Kingdom, and too far for any of my brother's scouts or outriders to have given chase from Rampart.

Not too far for Zaxx to find us, though, I thought darkly as we spiraled and spiraled down, before the dragon was hopping and stepping awkwardly across the brown stubble of the field, her landing awkward as she clutched protectively at Char.

"There, there now, thank you, Pax, thank you," I said when we had finally slowed to a stop at the end of the field where, on the other side of a line of straggly trees glittered the waters of the lake. The dragon had barely stopped moving as I scrambled down to her claw, gently teasing at the large talons to open and reveal my friend inside.

"Oh, Char!" I murmured in shock, as Paxala carefully laid her open claws on the ground and allowed me to carefully lift my friend out and onto my spread waxed cloak. She was deathly pale – even more so than usual – and her lips had a distinct bluish cast. From her shoulder, just under her collarbone, there extended the squat and ugly shaft of a black arrow, already broken off.

"Urh…" Char groaned weakly, trying to shift from her position but suddenly moaning in pain.

"She's alive. Thank the stars she's alive!" I said, although the dragon had already told me so. It meant all the difference to see it with my own eyes.

Right. Arrows. Arrow wounds. My mind raced. This was *definitely* something that I had been taught by my father, as it was something that he himself had been hit with on more than one occasion. *But what was I to do?* I didn't remember anything, my mind as blank as a cloudless sky.

"Neill. Calm. Help Char." My head buzzed with the angry command of the waiting dragon above me, and I nodded.

"Yes. You're right, Pax, of course." I took a deep breath, let it out slowly, and let my hands do the work that they knew, even if my brain couldn't find the words.

I felt for her pulse at her neck and at her wrist. Weak, but steady and regular. That was good. Next, I shifted her ever so slightly so that, if there was any danger inside of her, then the blood would not be inside her breath or her mouth. As soon as I was working, the memories started to come back. "The bolt," I muttered, knowing that I had to see if the arrow had gone all the way through my friend. With great care, I eased my hand underneath her, to the smooth and pale skin of her back, terrified of what I might find.

It wasn't wet, and the skin wasn't broken. So that meant that the arrow hadn't gone through, but was still inside of her, which would cause a whole lot more problems.

"But she's still bleeding," I said out loud, once again turning to my friend's front. There was a large dark area of blood, and it was still horribly wet and spreading. The arrow must have caught something inside of her, and, if she didn't stop bleeding, then she would spill her life's essence right now, before we ever got as far as the Dragon Monastery.

I had two options. To bind her as is, and just hope that my bandages would be tight enough to stop her blood loss. *Not going to work, Torvald!* I barked at myself. *Char is already injured inside. No amount of bandage wedged on top will stop that!*

Then my only other option was to take out the arrow, clean the wound, and hope infection didn't set in. I gulped. I had never performed that task before, but I had seen it done. I felt my stomach lurch once more and the ground tip underneath my feet, even though I was on solid ground.

"*Neill. Please. For dragon-sister. For Char,*" Pax said, lowering her head to gently push beside me.

I looked into the dragon's large and golden-green eyes and nodded. "Then I'm going to need fire," I said, and Paxala immediately turned to strike down some of the scraggy trees at the side of the field, stamp and scrape them into a sort of heap, and, with a cough, sent a spark of bright and hot dragon flame to set them.

"Thank you. And, I'm going to need…" I looked around the remains of the hedge, running quickly to pull aside roots and weeds and leaves until I found what I needed. "Self-Heal." I pulled a large clump, with its small and feathery leaves and delicate blue flowers. "Can you find this, Pax? As much as you can?"

"Skree-yip!" Paxala chirruped, at once leaping boldly over our heads to land on the other side of the field, snouting and pawing at the field verges for the precious herb. It was a common weed in all parts of the Middle Kingdom, but few people knew that it also made an excellent compress for wounds, as it helped staunch blood and fight infections at the same time.

While I waited for my supplies, I took out my knife, our watering pouches and the small nest of wooden bowls that we all carried, just in case we needed to eat or do things like this. With a grim shake of my head, I shoved my knife into the edges of the fire until my hand started to bake from the heat, and the blade burnished a bluish green.

And then, I set to work trying to save Char's life.

CHAPTER 18
CHAR, WAKING UP

"We haven't got a lot of time," the voice said, and I was sure that it was a voice I knew, although I couldn't quite remember exactly *whose* voice it was right now.

It was dark, I felt sleepy – and in pain.

"I know we haven't got a lot of time! But what do you want me to do? I'm not leaving her." That was definitely a voice I knew. Neill.

Neill. Rampart. The army. Suddenly, it all came rushing back to me in a flood. The dark sea of people, angry, shouting, jeering. The buzzing flight of arrows as they flew towards us, the quick and powerful wingbeats as Paxala turned – but not fast enough, as I had been hit…

No, I hadn't been hit by an arrow, not while flying. I was sure that wasn't the case, as I knew that Pax would never have let me get hit. Pax was my friend, my sister, and I should say my closest nonhuman friend, as Neill was my closest human friend.

Thock. I heard a dull thump, like someone knocking on a door, but to my mind it sounded like the noise that an arrow might make as it hit wood. *I did get hit,* I thought muzzily, and in an awful flood of nightmare images I remembered the anguished woman at Rampart, her pleading eyes as she started to say something to me, mouthing words without sound…

"Run." Was that what she had been trying to say to me? Why?

Because, in the next instant I recalled how the woman had been grabbed and thrown to the floor, as another, angry, hate-filled man had stepped forward, his bearskin cloak ragged and fur lining his gloves as he had raised the short bow almost straight to my chest. I had managed to dive – but not fast enough.

Thock.

"Who's there?" It was Neill's voice once again, and then I heard the creak as a door opened, and muttered, whispering words from the other side.

"No. Tell them that we cannot yet. That we're not ready."

"Neill, you have to…" said the second almost-familiar voice, a man's voice, young but older than we were. Who could it be? "If we wait any longer…"

"I told you, Jodreth, I'm not leaving Char's side! Prince Vincent can bleeding well wait!" Neill exploded, and I tried to tell him that it was all right, that he didn't need to stay here, but all that came out of my mouth was a dull groan, and with it, the sharper pain that brought me up, through the layers of sleep that had been hovering, and into painful, awful, consciousness.

"Char? Is she awake? Can she hear us?" a worried voice—Neill's —said suddenly.

"Thank the stars, she's waking–but give us some room! No more hovering!" Jodreth muttered, the older man's shadow falling over me as I blinked the sleep from my eyes.

I was in a dark room, cool with the scent of fresh mountain winds over the cold slopes. Somewhere, there was the scent of fresh bread and wood smoke. The monastery? I thought. I was suddenly ravenously hungry, and tried to push myself up on whatever I lay on, before another spear of pain lanced through my chest.

"Ach!" I hissed.

"Char-sister!" The voice of the dragon in my mind was suddenly close and enfolding, as I felt Paxala's presence purring and cooing over me. It wasn't her real body, of course, but she had thrown her mind at mine.

"I, I'm okay, Pax," I murmured.

"You're not. You're hurt. But the wizardling said he can help you," Pax rebuked me gently.

The wizardling? I thought. *Oh, she must mean Jodreth.*

"She's delirious," said Jodreth's voice, as I opened my eyes again to see him looking at me worriedly. His clear eyes were moving in front of mine, moving from eye to eye, to see if I could focus on him.

"The problem isn't my eyes, Jodreth," I said with an annoyed grumble. "I think it's the great big hole in my chest." I looked down to where, thankfully, I could see that there was no arrow sticking out of me, but my entire left shoulder was thickly bandaged. "I was talking to Pax, actually," I said. I was lying on a simple bed in one of the small rooms of the Dragon Monastery (I could tell from the pale, almost yellow stone, and the window that looked out onto the edge of the dragon crater beyond).

"Oh, of course, sometimes the herb can cause strange dreams and visions," Jodreth was saying, putting a calloused hand on my forehead and nodding as if pleased. "A little pale, but you haven't a fever. There shouldn't be an infection."

"The herb? What herb are you talking about?" I said, as another shape moved into view over my bed.

"Char? Thank the stars..." Neill breathed over me. He looked pale and haggard, with shadows under his eyes as he regarded me. He was wearing different clothes now, what I knew was his 'best' Torvald purple tunic with the drawstrings at the neck, over dark tan breeches.

"Neill, you look terrible. But you didn't have to put on a shirt for me," I tried to joke weakly, smiling. Even my face felt like it ached. How can one injury make the whole body hurt? I thought.

"Uhr, well, you're not exactly looking too hot yourself, Char," Neill said with an answering ghost of a smile. "But I'm glad that you're awake. We were all so worried."

"Not as worried as me," Paxala confided in me. She didn't recede from my mind as she usually did after our conversations, but instead she kept her awareness wrapped around mine, and I could even feel her looking out through my eyes.

"Okay, well, it seems that I am awake now, even though I

have no idea how I got here, and I haven't a fever, and you guys have been giving me strange herbs from the sound of it..." I muttered, as Neill got me some water to sip. After I swallowed, everything became a little better by a fraction.

"It's called Magewort," Jodreth told me. "When taken by a healthy mind, it induces a sort of trance, but it also is an amazing restorative. It can keep people on their feet for days at a time, without needing sleep or food, and it can help a sick person fight any ill or injury in half the time..." Jodreth said, looking proud at himself. "But if Neill here hadn't removed the arrowhead, and treated your wound with Self-Heal right after the attack, I don't know if you would have ever been strong enough to get this far!"

"Neill?" I turned to look at him wonderingly. I had no idea that my friend knew how to do such things, and also no memory of him treating me at all. Just the *thock* and then – blankness.

"I helped," Paxala swished her imaginary tail in the back of my mind.

I'm sure you did, my sister, I thought at the dragon with real affection. Pax had never displayed any jealousy towards Neill before, but I think, given the circumstance, a small amount was acceptable right now.

"I did what I could." Neill shrugged, suddenly looking at his feet.

"Thank you," I said to him, feeling amazed. *He has no idea how good a leader he is.*

"Here," my friend said awkwardly, suddenly rummaging in his breeches pocket to pull forth something small and pristine silver-grey, attached to a coil of leather twine. An arrowhead, cleaned and fresh as the day it had been forged. "It's a clan custom of the Middle Kingdom," Neill said through great embarrassment, "to keep a token of the first thing that almost killed you."

"Who says it's the first?" I made to joke, but, on seeing Neill's mouth drop I hurriedly reassured him. "I love it. Give it to me." I tried to lift my left arm to reach for it, once again feeling the pain there, but gritted my teeth and forced myself to do it.

"Ach!" I winced.

"Steady…" Jodreth counselled.

Neill dropped the arrowhead into the palm of my hand. It was a dart of steel, barely bigger than my thumb. "Hmph," I groaned at it. "Such a little thing, huh? Well, I'm glad that it's on the *outside* of me now, rather than the inside!"

"So are we all," said Jodreth seriously, before straightening up to uncover a towel from the table side, under which sat a warm bowl of stew, a hunk of Nan's bread, and some cheese. "You'd better eat, get your strength back, Char," he said, before pushing across the table another, smaller clay flagon which smelled like fresh herbs and something bitter underneath it. "And when you've had some food, drink this. It's more of the Magewort, and it will aid your healing dramatically."

"Do I have to?" I said with a frown.

"*Yes!*" I was surprised as both Neill, Jodreth, *and* Paxala in my mind commanded me to.

"Fine! Okay, I get the idea," I said.

"Now, Char, would you mind if I take this young man with

216

me and leave you in peace? There is some business we have to attend to." Jodreth was scowling at Neill.

"What business?" I said, managing to push myself up this time and reach for the bread and cheese. I was a little clumsy and slow, and my shoulder ached terribly, but my mother's tutelage came to mind. We mountain folk were supposed to be tough. We had to endure winters the like of which these Midlanders and Southerners had never seen before. I could handle a little wound like this! I dipped the bread in the stew and started to gnaw on it hungrily.

"Char, really, you don't have to worry yourself right now…" Jodreth was saying, tugging at Neill's arm to pull him out of the room, although Neill clearly didn't want to go.

Rampart. I thought in shock, almost dropping the bread. "Is it Rampart? Neill, we have to go back! That woman didn't want to be a part of their plan—I'm sure they're being held hostage in there!"

Neill furrowed his brows and looked off into the corner for a moment, which I knew meant he was struggling to think for himself and ignore what the others around him were impressing upon him. Another good sign, I had to admit.

"You can't go now, Char!" Jodreth said. "Maybe in a few days, if you do well, but I don't know if I have enough Magewort to last much longer than that…" the older man was saying.

"Neill?" I asked, ignoring Jodreth.

"Jodreth might be right." Neill frowned, turning his gaze to look back at me this time. "But so are you as well, Char. The problem isn't *just* Rampart, however, it's your uncle."

217

~

"What?" I looked from Jodreth to Neill. "What has Prince Vincent done now?" It could have been anything, knowing him, I thought gravely. Not that I did know him. Even calling him 'uncle' felt farcical to me, as he had never once showed an iota of interest in me or my upbringing.

"He's set up court, here, in the monastery," Neill glowered. "And even managed to get more of his people, his knights and his servants in here while we were away."

"What!?" I exploded, making my shoulder twinge with pain. "But we expressly forbid him to bring any warriors inside the gate! Who let them in?"

"Who do you think? It was Berlip." Neill rolled his eyes. I remembered the older monk. He was one of the monks of the old Draconis Order, one who had graduated from the Abbot Ansall's training and become a Scribe, without any magic and so unable to add the 'Draconis' after his name as Jodreth did. Berlip wasn't outright corrupt as Ansall, Olan, and Greer had been. No, instead he was just set in his ways, and self-righteous. He cared about the scrolls and the books of the dragon library, but little more… At least, I hoped that was the case, anyway.

"Berlip managed to get some of his faction on wall duty, and must have already been talking with the prince inside the walls, as, apparently"—Neill paused to run his fingers through his hair — "when we got back we found that Vincent has set up a court in the main hall, with a marquee outside in the training yard, and

Berlip's been given the position of Trusted Advisor to the throne!" Neill shook his head.

"The man is a weasel," Jodreth said. "I remember him when I was here. He disliked me because I was doing so well at magic, and he would refuse me access to the library," Jodreth growled angrily.

Neill nodded. "I'm afraid that you might be right, Jodreth. Berlip's acting like *he's* the one in charge, telling the other students and monks what to do, and how to study, and that they have to follow the prince's commands and the prince. Vincent has been handing out peerages and rewards like it's going out of fashion!" Neill sighed.

"He's trying to win over the students," I muttered, seething. "He needs to leave us alone."

"He's looking to save his own skin, more like," Neill said acidly. "You've seen my brothers' army at Rampart, Char. It's big enough to give Vincent's armies a tough fight, and I think the prince only came here so that the monastery would fight for him. Mount Hammal is one of the most defensible places in the Middle Kingdom."

"Yeah, you're right," I sighed, making up my mind. No time like the present, I thought, tearing a great hunk from the bread, before chasing it with the entire cup of Magewort.

"Woah there, Char, you're meant to sip it..." Jodreth was saying, as I felt the strange herb's effects start to course through me.

It started as a sort of comforting warmth, one that spread out from my belly, up to my shoulders and down to my legs, numbing the pain in my shoulder until it was little more than a dull, 'hot' feeling. My skin tingled like I had just emerged from one of the mountain folk's ice baths, and gone straight into the hot, steaming sauna. I could feel a quickness and taut energy in my limbs, making me want to laugh and shout and stretch.

"Better," I said with a grin, swinging my feet from the bed to push myself up into standing. It was a little awkward at first, as my body was still stiff and ungainly, but it was suffused with a warm numbness that eradicated any feeling of injury. *This was good stuff!*

"Char, I have no idea what you are about to do, but I am certain that this isn't wise." Jodreth held his hands up, as if pleading for me to reconsider whatever it was I was going to do.

"We fly, my sister?" Pax said inside my heart.

"You won't change her mind, not when she's got that look in her eyes," Neill murmured and I laughed. At least *one* of these people here knew me well!

"Come on, you two," I replied with an angry and ebullient self-confidence as I tottered towards the door, snatching up my short sword as I did so, and my black cloak. "I'm going to go tell *Uncle* Vincent that he's not welcome in *our* academy!"

"Oh, hell," Neill said behind me, probably reconsidering his decision to tell me the bad news.

CHAPTER 19
NEILL, WHO LEADS?

I buckled on my own sword belt and cloak as I followed Char down the spiraling stone steps. We had put her in one of the tower rooms, (Nan's suggestion, to get the fresh air and to 'keep us busy-bodies out of the way' – I rather think that she had been right), and so there were a lot of steps to get to the ground floor, but Char took them all without a grumble or a groan.

What is in that stuff? I wondered in alarm. And why hadn't Jodreth offered it to us before, if it was so powerful? I resolved to ask him about Magewort when we had the chance. My friend appeared joyous at the same time as being ferociously angry, and I remembered my father talking about the rare 'berserkers' who occasionally cropped up in his armies – warriors who could fight and fight past the limits of normal human endurance, seeming not to care at all how many injuries they sustained.

He also said that while they were great skirmish troops, they were a liability in the long run... But although Char's endurance and mountain heritage was strong– 'going out on the mountain' and not seeming to care about the cold—I didn't think that she was a true berserker. *It's that herb. It's causing her to act stronger than her body really is.* Fearful, I hurried after Char as she hit the ground floor and pushed open the door with a heavy squeal of the old hinges.

Sunlight flooded in, blinding me temporarily as I hit the ground floor and hurried out, with Jodreth racing along behind me.

It was busy out in the courtyard, busier than the academy had been, ever, since we had taken over it. If I didn't know any better, I might even have looked on the scene that confronted us as healthy; there was the giant black and gold marquee of the prince occupying one entire side of the courtyard; there were the hurrying forms of servants in similar black and gold and dark blue tones, bearing baskets or crates back and forth from the main hall and back. Someone was whistling briskly, and up on the wall there stood a trio of Royal Knights, their armor gleaming in the sun as they talked and joked beside a couple of younger dragon students.

The academy *looked* like it was working, only, it *wasn't*. Not if you looked at all closer.

There was the fact that no one was training, not with their padded practice weapons or with the prototype saddles we were making – there was just no room, now that the prince had his marquee here.

There were also no dragons roosting on the walls, which they had taken to doing once Zaxx had gone. Even though they scarred the stone work and even caused terrible damage to some of the roofs, both Char and I had permitted it until we could come up with a better solution for their roosting and guarding habits. When asleep, a dragon liked to be underground, but when awake, they liked to be up high. Like training a pony, that's what I reasoned, anyway – I mean, what good is a Dragon Academy if there weren't even any dragons on the walls?

But then, of course, there were the subtler signs of problems: the trio of Royal Knights on the walls appeared to be rebuking the students who really *were* supposed to be on guard duty, and I saw one of them pointing back down the stairs as he barked at them to leave the 'more experienced' knights to it. There was, over by the main hall, one of the older black-clad monks whom I recognized as belonging to Berlip's faction standing watch by the door, and glaring at us as we marched across the courtyard.

Like he is spying, or keeping tabs on what the rest of the academy is up to, I thought, which wouldn't be such a bad idea with Prince Vincent here, except whatever information he might have gleaned had never yet been reported to me. As I walked, he slunk into the main hall.

"No doubt going to scurry off to tell Berlip what we're doing!" Jodreth muttered beside me, making the sign against the evil eye back in the direction of the monk.

"No doubt," I agreed. I didn't like it. Not that anyone had done anything to outright challenge me and Char and the other student leaders of the new academy, but it felt all of a sudden like our grasp of the situation was slipping from between our very fingers.

Maybe Uncle Lett had been right, I should never have let that prince behind these walls. For a moment, my heart ached as I thought about how our parting had gone. Uncle Lett was surely leagues away by now, heading south, and he must think that I was betraying the family honor in favor of the Dark Prince.

Maybe he's right, I growled to myself, as Jodreth gasped beside me.

"Sweet moon and stars, she's going to get us killed," Jodreth said with a groan. A little way ahead of us, Char had raised her short sword again, bringing it down with a mighty swing to chop at the ropes that anchored the marquee to their wooden stakes.

She'd already managed to successfully cut two, and with a second blow, the third snapped as she moved onto the fourth stake, now causing a visible sagging in the tent.

Oh great.

The fourth line severed easily with a twang, and Char moved with all of the energy and vitality of a woman possessed, which, given that she was pumped up on Magewort right now, I guessed she was.

"Hey! Here! What are you doing down there?" One of the three of the Royal Knights up on the walls had noticed, and was pointing down at Char as she moved to the next stake, and the last on this side of the marquee.

The closest wall of the marquee suddenly started to sag inwards, causing a muffled shriek from inside, and servants and monks and knights started pouring out, looking all around to see what had happened.

"We'd better go to her," I said to Jodreth, who nodded.

"Hey! You can't do that – this is the prince's property!" One of the servants shouted, outraged as Char continued working at the back of the marquee. More ropes were released from their terrestrial duty, and the entire, grand marquee made of the finest dyed and embroidered panels of waxed linen, hand stitched, started to billow on its central poles.

"She's mad! Stop her!" someone yelled as I reached Char's side. I reached out a hand to grab her shoulder but something inside stopped me. I *wanted* to see the prince's fineries pulled down, I realized. *This was Char's home too.* She had a right to do this.

Twang! Another cord sprang away from its mooring.

"In the name of the prince!" There was a shout, and a hiss as a sword escaped the confines of scabbard. I looked up to see none other than Sir Rathon, not wearing his full plate but still enough chainmail and leather greaves to turn any of my thrusts, marching towards us, his great sword held in two hands.

With the rustle of fabric and a dull *whumpf,* one entire half of the tent collapsed, and one of the poles holding up the middle shook and then slid against its neighbor. There was a creak as the center pole slowly fell to the ground in a muffled tear of linen.

"You have to admit, it *does* look pretty good like that," Jodreth whispered at my side, and he shared my mischievous grin.

"In the name of the academy!" Char retorted, her face bright red and flushed from her work as she turned and strode past me to stand boldly before Sir Rathon. "This is *our* land. *Dragon* land, sir knight – and you would do well to understand that dragons are quick to temper, and you had better mind your manners before you start commandeering academy space!" She gesticulated with her short sword at the knight.

"No *dragon* seemed to mind, Miss Nefrette," Sir Rathon growled.

"Oh no?" Char cocked her head and smiled up at the sky, just as there was a deafening scream of dragon-shriek.

Paxala flared her wings as she plunged into the courtyard, almost knocking all of us from our feet, before dropping, with a heavy and pronounced thud onto the remains of the tent. I heard the sound of tearing fabric and the splintering of wood as precious barrels of southern brandy must have been destroyed, chairs and tables broken, fine foods squashed under her talons.

"Why, you impudent little..." Sir Rathon growled, leaning forward, as if to step at Char. I snarled and lunged, raising my own blade.

"Don't touch her!" I shouted, suddenly furious.

"Ignis Fulgur!" Jodreth shouted, rolling his staff across his body just as there was a crackle of thunder in the clear sky and a sudden flash.

A wave of noise rumbled deep in my chest, like being close to a dragon's roar, but Paxala hadn't spoken. My ears rang and my eyes blinked away the after image of a brilliant flare between us and Sir Rathon.

"Ach!" the knight cried, shaking his head and staggering just as we were, looking at the large blackened circle, as big as a barrel top steaming and smoldering on the ground between us.

"Jodreth?" I asked hesitantly. Even Char, in her intoxicated state, looked stunned. I felt unsteady, and it wasn't just because of the lightning strike. It should have been me to put a stop to Sir Rathon and Prince Vincent, I thought shamefacedly. But even so, I couldn't find a gram of guilt in me for having jumped to protect the beautiful mountain's daughter, Char.

But I cannot control lightning like Jodreth can, and I cannot hear dragons in the way that Char can. What was I doing here, other than trying to look after my friends?

"Lords and ladies of the Dragon Academy," Jodreth growled to all of us, "my noble Lady Dragon," he nodded at Paxala, "and Sir Rathon, let us stop this argument before any of us does anything regretful. I suggest that the prince comes out here, and Monk Berlip, and any dragon as wants to negotiate, and we settle, once and for all the guardian-ship of the dragon crater – and *then* we can start to talk sensibly about what we're going to do about our *shared* enemy!"

Sir Rathon flushed, looking warily between the giant Crimson Red dragon looming over us, and the Dragon Monk Jodreth, able to apparently call lightning from the skies. "As you wish," he said simply, retreating with slow, backwards steps towards the main hall.

"Someone should have done that when Vincent first walked inside that gate!" Char said to Jodreth with a pleased smile, but all I could feel in my heart was panic.

They're going to decide who protects this place, and it can't be me. I couldn't even protect my own father and stop Ansall from killing him. I knew Jodreth was right, *someone* had to be responsible for this place, but what good was I, after I had allowed Char to get shot right in front of me?

~

"Master monk, you certainly have a way with words," Prince Vincent purred from where he stood before us, an icy warning sort of purr. The sort of sound that a cat might make moments before it decided to attack.

The Dark Prince had come striding out of the main hall in a flurry of servants and swords-drawn knights, flanked by Sir Rathon and Monk Berlip.

You've made your bed now, Berlip. I scowled at him. *You'd better just pray that Vincent manages to win this argument, because if he doesn't, you won't be welcome here!*

"This situation cannot continue." Jodreth said, looking at him. I realized then just how young Jodreth was, and Prince Vincent appeared to be only a handful of years older– which didn't make sense to me, as Prince Vincent was already an uncle to Char.

"You are right, master monk, this situation appears untenable. But I have offered my support to Monk Berlip here, and he has seen the need for a strong hand here at the academy. A *royal* hand." The prince spoke in that assured authority that only royalty has.

"The academy doesn't need the throne!" Char said vehemently, still impassioned with the effect of the Magewort.

A suspicion formed in my mind as I looked at the young and

handsome prince, and it was the very same thing that I had begun wondering about Char's very own father. *Had the entire royal line benefitted from Ansall's stolen dragon magic?* Everyone knew that Old Queen Delia had been hundreds of years old by the time she had died, with Ansall older still. The thought gave me the creeps, and only affirmed my determination as I found myself stepping forward to speak.

"The academy will not suffer direct rule from the throne of the Middle Kingdom, or *any* of the Three Kingdoms," I heard myself say.

It was what my father had wanted, in a way. My father the clansman, my father the commoner who had risen with his people to become Warden of the Eastern Marches.

All of a sudden, I had a vision of how things *could* be, and I knew that this was exactly what Garf, my father's sworn bond-warrior, had been hinting at back at Fort. My father had a vision of the lands ruling themselves, putting their trust in those whom they could understand, not some distant kings kept alive by dark magic.

Prince Vincent turned his attention to me as if seeing me for the first time. "*Master* Torvald," he said in clipped tones.

Not calling me a lord now, are you? I thought wryly.

"You have traveled to Rampart, you have seen the forces that are arrayed against us all. Are you suggesting that you can face them alone, without my army's help?" the prince said conde-scendingly, his voice heavy with threat, and it was clear that he was trying to paint me a fool in the eyes of the fast gathering crowd of students, monks, and servants who lived here on the

mountain. "Or, are you throwing your lot in with your treacherous brothers and the remains of the old Draconis Order? Would
you bring all Three Kingdoms into civil war for the sake of
your pride?"

There were muttered gasps from the crowd, and I could tell
what they must be thinking. That everything that I had said had
been a lie.

"You are the son of Malos Torvald, a man I knew was plotting against me for years," the prince argued. "And you have
worked tirelessly to disrupt this academy and put yourself at its
head. We must ask – has this been your task all along?"

Well, it was true – I *had* been sent here to discover the
secrets of the dragon magic, and my father apparently *had* been
preparing for the day when both the Draconis Order and the
throne it propped up fell. Was I really just as bad as my
brothers?

"Neill," I was surprised when my head buzzed, and Paxala's
voice broke into my thoughts. *"Do not see yourself with his eyes.
Hunt for yourself!"*

I was shocked at how articulate and wise Pax's words were –
were all dragons this philosophical? But she was right all the
same. I lifted my head to look around the crowd watching. It was
true that some were looking at me warily, and in alarm, but there
were others who were shaking their head.

"Not so!" said a voice, and Dorf Lesser stepped out of the
crowd. "I know Neill, and he has been a faithful friend to the
dragons and to the students for as long as I can remember." The
small, rounded form of the navigator walked across the open

space to stand beside Jodreth, Char, Paxala and me. "I stand with you, Neill," he said out loud.

"Treachery…" Sir Rathon glowered, readjusting his grip on his great sword.

"As do I!" called another voice – this time from the handsome Terrence Aldo, son of the Prince of the Southern Kingdom, Prince Griffith, striding across the floor defiantly. "I know this Neill Torvald, and I know this *Princess* Nefrette. I know that both of them mean to protect the dragons of the academy, and all of us!"

"And your father, my brother?" Prince Vincent snapped, and I could see that he sensed the situation sliding away from him. "Is this war, now?"

"I renounce my claim to the Southern Kingdom so that I can do my work here, *uncle*," Terrence said loftily, taking a stand, unarmed, beside Dorf.

What? I looked at Terence, once a younger princeling, in astonishment. "Terence, really, you don't have to do this!" I said.

But Terence Aldo turned to regard me with more nobility than I had ever seen in the Dark Prince's eyes. "I do, Neill. My own father told me to be the best I could, because the people will only follow the best." He nodded to Char, and then to me. "And I have found two people who are better– even than me," he added with a small smile as he joined my side.

After that came another – Lila Penna, of the Raider Clans of the southern seas—and another— Sigrid Fenn, of Clan Fenn. Each of them recognized me and Char in some small way or phrase, and it felt like dawn breaking for the first time. I knew

231

that they were our friends, but I had no idea that they saw me like that, at least. And last but not least, little Maxal Ganna, with no noble or clan blood in him that I knew, but a family name that had been tied to the monastery and the mountain for generations, stepped forward.

"I stand with Neill and Char," he said simply, as if this were as obvious and natural thing as talking about the weather.

I felt touched at their willingness to support us. How had they that much faith in me? I thought.

"Because you showed them your heart." Again came Paxala's voice, and I turned to see her regarding me with her great and golden eyes.

"What is this?" Prince Vincent was confused that he could be defied so openly, and yet we were not asking to oust him from the throne. "You are *all* traitors? Is *that* what this is? You would rather ally yourself with the Sons of Torvald, and the very Abbot whom you overthrew not so long ago?"

"Prince," I found my voice, emboldened by my friends. I was weary, and tired of his overt or underhanded attempts to control the dragon crater. "We do not want your throne or your kingdom. We merely want to live in peace, with the dragons, and do what good we can in the world." To my surprise, there was a loud cheer from the crowd.

"Yes!" Char gave me a loud clap.

"But, my prince," Berlip said, "I am sure that what *Master* Torvald here is trying to say, is that we would gratefully accept any aid that you can offer…!"

"No!" I flashed with anger. "That is *not* what I am saying,

Berlip – and you would do well to keep your own counsel, and not profess to know mine!" I glared at him until he fell silent. "What I *am* saying, Prince Vincent – is that we will *grant* you our aid, if you give your oath to rule your people justly and well."

I didn't even know what I was going to offer until I had already offered it. But it made so much sense now. I didn't want to topple the king, or plunge the Three Kingdoms into a civil war. I wanted the Dragon Academy to be free, and, just as my father had envisaged, *we* would be the guardians that kept the nobles and the warlords in check. *We* could fly the dragons. *We* would keep them honest.

"Do you dare threaten the prince, boy?" Sir Rathon growled, and the knights around the prince reacted to their captain's words organically, shifting their stances, readying themselves for a bloody battle.

"It seems to me to be nothing more than a statement of fact, Sir Rathon," Jodreth said with a shrug and a smirk. "We do have a mountain packed full of dragons…"

Prince Vincent scowled, his mouth a thin line of fury as he digested our words. He wasn't used to being denied this way, and took his anger out on the monk at his side.

"I have been clearly misinformed about the *needs* of the academy," he said haughtily as he regarded Berlip. "You are stripped of your titles, and I have no need for your services."

Berlip opened and closed his mouth in panic and fear as the realization dawned on him that he had now made enemies with a prince, a dragon, and the majority of the Dragon Academy.

"Best if you leave, Berlip," Char said with deep satisfaction. "You and any who want to go with you." There was an awkward, flapping moment from the older monk, before he hissed like an angry cat and turned and ran, out into the crowd which parted around from him like he was an infected man. A few other of the older monks, the ones who had been as cantankerous as he was, and had jockeyed for position under the prince, slipped quietly from the edges of the crowd as well.

Well, that makes things certainly a lot simpler.

"So, you will help me defeat the rebel army?" Prince Vincent demanded of me. Char bristled at the prince's tone, but I let it slide. I had spent a lot of time when I was younger learning how to work around obstinate and short-sighted men.

"We will stop the rebel army from hurting the people of this land," I offered, and Char nodded at my side.

"Good." The prince motioned to Sir Rathon and his men. "Pack up our things. We will move my personal retinue to the army, and there, we will prepare to meet the foe."

Sir Rathon shot me a dangerous look, and I was sure that if I were ever to encounter him alone, without witnesses, then I would be sure to face consequences for daring to make his master look weak. I stood still, with my friends at my side, watching as the prince and his forces hurriedly packed their things, and left the confines of our academy.

When it was finally done Char turned to me and set a hand on the side of my forearm. "You did it, Neill. *You* did it."

"I didn't do anything. You had the guts to start taking down his tent and kicking out his men." I shrugged with a laugh. "I could never have done that!"

"No, *you* found the way through," Char insisted, as Jodreth, Dorf, Lila and Sigrid and Maxal all stood around us. "You found a way to keep the Dragon Academy safe, without starting a war. *You* are a true leader, Neill."

"Your father's son," Jodreth murmured as the others were loudly congratulating me, but when I looked to catch his eye, he didn't say anything.

CHAPTER 20
NEILL, FRONT AND FOREMOST

The rebel armies of my brothers and the Abbot Ansall would have been crazy to give up such an easily defensible position as the town of Rampart and so, unsurprisingly, our scouts told us that they hadn't.

I had been musing on this as we flew back north-eastwards, catching the high and cold northern current of air that came down from the tops of the northern mountains and shivering in our waxed cloaks. Behind me flew Morax the Sinuous Blue, Socolia the Stocky Green, as well as a handful of other dragons that we could find riders for: Veserpal, Jhokar, Haxar, Zhukis, Varo, Tchakka and Siuella. Ten dragons, I thought, fear rising in my chest. Surely, we would need more if we were going to fight the biggest army ever to walk across the Middle Kingdom!

And Zaxx, the thought crossed my mind like a shadow.

But I had been assured again and again by Char (relaying

Paxala's own counsel) that the other riderless dragons *would* follow and come to our aid if need be, and that they would do so under the watchful eye of the young White called Zenema. I still hadn't really met the young White yet, but I had seen her strong and lithe form staying defensively around the nesting caves. She may have been young, but the Great White dragon was already larger than even Paxala and any of the other dragons of her own age.

What a strange bunch we make, I thought, looking over my shoulder at Terence and his fellow rider Lila on Morax, and Sigrid and Dorf on Socolia. Sigrid had been having troubles working with the large Green all by herself, and she had been overwhelmed by the dragon's emotions – but Socolia had apparently taken a shine to Master Lesser, and so we had hurriedly schooled him on the use of the dragon harness and the saddle, and now Socolia and her two Dragon Riders appeared to be flying much smoother than before.

As with all of the other riders, it had been the *dragons* that had chosen which human they would like to be friends with–if any–after Char had been slowly encouraging the students to go down into the dragon crater under the watchful eye of Paxala or herself, and there seeking to offer the younger dragons strips of meat or, if they were really lucky, fish!

"Skrech!" Paxala underneath us made an anguished chirruping sound, which I took to mean that she had picked up on my memory of her last delicious morsel.

"So soon after lunch, Paxala? After the battle, we'll all feast like never before, I promise you," I said, not raising my voice as

I knew that the Crimson Red would easily hear my words anyway.

"What did you say? Did you spot trouble?" Char was calling as I shook my head, pointing down at the scales below us to indicate that I had been talking to the dragon, not her.

"I see!" Char gave me a mock grimace as if jealous, before breaking into a wide grin. Even though she was very protective over Pax, she wasn't covetous of her company or the dragon's affections at all. In fact, she encouraged Pax to try and share her mind with me, perhaps eager to share with another human what she experienced every day.

I studied my friend for a moment longer, her pale hair bouncing on her back in a tight and severe warrior's tail. She was peering ahead of her in determination, even though we were so high as to see nothing but the dark and indistinct haze of landscape far below us. She came alive when she was flying. I saw her eyes bright, her smile quick – even when we were flying straight into danger!

Neither of us had talked about the possibility of encountering Zaxx. The *inevitability*, I corrected. On the parchment paper Maxal, Dorf, and I had briefly sketched out tactics and strategies. It had certainly *appeared* as though ten youthful dragons should be enough to defeat even the giant Zaxx, but I knew that when it came to the golden bull, all bets would be off.

Who knew what strange powers he could have? I allowed myself to worry for the moment. That book Char and Maxal obsessed over, *Versi's Voyage,* seemed to claim that the older a dragon got, the stranger abilities it could display – not just the ability to breathe fire but to command fire, or to create ice, to read thoughts, to control thoughts…

Was that why Pax couldn't sense Zaxx's presence earlier in Rampart? It had to be, surely? And it was also the most worrying part of our mission, a topic Char had brushed aside as if it were of no importance when I'd tried to raise it with her.

"We are ten dragons, and twenty riders," Char had reassured me. "Ten voices of dragon-flame. Over forty throwing spears!" I looked down at my side to the short javelin-like spears that all the riders now had, one on each side of their saddle. It was longer than my sword, but about half of my body length, made from strong and straight ash wood, with long metal points fashioned by one of Nan Barrow's brothers. To me, the weapons looked flimsy and thin when compared to the imagined bulk of the golden monster that was Zaxx.

Ahead of me, Char rested her gloved hand on the edge of her saddle, and I wondered if I were imagining things or if it was trembling just a little. I told myself it was the cold because I didn't want to believe that it was the effect of the Magewort that Jodreth had dosed her with, or—worse—fear. Char certainly was optimistic, I thought, before once again feeling cautious. She was still injured, really, and I worried the Magewort was giving her a false sense of strength. I resolved to find a way to keep Char out of the direct combat if I could.

BWAR-BWAR! The distant and tinny sound of the dragon pipes rose in the air beneath us to catch even my stubborn ears, but Paxala was already wheeling down, leading the diamond-like flight of dragons in a vast turning circle like a flock of seabirds.

Far below us was the source of the sound, and I could just make out the dark column of riders that was Prince Vincent's advance guard. This was the agreed sign that we had between us before we would start our last swoop to Rampart itself. As Paxala let herself plummet down, the land rose up to us in dizzying speed, making the wind tear at my clothes and my eyes tear. Her speed was phenomenal, and the strength and power that she had in her wings and arms to catch her plummeting flight and swing over the mounted knights was incredible, giving me a little hope that maybe we *could* defeat the monster Zaxx.

Beneath us, the double line of mounted knights stretched back almost as far as my human eyes could make out. What had the prince said, seven, eight hundred mounted knights? We were still outnumbered easily ten to one in that case by the rebel warriors alone, but the prince also had a larger force of infantry soldiers following.

Our combined role was simple, if somewhat difficult to execute: the mounted troops and the dragons were to harass and draw out the enemy from Rampart with lightning-fast raids and strafing air attacks, testing and holding the much greater rebel force as we awaited the arrival of Prince Vincent's large infantry force.

But we also had Zaxx to contend with, I thought, searching the skies overhead. If he showed himself, then I had given orders that the most experienced half of the dragons would split to challenge him directly (Pax, Socolia, Morax, Veserpal and Jhokar) while the other five would do what they could to call to the dragons of Mount Hammal. We were a long way away, far out of earshot of any normal creature, but once again, Paxala assured me that Zenema would hear of it if they came under attack.

I just hoped that she was right.

~

"Torvald!" barked Sir Rathon, at the head of the mounted column. He looked in his element, surrounded by his largest knights, and caparisoned in full plate armor. Assured of his superiority, I thought – although his fellow knights appeared somewhat *less* sure of the ten dragons landing in the meadows around the roadside. There was a river a little farther away, and Char nodded toward it.

"I'll let the dragons drink their fill, before..." she stated, and I agreed gravely.

"But Char.... How do you feel? Your shoulder?"

Char gave me reckless smile. "Jodreth gave me more of that Magewort, so I don't feel a thing!"

"Still, please be careful," I said. "I, I don't think I could stand it you were hurt again..." I whispered.

"Neill." Char's grin faded, momentarily serious. "Thank you. But what we're doing, where we're going and who we're facing..."

There was no need to finish the sentence. We all knew what was coming. There were no guarantees that any of us would make it.

"Go on, dismount and see what that oaf Rathon wants," Char said in a lighter tone, pushing me on the shoulder. "We both know that it's going to be *you* who gets hurt before me, anyway," she said with a grin. With a burst of air and force, Pax and the others leapt into the air to fly-hop the short distance to the river, there to submerge themselves almost to their wings, throwing water up into the air and over their beak-snouts.

"At least they don't seem skittish," the general said heavily, but I ignored the intended jibe.

"Are you all prepared, Sir Rathon?" I said. *Remember that you are equal in this,* I counselled myself. Even if I didn't want to be, I was the representative of the Dragon Academy, and I wouldn't be cowed by this man and his legion of knights.

"Of course," the general scowled. "Are you?"

"Aye," I nodded.

"And the dragons? Do they, erm, do they have their fire ready? This will be a difficult fight, you understand. And you riders are so young," the general said.

"You do not need to be afraid for us," I said. "Some of us have had not a little experience at this."

"Hmph." The general's frown deepened, shaking his head as if to discard the niceties of the conversation. "Anyway. This road leads us to the north-westerly approach to Rampart."

"The side that the armies are on." No one wanted to get bogged down on the other, river-village side of half-broken buildings.

"I want you to strafe them first," Sir Rathon mimicked the dragons swooping down low over the armies. "Soften them up, and then we'll make a direct charge. But we'll get one good frontal attack, and then the rebels will see that they have more numbers. It's impossible for them not to."

"We have the dragons; we can keep them occupied," I said.

"Well, you'd better – because after that, I intend to lead my men back down this road, giving time for the infantrymen behind us…" Rathon glowered at me. I could sense that there was something more going on here under the surface. Maybe it was just the man's way before battle, of course, or maybe it was just the fact that he didn't want to fight alongside someone he deemed 'inferior.' I couldn't be sure.

"And the prince?" I asked. "He is leading the infantry, is he not?"

"Of course!" Sir Rathon said. "He is safer surrounded by them, and they will be pleased that their great prince is with them as they march into battle." But Sir Rathon looked askance for a moment, as if worried. Was he worried for the prince? Was that what this was? I thought, before deciding that the hour was too late for me to do anything about the general's anxieties.

"You do your job, general, and I promise that the Dragon Riders will do ours," I said.

The general made the same harrumphing sound once again. "You'd better," he muttered, before turning and stalking back to his own steed. "My lance and shield!" he shouted. "Sound the horns! We ride! We ride for the Middle Kingdom!"

I stepped down off the roadway to let the column pass as the war horns of the prince's knights blared harshly around me. As they rode, I saw the loyalty and the grim determination that Sir Rathon inspired. Is this what you have to be, to lead the hearts of men? I thought. I didn't want to turn into a Sir Rathon. Why, if I were ever a general or even a ruler, I would never sit at the back, surrounded by thousands of soldiers like the prince does! I thought. I would ride at the front as Sir Rathon does. Because, I suppose that was one thing to be said for the general. At least he *led* his people into battle. What sort of prince hides at the back?

The war horns sounded again as I turned to start jogging to the river, where the ten dragons of the academy were starting to climb up out of the river and shake themselves off, their scales making many clattering sounds like a forest of dead branches in the winter storms.

What ridiculous thoughts I am having, I thought. I will never be a general, and I will never be a prince!

Even though we waited for Sir Rathon's mounted cavalry to pass us, cantering up the last stretch of road before the bend in the hills that led to Rampart, we still easily outpaced them as soon as we were in the air.

"We go high!" I counselled Char, raising my hands up to the layer of clouds above us. "We go high like an arrow, and then…" I mimed bringing my hands down in a deadly swoop. I knew that the dragons would love that maneuver, but I also wanted to keep them out of the way of the rebel's arrows and catapults and whatever else they might have to counter us.

Because I didn't dare forget that Ansall and my brothers, at least, would have *some* tactic to try and counter the dragons of Mount Hamal.

"Neill? These clouds... They're odd..." Char said as we rose, higher and higher. Around us spread the flight of dragons in a large V formation, with Paxala, Char, and I at their very apex.

She was right. The clouds were heavy and thick clouds, a dark curtain of a deep freezing cold storm grey. I had tried to keep sight of the land below us, and the column of knights turning toward the long, elongated bowl of hills. There, at the other end of the valley was the line of the fortified Rampart wall, standing head and shoulders over a deep pocket of mist, the glimmers of what must have been the armies' cook fires barely visible.

It was going to be murky down there between the hills, but I tried to tell myself that it was all for the better, that the rebel army would be just as disoriented as we were.

"Just stick to the plan!" I shouted to Char, wishing I had brought some sort of war horn like Sir Rathon had below, or something to be able to signal to the other Dragon Riders, presumably still following our lead but unable to see us, just as it was impossible for me to see anything other than Pax and Char. As soon as we'd flown into the thick slate grey clouds, we had been plunged into a weird, muffled quiet, where the sounds of the other dragons and the armies far, far below us appeared out of sync with reality.

"Srech!" A dragon on my right chirruped in a concerned fashion, but I couldn't be sure if they were closer than they should be, or farther away. Somewhere, too, came the jangle of harnesses and the stamp of the warhorses.

"We must be near our descent now, surely?" I called to Char, who had doubled over Paxala's neck, out of the cold.

It wasn't the cold though, as she turned around to me and said in anguish, "Neill! Something is wrong! Paxala cannot sense the other dragons. She cannot sense Rathon's knights below, she cannot sense the rebel army."

"What?" I said with a frown. "Is she mistaken? Maybe she's frightened of the battle—"

"She's a Crimson Red dragon! She doesn't *get* frightened, Neill." Char shook her head and once again turned to put her hands on the sides of Pax's broad and strong neck muscles. "No, there's nothing, she says. She doesn't know where the other dragons are at all— and it happened as soon as we went into these accursed clouds."

"Ansall," I snarled. It had to be. Only he and his other treacherous Draconis Order had the sorts of magical power able to do this. "Dive. We dive, now," I said. "Ask Paxala to light the way."

"But the other dragons!" Char cried, even as Pax started to hold her wings in that gliding gesture I now knew so well – just before tucking them together and diving forward. Stars keep us from colliding with any of the other great dragons, I thought, dreading what could happen when two such large and dangerous creatures hit each other in mid-flight.

"We should already be in the lead, Char," I argued. "And we have to do something!"

I sensed that buzzing in my head as Char conveyed her

thoughts to the dragon below. Whatever she had said, Paxala responded by angling herself to dive faster. She wanted to be quick. She wants to be the first, I thought, as orange light flared ahead, coming from the mouth of the Crimson Red. She hissed small gobbets of fire, causing the clouds around us to suddenly glare with red and orange, revealing her ruby red body in flashes. I hope this works, I thought, seeing how she had turned herself into a living lantern.

"Skreayargh!" We plummeted out of the sky like a burning arrow, the flames that Pax was blowing flowing around us in thin, fast-evaporating sheets. I wondered what the rebel army would think when they saw us. We would look like an incandescent, falling star!

There was a sizzling sound as the flames revealed a dark, draconian shape just behind us on our right. It was Morax! Another flare of flame and there, right behind us was Socolia, copying Pax's example.

"Char?!" I managed to shout over the howl of the rushing wind. "There is the land to think about..."

"She knows what she's doing!" Char said angrily, though her face was tight and pinched with worry. She didn't like what Pax had told her, I could tell. The Crimson Red's sudden inability to sense was something new and unsettling for all of us.

WOOOSH! With a sudden flare of Pax's wings, we broke through the low-lying cloud and into the rounded, broad area in front of Rampart. We were traveling fast, straight for the wall itself.

"Turn! Turn!" I was shouting, struggling to signal to Morax

at my side as Paxala shrieked, and threw herself into a curving roll.

My stomach lurched and I groaned as I was lifted bodily from the saddle and thumped painfully back down into it again to see, for a split second, the ground racing past above my head as Pax flipped herself over again, pulling herself out of her flaming death-dive headlong at the reinforced, gigantic wall of Rampart.

"Shrekh! Sckreayargh!" She and the other dragons called in alarm, peeling off in all directions so as to avoid the wall.

"It was Ansall," I breathed, my heart thundering a hundred beats a minute. "It had to be. He must have made that magical smoke and clouds above, to lure us in…" And, it would explain why Pax couldn't sense Zaxx before – was it because the Abbot had used the same, nullifying clouds? Hadn't there been a low river fog hanging over the river-village outside Rampart before?

Paxala shot out along the lip of the bowl of hills in a wide circle, allowing us to catch our breath and begin our first strafing run – only, something was wrong. *Very* wrong.

There was no rebel army here waiting for us.

CHAPTER 21
NEILL, AND THE DARKENING

There was no rebel army here. No matter what my eyes reported, my mind refused to believe. But what could that mean? Where were they, if they weren't here?

We flew, skirting the hills, away from the walls of Rampart and its heavy blanket of low, magical grey clouds just overhead. The clouds had lowered to entirely cover the tops, forming a hollow where the light below was dingy and grey, and the sound curiously echoing. It was like a cave, with the back of the cave being the tall wooden walls of Rampart with its sharpened stake wall tops.

The ground beneath was churned from the passage of many, many feet and hooves, and, as I looked down I could still see the many small flares of campfires, the pitched tents – both individual and large, as well carts and vehicles standing in small huddles like they were old friends in a market place.

"Neill?" Char was clearly as disconcerted as I was. "Where are they? Where are the rebels? Your brothers?"

"It's a trap," I said, stating the obvious, probably. "We have to warn Sir Rathon!" I said, just as I saw, amongst the discarded remnants of the encampment another batch of wagons and carts, sitting on their own. These different carts were long and bore about six wheels on either side, with long wooden arms stacked carefully along their body. "That makes no sense – those are catapults, I am sure of it." I pointed to them. They were, as far as I could guess, the only weapon that the warlords and clan armies had against dragons. They were also one of the few weapons that an army had against a walled or fortified enemy. "If the rebels had meant to march on the academy, or the prince's own palace, they would have taken those catapults with them," I said. At least, I was sure that was what my *father* would have done, and would have expected Rubin and Rik to have followed suit.

It's not like the sons of Malos Torvald to throw away any weapon that they're going to need in the future, I thought in alarm.

The sudden blaring of horns made me look up as the double-column of Sir Rathon's knights of the Middle Kingdom marched into the valley, their plate and chain armor catching the reflected glimmers of the cookfires, and their proud banners and pennants flailing and flapping with the force and fury of their charge.

We flew towards them as we watched their column break apart in practiced and tried maneuver, their two-rank lead (with Sir Rathon and his trusted second right hand at the front) to become a line of four, eight, sixteen, and soon it was an outpouring of what must have been over a hundred mounted lancers, and still room for much more in the empty battlefield. They charged at nothing but churned mud, their furious clip faltering and slowing, as their tight formation started to fray in confusion.

"Sir Rathon! Sir Rathon – go back!" I stood up in my stirrups to wave both of my hands at him. "It must be a trap – go back!" I hollered, but my words either could not reach him or went ignored. Instead, the general slowed his troops' furious charge to a slow trot, before calling for his forces to form a dense cube.

BWAR! BWAR! Another wave of flash of the banners over-head as Sir Rathon was summoning me closer to give counsel.

"Neill? What should the other dragons do?" Char was saying.

"Can Pax tell them to keep circling the hollow, but stay *well* clear of the Rampart walls?" I said quickly. "And stay *under* the clouds, if they can."

Char nodded, as Pax gave out a series of whistles, shrieks, and clicks of bird calls. "Hey!" I heard Terence call out as his blue Morax suddenly changed direction and hugged the hills of the hollow, but Lila saw me waving, and gave us a thumbs-up sign.

"Is Pax okay now? Can she sense the other dragons? What about Zaxx?" I said hurriedly as we peeled off from the other dragons and started flapping down towards the knights.

"Yes." Char nodded, white-faced with worry. "All is back to normal, and yes, she tells me that Zaxx has been here, as well as a good few thousand or so human warriors, but neither are here now."

Then, where are they? I thought. And were the dragons' senses restricted to what was here in this hollow, underneath that cloud? That meant that we were sitting ducks…

I didn't like it. Not at all. Not one bit. I made to stand up again, to try and signal to Sir Rathon that he should wheel his knights out of here, just as I intended to do, when there was a *change* in the air.

A cold breeze. No, to be more accurate, it was a freezing wind, and it was coming from over the top of the Rampart wall. "Wait," I murmured to Char and Paxala both, and we slowed our flight, pausing to beat Pax's wings in the air above the deserted plain. There was no way I wanted us to be vulnerable and on the ground whenever the trouble came. Dragons needed to be able to *fly*.

"There, what is that?" I saw something on top of the Rampart wall. A speck, barely bigger than a thimble. It was a man, and even from this great distance I swear that I could recognize the proud stance it took, unbowed and unbroken in the very center of the wall, before stepping forward boldly, right to the very edge.

"Draaagon Ridersss," the voice of the Abbot Ansall found us through the wind, sounding strange and with hissing sibilants. I thought that it must be a strange effect of the clouds above. As I watched, I could see the same austere black garb, the same gleam of a hairless head (the beard appeared to be gone) and he even still had his cane at his side which I saw him rise to point down at the knights below us.

"Knightsss of the prince," the Abbot croaked, and I thought that we would never have been able to hear it were it not for the strange echoing amplification of the clouds around. "Sssuch a shame that Vincent couldn't make it. I have an offer for him. One that he sssimply cannot refuse!" The man started to hack and cough where he stood, and Sir Rathon spurred his horse forward and called up to the great wall and his enemy above.

"Abbot Ansall! Oath-breaker! Heretic! Traitor to the rightful throne of the Middle Kingdom. You have been charged for your crimes and, before the eyes of the world and in the name of the prince, I order you to give yourself up to his judgment, now!" Sir Rathon barked in a voice used and suited to battlefield chanting.

"Sssilly little man. Why would I give myssself up?" The Abbot finally stopped choking and coughing, but appeared to be laughing instead.

"Your armies have clearly abandoned you – as well they might when they saw our dragons," Sir Rathon barked. "You know the might of Prince Vincent's armies. Give yourself up now."

"But, why little general – my armies haven't abandoned me. No, far from it – they are all around!" He raised his staff and emitted a cry, and I saw a spark of electricity flare from the top of his cane and up to bracket along the bottom of the lowering clouds.

"Dragon Riders? Ready!" I called, reaching for the first lance which I intended to throw straight at the heart of the Abbot. I didn't know where the rebels were hiding, but unless the Abbot was lying, they had us surrounded.

And then something really weird happened.

The dark and heavy clouds above started to wisp downwards.

Small tufts and tendrils of smoke fell, insubstantial and wavering from the sky. There were a hundred tentacles of smoke, and a hundred, hundred more.

"What is this...?" I said as drips of the cloud-smoke fell past my shoulder, puffing and evaporating right there in Paxala's wing to regather and coalesce in its same column of smoke on the other side, continuing its fluttering way down to the ground.

"Enough of your games and theatrics!" Sir Rathon shouted savagely, swiping his lance across the nearest column of smoke that stood before him, scattering it into wisps. He spurred his horse to charge through the next, scattering that one, too.

"I don't like this, Neill – I think we should get the dragons out of here," Char said.

"I don't know what the Abbot is playing at, or whether he's just buying himself time, but you're right," I nodded, standing once again (shirking away from the nearest column of cloud-smoke as it flowed off my shoulder) to shout, "Dragon Riders! Ride!" Paxala wheeled, but, as we did so there was a sudden scream from below, halting our escape.

"What was that?" I looked down. We couldn't leave Sir Rathon and his men down there if they were under attack! I peered, and saw that one of Prince Vincent's mounted knights was on the ground, dead, and standing before him was a shadowy, insubstantial figure.

More screams erupted from the mounted knights as the columns of cloud-smoke coalesced into pale warrior-like forms, barely human, but each holding the shadow blades and weapons as they must have done in real life.

"What has the Abbot done to his army?" I asked, aghast at what I was watching. I watched as more of the cloud-warriors formed, and struck, before collapsing and tattering into mist whenever they were struck. I didn't know if that meant that the specters were banished, or dead, or whether they would only come back again, but I could see our knights were surrounded, and that they could be attacked from anywhere, any angle, at any moment.

"Sir Rathon!" I screamed. "Get them out of there!"

"How do you like my new army, little general?" the Abbot cooed and purred. "The mighty Zaxx has been very kind to me. He has been teaching me so many ancient and forgotten things. Magics forgotten by humanity that, with a little tinkering of my own, I have used to make us *invincible*!" The Abbot cackled at us. "You fools fell for every part of our trap!"

Hsssss.... Behind the Abbot, there came a deep, hissing groan, that seemed to shake the very walls of Rampart itself.

"Char? I think we've just found out where Zaxx is…" I said hesitantly as the deep grey clouds *behind* Rampart started to deepen, as if a great shadow were moving toward us.

"Behold, your god!" The Abbot started to gibber as twin patches of glowing red eyes winked on in the clouds above him.

He's insane, I thought, hefting the throwing lance up to my shoulder. "Char – I want a clear shot – but I want all the other dragons to get back to the academy. Now."

Char nodded grimly, conveying my wishes to Pax who twittered and shrieked her suggestions to Morax and Socolia and the others, while beneath us, the knights were being butchered.

"Skreyargh!" Paxala beat her wings furiously in tight circles, trying to not only blow away the cloud-warriors but also to gain enough momentum for a charging attack. Just one shot, I thought. That is all I need.

Above us, however, the Abbot cackled as the great, flame-filled eyes of Zaxx drew closer. "You see, before I only wanted to be immortal, for myself. I gave that knowledge to the Old Queen Delia, and helped lengthen the lifespans of the princes… but what the great and mighty Zaxx has showed me? He has showed me a way not only to live forever, but to be *everlasting…*" He doubled up in some sort of hysterical joy as Paxala swooped, and I raised my arm…

"You just have to want it badly enough…" the Abbot said, throwing out his cane and pointing it at *us*! My heart quailed, but Paxala's did not, and she flipped her wings to her side, curving her flight around the bolt of electrical light that shot past her, and hit the knights beneath and behind us. There was a sound like sizzling water, and I looked over my shoulder to see knights and horses *evaporating* into the same shadow, cloud-smoke as the Abbot had called.

He's only adding to his army of darkness, with every kill his soldiers make, I thought in horror, seeing the wisps of the human knights rising upwards, upwards to the strange clouds above.

Hsssss…. The glowing eyes were joined by a snout, and horns, and tufted ears as a great head almost the size of Pax's entire body emerged out of the mists. Zaxx had grown huge in his exile.

"Neill, now! Now!" Char shouted, using her own stirrups to

help Paxala turn in a tight curve in front of the walls, leaving me with just one, crystal-clear moment—

The Abbot had lowered his staff and stood, not twenty feet from me. He looked different, changed. Gone was his wispy and wiry beard. Gone were his eyebrows and any sign of hair. Just a wizened, ancient head with sunken, glittering eyes. And it wasn't only his eyes that glittered, but the skin around his brows, his cheekbones, under his eyes and lips was also oddly reflective, like, he had *scales.*

"Yargh!" I threw the small lance, and watched as it arced over the distance between us, as fast as thought and made all the speedier by the momentum of the dragon upon which I sat. The Abbot looked astonished and confused for a moment as it shot straight at him, thudding into his body.

"Oof!" the Abbot exhaled at the same instant there was the *crack* of splintering wood as the lance shattered on impact with the old man's chest. Although the force of my throw bowled him over, the throwing lance was in pieces all around him, and the Abbot was coughing and pushing himself back up again.

"It didn't kill him. It didn't even injure him!" I said, mortified as Paxala flashed past and upwards, flaring her wings and claws at the rising maw of Zaxx, the monstrous golden bull.

"Skreayargh!" Pax roared her defiance at the dragon that was her father, and, in response, Zaxx opened his mouth and shot out a torrent of flame.

"Dive!" Char shouted, but she did not need to tell me to clutch Pax's neck, nor the dragon to suddenly spin in the air and change direction, avoiding the boiling firestorm that erupted from Zaxx's mouth.

Great claws, each talon as big as my entire body seized the top of the Rampart wall, breaking it apart as Zaxx hauled his bulk onto it, ready to launch after our much smaller dragons.

"Arise, my god! Arise, my army of darkness!" The Abbot was capering where he stood, as more and more wisps of shadow smoke rose from Sir Rathon's fallen knights. I watched as the Abbot once again gestured with his cane, pointing south. "Fly to the Dragon Mountain, and punish those who would stand in the way of our birthright!"

At his command, the clouds boiled and parted, as the shadow-soldiers melded into it, and the clouds broke away from their more natural fellows, and raced southwards, towards Mount Hammal.

"Uh, Char…?" I called.

"I saw! And we're not staying!" Char shouted.

Thank the stars, I thought, as I saw the tails of the other Dragon Riders vanishing out of the head of the valley. We have to catch that shadow army, somehow. We have to stop it from falling on the academy as it had here. Behind us there were screams, and another bolt of terrible power as the undying Abbot turned more of Sir Rathon's living knights into his army of shadow darkness.

CHAPTER 22
CHAR, FLYING

We flew as fast as we could, though no words passed between the riders. We all just knew that we had to get back to the dragon crater and our friends.

The dark armies of the Abbot were heading there. How fast did they travel? How could we warn the crater and the academy before they got there? I kept thinking again and again in alarm. We had been unprepared. Woefully unexpecting the dark magics that the bull dragon and the Abbot could utilize. Behind me, Neill's face was pale and pinched with fury, his eyes far away.

"There was nothing you could have done to prepare for that," I said to him. "Nothing any of us could have done."

Neill blinked, looking at me as if for the first time. "I know that. But it's not just that. It's Rubin. It's Rik. It's all the other clansmen of Torvald whom I have stood beside, trained under..."

The realization hit me of what he meant. "Oh stars, Neill, I'm so sorry." They must have been killed by the Abbot, killed and transformed into those shadow specters that were even now racing towards our home. I couldn't imagine what that must be like. Never to see your family again was devastating enough – but knowing that they had been trapped for eternity as some sort of evil spirit?

"We'll stop the Abbot," I promised him savagely. "We'll make him pay for everything that he has done..." Somehow, I thought.

"If it's the last thing we do," Neill said, before his eyes widened and he pointed behind us. "Look. It's there!"

I turned to see that he was right. Racing ahead of us, moving of its own steam and apparently independent of any current of air was the dark, boiling cloud of the Abbot's shadow-army. It was flying low to the ground, heedless of the trees, hills, buildings or even villages that it flowed over and through. I watched it speed past an open country trail, upon which had been moving a cart and horses. As it eclipsed them, there was flash of light, and then the cloud was gone and the cart upturned on its side, abandoned. No sign of the drivers, or of the horses.

"It's like it just consumed them," I murmured.

"The darkening is death. It is beyond death," Paxala snarled into my mind, making me wince with the force of her anger. *"That is everything that the dragons stand against. The dragons are fire and warmth and light – and that shadow is cold and dark and death."* I sensed her deep disgust and fury at what her own father, Zaxx, had apparently done. The bull had moved beyond being a mere monster, or a mere tyrant to her – he was now an abomination.

"I will kill him. I will end his evil." Paxala lashed her tail, exploding a stand of trees as we flew.

"I know you will, my sister," I reassured her. "But first we have to outpace that thing, if we are to ever see our friends again."

"Nothing can fly faster than a Crimson Red!" Paxala growled, and felt the thrust of energy as she threw everything she had into her flying. Her wings beat so fast they blurred, and I saw her making tiny adjustments all the time to catch the breeze, to make the most of that current of air.

And little by little, we started gaining on the dark cloud.

~

"Yes! Fly Paxala! We're gaining on it!" I shouted as the cloud seemed to grow larger ahead of us. We had already passed and pulled away from the other nine dragons, as if the Crimson Red was trying to prove her point that we were indeed the fastest thing in the skies.

We were close enough now that I could see more detail in the dark cloud's surface, the way that its body was constantly shifting and moving, and, I swear, I could make out the impressions of bodies, limbs, even faces.

My heart quailed at the thought of it – so many lives contained within that one shape. How many had there been in the rebel army? A thousand? Two thousand?

"Take heart, my sister," Paxala roared into my mind, and I could feel within her the unquenchable fire that felt like the pulse

of life itself, filling me with confidence and courage. It made me forget the ache in my shoulder, and the energy that the dragon was giving me felt stronger even than the Magewort potion that Jodreth had supplied me with.

The dragon's powerful wings weren't blurring with speed now, but beating vigorously and slowly, powerful beats that, with every downstroke powered us closer to the dark cloud.

"Char, up ahead," Neill said, and I refocused my eyes, not on the cloud, but on the horizon where there was a pinnacle emerging. How fast were we going? We had covered more distance now, at the top range of the Red's abilities and in less time than we ever had before.

"There's our goal, Pax," I whispered. "Take us home." I lifted my legs from the stirrup-levers and nodded for Neill to follow my example. There was little that either of us could do now that would help the dragon in a straight race, and, without our insistent guidance, Pax roared and shot forward like a dart, skipping ahead of the cloud, barely meters above it, before arcing downwards into one long swooping flight, straight for the mountain. The wind filled Pax's wings and pushed us even farther ahead.

The cloud receded behind us. We were going to make it! We were going to get there before the Abbot's dark army! I exulted.

But we wouldn't have long when we got there before we were engulfed.

CHAPTER 23
NEILL, THE CONFRONTATION

"What is the meaning of this?" I shouted. "They were meant to follow on behind! To advance to Rampart!" I demanded when I saw what was below us.

Prince Vincent's foot soldiers hadn't left the slopes of Mount Hammal. They had, if anything, dug themselves in deeper, advancing in terraced waves of trenches up the slopes, almost half the height of the mountain itself. *But their walls and defensive lines were facing outwards, at least,* I thought. They hadn't meant to attack the academy – for now.

"The prince has to come out and fight!" I called to Char as we rocketed closer and closer. "Land me before the walls. I will see what is the meaning of this treachery."

"Not on your own! We'll go with you? Paxala and me?" Char said, casting a worried look behind us at the dark cloud that was still advancing, growing larger and larger on the horizon. And beyond that, somewhere back there, were the nine other Dragon Riders.

"No," I said, as Paxala started to flare and beat her wings to slow enough for a brief landing on the barren slopes of the mountain. "You need to warn those inside the academy. Get Maxal, Jodreth. Anyone with any bit of magical training–maybe there's *something*, anything you can pull together to help us defeat this thing."

"I'll try," Char said, frowning, holding my gaze for a moment as Paxala turned to take off once more. "Stay alive, Torvald."

"And you," I said, feeling as if one half of me was being ripped apart as I watched my friends leap into the sky, to acrobatically flip in the air over the walls of the Dragon Academy itself.

No time, I thought, turning to run down the slopes of the mountain toward the dark black and gold tent, surrounded by wooden stakes and archers that belonged to Prince Vincent.

My sides burned as I ran as fast as I could, but the sight of evil shadow that was gaining size on the horizon made me forget my human frailties. I sprinted, ignoring the collection of Middle Kingdom scouts who stood up as I ran past.

I charged through the ad hoc lines of trenches, and gathering soldiers and militia, tough men and women who lived and died by the sword and had already spent weeks on the road.

"Here! Stop him!" their captains shouted. I managed to shove the first to try and tackle me aside, and knock down the second.

"Take me to the prince!" I bellowed. "I am the first Dragon Rider and I must see your prince now, our very lives depend upon it!"

I threw a glance over my shoulder and saw the cloud was growing in size, now occupying almost a quarter of the northern sky. When would it reach us? Where were the other Dragon Riders? I wondered in anguish. The cloud had traveled fast. Faster than any normal weather front. Almost as fast as a dragon!

"Bring him forward," an imperious voice sounded past a line of very large and very surly looking infantry. As they parted, I found myself staring at the Dark Prince himself before his fine black and gold tent, dressed in chain mail over a stained, dark-leather cuirass. At his arms and legs were finely tooled greaves, and at his hip was the finely made sword. He had braided his long, dark hair into one long warrior's plait, although I thought that a helmet might be more sensible in his position. He was also looking at me with suspicion.

"*Master* Torvald? Where is Sir Rathon? Where are my knights? Have you won the battle so easily?" he quizzed me.

"You betrayed your oath to join us as our rearguard!" I said hotly, wishing my arms were free so that I could at least point a finger at him. "Sir Rathon knew it," I said, my heart finding the words as I remembered the old general's wary, suspicious conversation right before the battle. "He *knew* you weren't going to back him up," I challenged him.

There were a few gasps and mutters from the heavy infantry around us, although I did not know if that was because of my accusations, or the tone of voice that I was using to insult their prince.

Their prince, I reminded myself. He has never been my lord. He has never been loyal to me, or to Torvald.

"What use would it have been if I marched thousands of men north, only to have the great Dragon Riders and my best knights defeat the armies before I even got there?" Prince Vincent purred. "Better to wait here and discover the sort of valor and skills that you Dragon Riders have in battle, before joining, I think."

"You sent us to die," I spat the words at him. "Either that, or you're a coward." I could see the type of man that Vincent was. One who was forever getting good people to do his dirty work. He had probably wanted me and Char to die in the battle, so he could once again try to take over the academy in our absence. He didn't care if Sir Rathon died, just so long as he himself didn't.

"How *dare* you call me a coward," *Schnickt!* There was a whisper-quick maneuver as the fine, straight-bladed sword that the prince wore appeared in his hand. I had barely seen his hands move, they were so quick. I reassessed my judgment of him – he might be a coward, but he was a *very well-trained one.*

"And, *Master* Torvald. You may be the First Rider. You may be the Chosen Warden of the Academy, as your father was the Chosen Warden of the East. But you are still my subject." The prince advanced on me, his blade still held out, and my hands still seized by the prince's men on either side. *Is this how it all ends?*

"And those dragons, too, are my subjects. If I choose you to die for the good of the throne, then you'd better well do it!" Vincent said coldly.

"Now's your chance to prove you are not a coward, Vincent," I snarled back, nodding over his shoulder at the cloud that was fast approaching over the plain. It would be on the forward lines and walls of his troops in moments. "That is our enemy. The enemy you swore to defeat. That dark shadow has been summoned by your old friend the Abbot, and it contains the unquiet souls of thousands of men, bent to the Abbot's will. The Abbot will also be here soon, with the monster Zaxx. Prove to us all that you can lead!" I demanded of him.

"What? That?" The prince was staring at the dark shadow in horror. "You mean that you *didn't* defeat the rebels? The Abbot? Zaxx? You mean that Sir Rathon and my knights—"

"All dead. All fed into that dark magic." I nodded, as the dark shadow engulfed the first line of the prince's troops.

~

There were terrifying screams, and flashes of muted lightning from inside the cloud as it devoured the crowd below us. As soon as the dark shadow had hit the mass of human soldiers it had halted as if busy, and even from this great height I could see the edges of the cloud starting to fray and dissipate, as shadows uncoiled and dropped to the ground, taking on almost human form...

"What – how do we stop it?" The prince said, aghast, as the captains on either side of me dropped their hold to stare at the thing that they couldn't fight.

"I don't know," I said. "Our spears were useless against it, and Sir Rathon's knights' weapons were too."

"Fire!" The prince suddenly commanded. "Bring up the fire-pots! Try to burn it!"

The command was passed down the slopes of men by shouts and waving flags, and we watched as small, fast moving teams of soldiers with heavy packs carrying little clay pots started to snake down towards the front.

It was a frontline that was rapidly collapsing under the sudden arrival and dissipation of ghostly, shadow-attackers. I saw some of the Middle Kingdomers start to abandon their posts, whilst others bravely held on, to be surrounded by strange shadow-beings.

"Clear!" We heard the thin warnings of the distant fire-hurlers, as the small teams threw their clay pots, lit on one end, at the enemy. They sailed harmlessly through the dark, exploding in a scatter of sparks and flames, to under light the shadow.

"Fire doesn't work," the prince said, wide-eyed, his entire demeanor changed from arrogance to panic. "Torvald, you *must* do something. You *must* have an answer to this!"

I didn't know what the answer could be. I had never faced anything like this before, and I had never heard of my father ever fighting a foe this strange. But there were people down there who needed guidance. Who needed some help, however slim it might be. My mind raced.

"Lead your men, prince," I snapped at him. "Let them see you. Guide them back up the mountain to the academy."

"What good will *that* do?" Vincent was almost hysterical.

"It's what they deserve," I growled back. "And then we find Ansall. And Zaxx. It's Ansall and Zaxx's magic that caused this, somehow – if we can stop them, then maybe, just maybe, their spells will unravel as well."

The prince nodded, his face pinched with fear and concentration as he signaled for his horse to be brought forward. "Guards! To me! We clear a path for the escaping soldiers. Help those who have fallen." He was saying as he leapt atop his horse. In the dark and flame-lit gloom, he appeared almost noble. "Torvald?" He pointed to another stallion that had been brought forward.

I might as well do some good, before we all die, I thought, vaulting onto the horse and wishing it were a dragon. "Easy fella, easy," I murmured to him, before starting to help the prince save what he could of his people.

The cloud was moving at a steady pace, no faster than a slow walk on foot, but implacable as it started to swirl around the slopes of Mount Hammal, and then, horribly, start to rise.

"Skeayar! Sckrrr!" The dragons whirled and called from above the academy and I raised a gloved hand, hoping that any of them would see me, and know that I was all right.

"Char knows." Paxala's voice, heavy and angry, broke into my mind. She seemed able to communicate with me much easier here on mountain soil. *What was it they said? That this mountain is sacred...*

"I will tell her what I see of you. She is busy with the lightning monk."

The lightning monk? I thought in confusion, before the

answer came to me. I smiled wearily. She must mean Jodreth. "Good. Just tell them to find a solution!" I said out loud, making the wounded soldier I had been helping look at me oddly. I rode beside the prince, giving orders for the soldiers to evacuate their positions and start moving up the mountain ahead of the cloud's advance. We were still losing hundreds of people down at the front – those who had either bravely stayed to try and fight the shadow-warriors or those too slow in running away.

It appeared that Char, Jodreth and the others had at least found a way to help as there came a sudden crackle of thunder behind us, over the Dragon Academy. Illuminated over the front gates a small gaggle of people, one of them—Jodreth—with his staff held high and another with a spark of bright hair caught in the reflected lightning.

Char, my heart beat. She was fierce and proud up there, just as she always looked to me.

I've never had much time for girls, I thought. It was always swords and fighting stances, but if there were ever a girl I'd happily spend the rest of my life with, it would be her.

Only now, it all appeared almost too late as the cloud was billowing up in front of the mountain, ready to engulf us all. I'm an idiot, I thought. I should have told Char what I felt about her earlier.

I looked back up at Char, and saw that her assembled group were doing something, raising their interlocked hands into the sky as the lightning crackled over the gathering clouds.

This is like what the Abbot had them do before, I remembered. When my brothers had attacked this mountain, the Abbot had managed to hypnotize his magical students into summoning a great storm, and now, it looked as though Char and Jodreth were attempting to do the same.

The storm clouds generating above the academy swirled and glowered, lowering their bulk over the slopes of the mountain in direct retaliation to the Abbot's spectral cloud. I watched in a sort of awed terror as these two titanic forces crept towards each other, a thin strip of blue-grey sky between them, and then, with a roll of thunder, the academy's cloud gave way to a gale of hurricane wind, straight down into the dark shadows of the Abbot's.

"Woah!" The soldiers around me suddenly slipped, gripping their helmets and each other as the gale force winds Char had summoned blew apart campfires, tents, blew spears out of soldier's hands.

But it was also forcing back the shadow-warriors. On the slopes below me, one of the shadow-warriors attempted to stride forward, raising his eldritch sword as more and more gobbets of shadow-stuff were pulled from his body. Through sheer evil will, the thing continued to march, even as it grew fainter and fainter, before eventually evaporating into darkness.

We might even be able to win this, I thought, watching the magical gales drive the dark shadows back. But how long before they re-incorporated and attacked again?

Just as I was starting to build my hope once more, there emerged over the darkening shadows the mighty bulk of our true enemy, and he was being harried by seven much smaller dragons.

Zaxx had arrived.

CHAPTER 24
NEILL, THE GREATEST CHALLENGE YET

Zaxx had arrived, over the skies of his old home, and he flew ponderously and slowly, like a mountain hovering in the air. His wings were ancient and much-tattered, and his golden scales had cracked and dulled so that he now appeared just yellowish, and with a hint of rust.

But he was immense. He dwarfed all of the smaller dragons, including Paxala. He was a thing out of legend. A nightmare of a forgotten past that was somehow still alive in the world.

"Seven dragons?" My mind caught up with my horror. I counted again. Yes, there were Morax and Socolia (I would recognize them anywhere) and there too were the other single-rider dragons of Veserpal, Haxar, Zhukis, Varo, and Tchakka. I watched as they each swarmed and mobbed their tyrant dragon like diving crows – swooping in fast turns to slash at the bull's wings, back, or belly. The bull shuddered in his flight and flared his great wings every now and again, but it was clear that he could withstand a lot of scrapes from these smaller creatures.

"Where are Jhokar and Siuella?" I said to no one in particular, too shocked to keep my thoughts to myself as I recalled the Green and the Blue who had accompanied us. What had been their riders' names? I remembered a quiet girl, a warlord's second daughter, as well as an athletic young man with blond hair, old to be a Draconis Order student perhaps, but still friendly and serious-natured. How could I remember their dragons' names and not theirs?

"Yes, Neill. They have fallen fighting my father. We dragons sensed their blood," Paxala informed me in my mind, and I could feel her rage; it echoed my own.

"Torvald!" It was the prince, already ahead of me and wheeling his stallion around towards where Zaxx appeared about to land, right in front of the academy gates. "You said I was a coward, and only killing that beast and the monster it carries would end this darkness. Well, we shall see about that – no one shall steal my kingdom away from me!"

I watched as Prince Vincent turned his stallion and spurred him towards the monastery, armed with nothing more than his sword and shield.

He's gone crazy, I thought as the small figure accelerated up the slope and the gigantic Zaxx thundered to halt, crashing into the gatehouse walls with his bulk and shaking Char, Jodreth and the other magical students from their ritual. Almost immediately the storm winds lessened and started to subside, as the dark shadow army coalesced once more.

"Char!" I called, urging my own steed into a gallop after the prince.

"I see it. I will save her," Paxala said, her thoughts as fast as lightning as I saw, up ahead, a glimmer of red in the dark skies.

Please, be quick Pax, be quick... I gasped, watching as Zaxx settled on his haunches and a clacking, guttural roar escaped his maw. He was laughing.

～

"Come closer, little prince!" Zaxx boomed at the charging Prince Vincent, and, to his credit, Vincent didn't hesitate. He charged on his steed straight at the monster, his sword held high—

With a roar, the golden bull lashed out with a paw, seeking to dash him and his steed to pieces. But the bull wasn't as quick a beast as Paxala was, and Vincent threw his horse into a kicking swerve so that Zaxx's talons only scored their deep furrows into the earth.

"Pax?" I shouted desperately on my own charge to the gates.

"Char is safe. I have her," came the Crimson Red's reply, and a moment later, she leapt into the air from behind the walls, to wheel over her father. The sudden appearance of his daughter drew the bull's attention and Prince Vincent capitalized on the opportunity, darting forward to swipe his sword at the bull's shoulder.

There was a metallic clank and screech, and I swore sparks flew, but no damage was done.

"Daughter. I should have crushed your egg when I had the chance, just as I killed your mother," the golden bull said clearly in my mind, and it seemed the prince also could hear the dragon, for he glanced upward briefly.

It was the wrong move for the prince. With a sudden snarl, Zaxx lashed his tail—a tail that was thicker than an oak tree—across the rocky ground, and I heard a *whump* as it hit both rider and horse.

Is he dead? I wondered for a moment, watching both bodies tumble aside to the rocks – but no time to check as now it was me, on a steed, before the Gold bull. The Dark Prince had given me a sword, which I hefted in my grip before the King of Dragons. It was a well-made blade, serviceable and sharp, not the thin finery of the prince's own.

Maybe I can distract him. Give Pax a chance to attack...
"Zaxx!" I shouted, spurring my steed into a leap over the tip of the Gold's tail as I leaned down.

Clang! I swiped as hard as I could at the beasts' forked tail, and heard a crunch as one of the aging scales was barely dented. What good was a sword against a beast of his size?

"Fool." The dragon spoke once more, although I didn't know if it was to me or the prince or Pax. He lifted his tail to swipe at me as he had at the prince, but before he could, there was a scream from the Crimson Red above our heads.

Defiant and angry, Pax shot down like a hunting hawk, scraping her claws across her father's snout.

He shouted in pain, and gouts of thick, dark dragon blood

spattered onto the ground. His attention turned to the more dangerous daughter, leaving me free to leap from my saddle, rolling on the ground before the beast. I'd not take my steed with me to death, and, at the sudden loss of its rider, the horse galloped down the slope, and hopefully to some form of safety – although with the Darkening cloud spreading up the slopes of Mount Hammal, I knew that might even be short-lived.

Paxala was swooping up, turning in her flight as Zaxx suddenly reached up, standing on hind legs to bat at her like an angry cat.

He missed. Paxala – with Char riding on her back – performed a whisper-quick aerial maneuver to dance out of the way of those dangerous claws.

Now was my chance. I ran to the bull's feet, leaped, and, with my sword in one hand seized onto his scaly leg. I clung on as the dragon shifted and moved, reaching to bat at the dancing Paxala above him. Zaxx was too busy fending off his daughter to notice me as I climbed. I could smell the heavy, bitter tones of soot and smoke pouring from the bull's mouth as he prepared his dragon flame against his daughter.

But there was one adversary who I had forgotten. The Abbot Ansall, himself clinging atop the monstrous Gold.

"Torvald?" he snarled from above me. I craned my neck to see the ancient looking man, still wearing his tattered Draconis Order black robes, barely clutching onto the tines of Zaxx's back. He did not have the harnesses and saddles that we Dragon Riders did, and instead was clinging on haphazardly as he tried to lower his staff in my direction.

"Sckreyargh!" Paxala's screech distracted both the Abbot and me, as the dragon dove once more, straight at Zaxx's snout. Zaxx's neck inflated horribly, and he roared his flame.

Pax! Char! I thought in terror, but I should have known better. The Crimson Red pirouetted on one wing tip avoiding the flame by the neatest of margins as the fire burst against the front gate of the academy, and shot hundreds of feet into the air behind her. Zaxx lunged after Pax, the sudden movement dislodging Ansall, and the bolt of purple-dark energy that he shot from his staff flashed over my shoulder to hit the ground in a sizzling display of destruction.

I climbed as fast and as high as I dared, clutching the spines of Zaxx's back as I moved. I didn't think, I didn't plan, but reacted on instinct when the Abbot lifted his staff in my direction once more. I swung around the spine one-handed, as another bolt of purple energy burst across the air where I had been.

"Dislodge this gnat, great Zaxx!" Ansall shouted as I climbed closer, but I was far more practiced in the art of dragon riding than the Abbot and the great beast had problems of his own. He turned to keep an eye on his daughter already wheeling back around for another attack, just as there was a cry from the ground.

"My kingdom! MINE!" It was Prince Vincent. Remarkably, he had survived the crushing tail blow and had done as I had, racing under the bulk of the golden bull while Zaxx was distracted with Paxala. As I watched, Prince Vincent leapt from where he had climbed up the foot of the beast, fine blade outstretched, to plunge it between the softer, smaller scales of the

dragon's lower neck, where the strange, inflatable organs of the dragon's flames were. I hadn't thought Vincent knew much about dragons, but aside from the eye or the mouth, the magical, chemical organs of the lower neck were probably the most damaging a target as could be found on an adult dragon.

Zaxx made an awful gurgling groaning sound as he suddenly convulsed, shaking his neck and head, sending Vincent, who had been hanging from his sword, flying to the floor, and shaking Ansall as the older man clutched onto the bull's shoulders. I only managed to stay aboard the dragon's back because I was already clinging to one of his spines with all my might.

Vincent hit the dirt, crying out as his leg collapsed beneath him, breaking at an unnatural angle, and sending the prince tumbling across the clearing in front of the gate.

Zaxx landed with both paws heavily on the ground, holding his neck crookedly, the handle of the blade, sticking from the side of the bull's neck. It looked deeply embedded, but too small to ever kill such a massive foe. Both Ansall and I were still on the dragon's shoulders, but only just.

"You dare to attack the Dragon God!?" Ansall screamed at Prince Vincent, hysterical in anger as he thrust the staff down at the earth.

Hsss! With a burst of purple and dark energy, the Abbot's foul magic hit the prince square on, washing him in waves of strange, glowing flame.

Prince Vincent shrieked as the flames overtook him, turning his once fine and handsome form dark, insubstantial, tattering away into the dark shadows. For a moment I thought I saw an impression of shadow and smoke, a figure of the Dark Prince trying to maintain his old form, as the shadow-thing whispered, *"My kingdom, miiiine,"* before dispersing.

It was a gruesome sight, but a moment I couldn't afford to waste. As the Abbot was busy, I clambered across the back of the beast, nearing the jubilant Ansall—

"I dare," I snarled, striking out with my blade at the Abbot's outstretched hand and staff.

"Urk!" My blow hit the old man's arm squarely, but there was a sudden crack as the sword splintered as if it had struck diamond. It might not have wounded him, but the blow was heavy enough to knock the Abbot's arm away, releasing his staff to spin and clatter to the ground below.

The Abbot fell back among the tines of his god, hissing at me like a, well, like a dragon. "You ingrate. You inferior little bastard!" he spat at me, and I could see from this close distance that the Abbot really *was* different. His brow was heavily scaled, and his eyes flashed a golden-orange, just like the dragon beneath us.

"What have you done?" I breathed, seeing for the first time the way the man's arms extended into talons.

"I have joined with the dragon," the Abbot sneered at me from where he still stood on Zaxx's back, proud of the fear that he was causing. "It started with the baby dragon bones, giving me magic, but Zaxx brought me wild dragon blood and flesh. I am becoming one of them. I, too, am a God!" Abbot thundered, striking forward to swipe at me with blackened claws.

I did only what I was trained to do, by my father, and at the academy. I fought the draconian abbot, using my broken sword to desperately parry and riposte the Abbot's slashing attacks, but every blow that I landed only skittered across the man's magical hide. His scales must be as hard as the dragon's underneath us!

"Ha! Little human. You cannot defeat a god!" Ansall laughed, kicking down at me from his shoulder-perch to catch me on the side. I lost my footing on the thrashing shoulders of Zaxx and fell, scrabbling on the scales as I clutched my arm around the bull's neck.

There! My fingers found the hilt of the Prince Vincent's sword, still embedded in Zaxx's neck. I hung from it as above me Ansall stepped forward, right to the edge of Zaxx's shoulder as the golden bull huffed and wheezed.

My hands started to slip, so I gripped tighter, only for the blade itself to move, horribly, in the flesh of the Gold bull. The wound pulled and tore, and thick, strangely green ichor seeped from the wound, covering me and the bull's neck both.

"Prepare to die, Torvald," Ansall crowed with laughter, reaching down ready to slash at me with his claws.

"Neill. Jump!" It was Paxala in my mind, her own mind feeling focused and fraught with tension.

"I might not be able to defeat you," I said through gritted teeth. "But I have friends who can!" I jack-knifed, pulling on the blade as I did so and kicking out against the neck of the spluttering Zaxx with my feet as I sprang – pulling the blade free from the golden monster's neck. With it came a spout of the green ichor, and then I was falling to what would be the death of me if I hit the hardpacked earth at the monastery gate.

As I fell, I was dimly aware of Zaxx howling in agony, as he writhed in pain from the gaping tear in his flesh, and the Abbot losing his footing, tumbling head over heels after me, but what I held to in the forefront of my mind was the glimmer of hope that Pax had not told me to jump only for me die at the same instant I defeated my foes.

Just as I thought all might be lost, that Paxala had commanded I jump only because she saw the opportunity to topple both Zaxx and the Abbot, there was a shriek of wind and a sudden knock as talons grabbed around my body, and a lurch as I was hauled into the air. Paxala had swept under the bull's head and neck – straight through the jaws of hell itself – to seize me before I was dashed to the floor. As she flew, Char shouted, "Now!"

There was a *whoosh* from behind me as some other of the crater dragons roared dragon flame at their tyrant. My stomach lurched with the quick aerial ascent, and everything was moving so fast as to make it difficult to see what was happening, but I felt heat against my back and my legs, and a deafening roar, which could only have been Zaxx. The bull's ichor, I thought. If the younger dragons had even set a spark of their own flames to it, then the whole messy lot would catch fire. It had been pouring out of the Gold dragon, and he would be lighting up like a fuse set to an oil barrel…

"Fly, Pax, fly!" Char called, and we shot upwards, upwards into the colder night air to wheel and turn high over the scene of devastation.

The dark cloud, is it still coming? I was thinking. "We have to save the people," I gasped from my ragdoll position in Pax's strong talons, meaning everyone: the academy students, the prince's soldiers, citizens in all Three Kingdoms had to flee before the evil that the Abbot Ansall had created.

"We *did* save them, look, Neill, look!" Char was shouting joyously as we circled high above Mount Hammal.

Down below, the scene was one of utter chaos and destruction; there were bodies on the floor, there were rivers of the prince's soldiers fleeing down the slopes of the mountain. The front gates of the academy had fallen, as had the back wall where last Zaxx had attacked. Worst still, a great purple, green, and orange firestorm was raging at the foot of the destroyed gates, a dark shadow of a titanic form in the middle of the flames – Zaxx.

I had been right. *The dragon flame ignited Zaxx's own ichor,* I thought with a shiver. The Gold tyrant had been destroyed by his own venom.

Around the firestorm flew the other crater dragons—Morax and Socolia, Verserpal and the others. The giant White dragon Paxala had called Zenema was already cooing and calling to the younger flying dragons, keeping them away from the chaos.

The mountain looked to be as close to a vision of destruction as I had ever seen it, but amazingly the main hall of the academy still stood, and the dragon crater was still safe.

"We've done it," I said, a little deliriously. "The Abbot, Zaxx, the rebel armies..." They were all gone. All of those who had threatened the dragon crater were dead. *Even the Prince Vincent is no more,* the thought hit me. *He had shown courage at the end.*

But what would happen to the Middle Kingdom now that it had no prince to lead it?

"Neill. You look so worried – but we've won. We did it *together*," Char said. "The dragons can have a future now. A real future."

EPILOGUE

TORVALD, A NEW ERA

Even though the enemies of the Dragon Academy had been vanquished in one terrible night, the fall of Zaxx, the Abbot, and Prince Vincent, all still left me with unsettling questions. Despite our attempts to quell the flames, the unnatural fire before the gates of the Dragon Academy raged for three days and nights; a great bonfire that I thought must be seen clear to the Eastern Marches and even to the edge of the Northlander Princedom itself.

"It's like the bonfires of old," Maxal Ganna, the owlish dragon student and now the Master of Magics confided in me, as we sat on the second fiery evening atop the high walls of the academy, watching the smoldering ruins. "Versi talks about them, how dragons used to work with humans to set ceremonial bonfires."

"Really?" I asked. "That's strange–why would the dragons do that?"

"The dragons would use them when they chose their dragon friends. It was called the Choosing Ceremony," Maxal said, and I nodded as Maxal's explanation seemed to fit. The bonfire below was a symbol of the edge of the old era, and the choosing of a new. Of humans and dragons working, training together in this new thing that we were going to create.

The Dragon Academy.

But my mind snagged on something— "The Choosing Ceremony? What's that?" I asked.

"I've got to do more research, but it seems to be the ritual that held the dragons and the humans together, that allowed them to act as one," Maxal said, and I filed that tidbit away as something to return to later, once we'd restored some sense of order.

In the days that followed, a strange sort of peace settled on the mountain. I think that it must have been the destruction and disappearance of the rebel army – turned to shadow and then dissipated when Ansall fell into the flames – and then the subsequent loss of Prince Vincent to the same foul magic, that made travelers wary of approaching the sacred mountain.

"The villagers below know you will do right by them, as I and my boys have told them just what sort of man you are, Neill, and what sort of woman Char is, and the rest of you pups up here. But the traders? The merchants?" Nan Barrow confided in me on the third evening of the burning Zaxx. Her large, sprawling family lived in the tiny scratch of a village around the southern slopes of the mountain, so she had a finger on the pulse of the community in the way we on the mountain did not. "They are scared of what evil is going to be born here next."

It distressed me, that the normal Middle Kingdomers would think this, although, with everything that they had been through, I couldn't blame them. And so,

on the fourth day, I assembled the Dragon Riders.

"We have a new charge," I announced. "We must fly out across the land, carrying simple supplies and assist any villagers or Prince Vincent's fleeing troops who need it. We must offer them protection," I advised the assembled Dragon Riders whose weary, dirt-smeared faces were no longer those of freshly recruited students.

"If they need food, offer them provisions. If they are lost, use your flight to guide them to the nearest safe town. If they are under threat of brigands and bandits, defend them. If they need medical help, then direct them here." We still had a lot of medical supplies from when the Draconis Order used to train healers and scribes, and I was determined that tradition, at least, would continue. "You will bear urgent messages, you will clear the roads if the storms have knocked trees across the path. You will make your camp by the hamlets and villages that have no leader, until they can appoint their own spokespeople," I advised.

It was a simple plan, and one I modelled on my own father's writings. Like him, I did not believe that the warriors of the clan should only protect the clan lands, but also keep the clans safe as they conducted their own affairs. Extended out to the entire Middle Kingdom, I foresaw a time when the Dragon Riders could protect and keep the towns and villages as they elected mayors and captains.

"The people are our clan now," I said to Char one day,

causing her to smile.

But there were still strange and troubling questions. Where had the Darkening cloud gone? Was its destruction really a matter so simple that when Ansall died, his shadow army dissipated? And what were we to make of the rumors telling of shadows in the northern mountains? Were these stories mere superstition or not?

Then, too, was the discovery, when the fire had eventually burnt itself out, of Zaxx's blackened and burnt bones at the foot of the academy gates. It came as a relief to know he was truly gone, but we did not discover any sign of the body of the Abbot Ansall, nor his magical staff. "Incinerated completely in the fires," Char said grimly, and I hoped she was right.

What we did find, however, right in the center of bonfire, and the very hottest place of the fire, was a blackened crater with three strange crystal-like orbs. Were these something that Ansall had been carrying with him when he fell? Were they the secret of his strange powers of invincibility and darkness? Or were they some strange remnant of a dragon-organ, fused together by magic and flame? Or perhaps, they were little more than the glowing earthstars that sometimes cropped up naturally in the ground, glowing, light-catching stones, somehow uncovered by the inferno that was the dying Zaxx?

"I have no idea what they are," Maxal Ganna had said doubtfully, turning them over to Dorf Lesser. My friend and roommate hefted them in his hands, each no bigger than a duck egg, blackened with soot, but shiny and smooth underneath. Dorf had become taller and broader in our battles, but he still had his boyish way about him.

"Pretty," he shrugged. "Maybe we should keep a hold of them, in case they mean something...."

"No," Char said vehemently. "They might be like the dragon bones. Corrupt."

Dorf suddenly grimaced, dropping the stones to the floor and looking to wash his hands.

"I agree with Char," Jodreth said in measured tones. "These dragon stones don't *feel* natural, but I also think it might be unwise to just throw them away. What if they bring back some sort of evil against us, in later times?" I was surprised when those assembled; Char, Dorf, Maxal, Jodreth, all turned to regard me for my opinion.

"Separate them," I said. It seemed the only reasonable solution. I looked to Char to see if it was acceptable to her and she nodded. "Keep one here at the academy, and Jodreth and Maxal can study it. But the other two? I say we give them to two dragons, with the express orders to take them far away and never reveal their location."

"Nothing is ever lost forever," Jodreth murmured, but an angry look from Char silenced him. It was settled. Whatever the real truth was behind these strange dragon stones, we might never know, but perhaps future generations would manage to decipher them.

The last – and greatest – change that occurred was the arrival of the princes, Prince Lander of the North, father to Char Nefrette, and Prince Griffith of the South, father to Terence.

They came, marching into the Middle Kingdom not a week from each other, and made their way to the makeshift camps at the base of Mount Hammal, left by Prince Vincent's forces. They were met by our Dragon Riders first on the road, and warned that we would brook no war here in the Middle Kingdom, but, amazingly, it appeared that they did not come to carve up their brother's kingdom for themselves.

"What use do I have of a soft, cold land like this?" laughed Prince Griffith when Lila Penn forewent all attempts at diplomacy and asked, the instant he arrived, what his intentions might be.

Later, as we hosted as grand a banquet as we could manage with our own stores and Nan's ingenious incorporation of the food and wine brought by the princes' own entourages, there was a chance to talk at depth about what was to happen next to the Dragon Academy – *and* to the Middle Kingdom.

"If the people of the Middle Kingdom wish to get out of this dangerous place and head south to mine, I won't stop them!" Prince Griffith said cheerily, and Char had to stop me from growling at him by kicking at my shins under the table.

"And you, Father, why bring your armies here?" Char asked of Prince Lander.

The Northlander ruler had looked old— both he and Griffith seemed to have aged since last we'd seen them, as it happened. It was as if once the Abbot Ansall and his foul magic was exorcised from the realm, then so too was the unnatural longevity that had been given to the royal line.

"Your brother, Wurgan," Prince Lander said stiffly, indicating the red-haired, red-bearded giant who commanded the prince's armies, "and your mother have made me see that the Middle Kingdom needs allies, not another tyrant. And I have enough problems of my own in the north, as the wild mountain dragons appear to be tripling in numbers this year…"

Despite the fact that he claimed to have come to help us, it was the Dragon Rider who agreed to give Prince Lander aid in his struggle against the ferociously dangerous shadow-blue wild dragons that lived in the northern wilds. Maybe there was even a chance that we could befriend them, eventually, although I doubted it.

"And what of the Middle Kingdom?" It was Jodreth who surprised me by saying, standing up amidst the banquet whilst we were discussing heavy matters. "I am sure that Neill, Char, everyone here is pleased to have help in rebuilding the Dragon Academy, but we need to think beyond these walls to the people of the Middle Kingdom. Who shall rule them?"

There was silence from the table, and my heart sank. I was dreading this difficult part of the discussion. I imagined that one of the warlords or lesser nobles would put their name forward.

"We have been discussing this, my brother and I," said Prince Griffith, standing up to raise a glass. "And we have come to a settlement, as neither he nor I want to govern this troublesome province." A rumble of disagreement came from the assembled Middle Kingdomers, and Prince Griffith spread his hands wide in a placating gesture and grinned at them. "I do beg your pardon, but you have to agree that no end of trouble has come from here in the last few decades!"

He was right at that at least, I thought, and the crowd seemed mollified by the inarguable truth of his observation. Although worried what the Southern Prince would suggest next, my eyes sought out the only two candidates I would pledge myself behind: Char or Terence.

"And we have determined who here has the skills to help govern the Middle Kingdom, if they agree," Prince Griffith announced.

I'll fight to the death for either of them, I thought as I looked at my friends, before realizing that actually, I would fight to the death for anyone here at the academy. In fact, I would do more than that – I would live for them as well.

Prince Griffith turned to me, to raise his wine glass. "Neill, son of Malos Torvald. You were raised by the Chosen Warden of the East, and you rose to be Protector of the Dragon Crater. You have the ear of the dragons here, and you have managed to train the Dragon Riders, the only force capable of holding the Middle Kingdom together at the moment. You clearly have the skills. You, along with Char Nefrette, daughter of Prince Lander, have—"

"And the Lady Red," Char said, nodding to the distant, but unseen presence of Paxala somewhere outside.

"And your dragon, of course," Prince Griffith continued. "You three are our choice as Wardens of the Middle Kingdom, in perpetuity, until such a time as your heirs – if they come–are of age. *Then,* there will be another Great Council meeting, and another choice appropriate for that time will be selected. Do you accept your duty?" The Southern Prince's voice was stern as he offered me the wine cup.

All eyes in the tent were on me, and a silent hush filled the room. Could I do it? I asked myself. *No,* I immediately, and instinctively thought. *I was not my father, I was not Malos Torvald. I couldn't do this alone.* But, underneath the table, Char's hand found mine, and I knew then that if I said yes, I would not have to face the task alone.

"I'll stand at your side, Neill Torvald," Char breathed as she looked into my eyes.

I couldn't do this alone. But I knew that I could do anything if I had this woman with me.

"Neill should be who he is meant to be," Pax's soft whisper of a voice sounded in the back of my mind. *"Warden. Protector. Guardian. And Char too."*

"Think of all the good you can do," Char whispered to me, a half smile starting to curl her lips.

I did. I thought of my father's writings on strategy, tactics and leadership. It had been those lessons that I had tried to impart, in what ways that I could, to help defend the Dragon Academy. But my father always had his hands tied with the rules of Prince Vincent, I realized. And he had never managed to send out Dragon Riders to help others as we have. My father had made me think like a good soldier, but Char and the dragons had made me become a good man.

"Think of all the good *we* can do." I smiled at her, suddenly awkward as I said, "If, that is, you will consent to govern this troublesome kingdom with me…"

"Of course I will, Torvald. I wouldn't want to be anywhere

else." Char smiled back at me. My heart lifted as if I were dragon-flying, and I stood up, with Char standing at my side and our hands held into the air above our heads. In front and around me were all of our friends, everyone who had ever stood for us and beside us: Dorf, Jodreth, Maxal, Lila, Sigrid, Terence – and they were all beaming with their support.

"I accept," I said, taking the offered chalice and drinking a deep draught before passing it to Char to do the same to the wild applause of all those gathered.

END OF DRAGON MAGE
THE FIRST DRAGON RIDER BOOK THREE

Learn more about the Kingdom of Torvald and its dragon riders in Ava Richardson's epic fantasy series, **Return of the Darkening Trilogy.** Keep reading for an exclusive extract from **Dragon Trials.**

THANK YOU!

I hope you enjoyed The First Dragon Rider trilogy. Please don't forget to leave a review.

Receive free books, exclusive excerpts and be kept up to date on all of my new releases, when you sign up to my mailing list at AvaRichardsonBooks.com/mailing-list

Stay in touch! I'd also love to connect with you on:

Facebook: www.facebook.com/AvaRichardsonBooks

Goodreads:
www.goodreads.com/author/show/8167514.Ava_Richardson

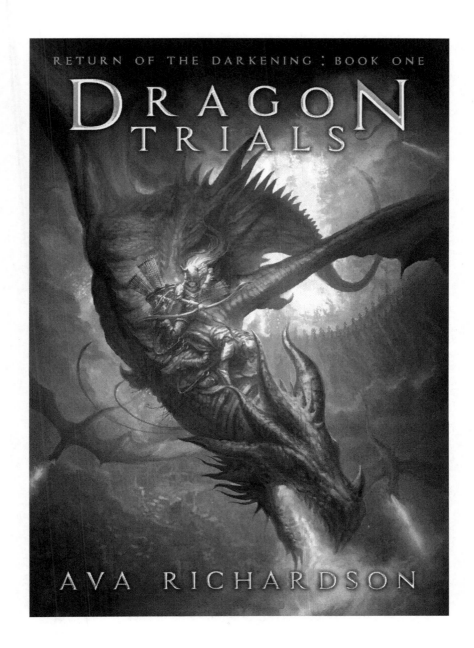

RETURN OF THE DARKENING : BOOK ONE

DRAGON
TRIALS

AVA RICHARDSON

BLURB

High-born Agathea Flamma intends to bring honor to her family by following in her brothers' footsteps and taking her rightful place as a Dragon Rider. With her only other option being marriage, Thea will not accept failure. She's not thrilled at her awkward, scruffy partner, Seb, but their dragon has chosen, and now the unlikely duo must learn to work as a team.

Seventeen-year-old Sebastian has long been ashamed of his drunken father and poor upbringing, but then he's chosen to train as a Dragon Rider at the prestigious Dragon Academy. Thrust into a world where he doesn't fit in, Seb finds a connection with his dragon that is even more powerful than he imagined. Soon, he's doing all he can to succeed and not embarrass his new partner, Thea.

When Seb hears rumors that an old danger is re-emerging, he and Thea begin to investigate. Armed only with their determination and the dragon they both ride, Thea and Seb may be the only defence against the Darkening that threatens to sweep over the land. Together, they will have to learn to work together to save their kingdom...or die trying.

Get your copy of **Dragon Trials** at
AvaRichardsonBooks.com

300

EXCERPT

Every fifth year, the skies over the city of Torvald darken as large shadows swoop over the city, dark wingbeats blowing open window shutters and their bird-like cries disturbing babes and sleeping animals alike.

The city folk of Torvald are prepared for this ritual however, as the great Dragon Horns—the long brass instruments stationed along the top towers of the dragon enclosure—are blown on those mornings. Farmers and market folk rush to guide their skittish cattle out of sight, whilst children flock to the narrow cobbled streets or crowd atop the flat rooftops.

Choosing Day is a time of great celebration, excitement and anticipation for Torvald. It is the time that the great enclosure is unbarred and the young dragonets are released into the sky to choose their riders from amongst the humans below. It is a day that could forever change your fortunes; if you are brave and lucky enough. It is a day that heroes are made, and the future of the realm is secured.

~

"Dobbett, no! Get down from there right now." Dobbett was a land-pig, although she looked somewhere between a short-snouted dog and a white fluffy cushion. She grunted nervously as she turned around and around atop the table, whimpering and grunting.

She always got like this. I wasn't very old the last time that

Choosing Day came around; I must have been about thirteen or fourteen or so, but I remember how my little pet ran around my rooms, knocking everything off stands or dismantling shelves. I couldn't blame her: land-pigs are the natural food of dragons, and if she even caught a whiff of one, she went into a panic.

"No one's going to eat you, silly," I said to her in a stern voice, making sure I picked her up gently and set her down on the floor where her tiny claws immediately clacked on the tiles as she scampered under my bed.

Good Grief! I found myself smiling at her antics, despite myself. Dobbett was a welcome relief to the butterflies I was feeling in my stomach.

Today was Choosing Day, and that meant that today would be my last chance. If I wasn't picked now, then by the time another five years rolled by, Father would probably have married me off to some annoying, terribly fat merchant or nobleman.

Memories of the prince's last Winter Ball flashed through my mind, filling me at once with the most curious mixture of disgust and hopelessness. The prince, and all the royal family, had been there of course, and my older brothers too—Reynalt and Ryan— looking splendid in their dragon scale jerkins.

They managed to do it, I thought. *They got their own dragon.* My two older brothers were chosen almost as soon as they were old enough to sit on the saddle—even though it is always the dragon itself that does the choosing.

"*As close as egg and mother, is a Flamma to a dragon,*" I mouthed the well-known Torvald saying desperately hoping it would prove true. I wanted to declare: I am Agathea Flamma, or more properly, *Lady* Agathea Flamma. Our household had sired Dragon Riders for the last hundred years, and the rooms of Flamma Hall were filled with the statues, busts and paintings of my great-uncles and grandfathers and great-great grandfathers who rode the mighty drakes into battle in defense of the city and the realm.

My brothers were chosen, why not me? Everyone had expected them to be chosen. No one expected me to be.

I am a girl. They say I am better suited to marrying well, running an estate, raising little Dragon Riders all of my own... "Ugh!" I snorted in disgust, throwing open the patio doors to the balcony of the tower and walking out into the fresh morning air.

The last of the Dragon Horns just finished their mournful cry. I could already hear cries and screams of excitement as the shapes flew out of Mount Hammal, the dragon enclosure far over the mountain from here. They looked so beautiful. Long, sinuous necks, powerful; each one a different colour. Today there are green, blue, black—even a red.

Get your copy of **Dragon Trials** at
AvaRichardsonBooks.com